DOUBLE-DECKER DREAMS

Also available by Lindsay MacMillan
The Heart of the Deal

DOUBLE-DECKER DREAMS

A Novel

LINDSAY MACMILLAN

alcove
press

Copyright © 2023 by Lindsay MacMillan

All rights reserved.

Published in the United States by Alcove Press, an imprint of The Quick Brown Fox & Company LLC.

Alcove Press and its logo are trademarks of The Quick Brown Fox & Company LLC.

Library of Congress Catalog-in-Publication data available upon request.

ISBN (paperback): 978-1-63910-282-2
ISBN (ebook): 978-1-63910-283-9

Cover design by Sarah Horgan

Printed in the United States.

www.alcovepress.com

Alcove Press
34 West 27th St., 10th Floor
New York, NY 10001

First Edition: June 2023

10 9 8 7 6 5 4 3 2 1

For my grandparents, Bill and Rita Vullo.
Your sixty-two-year marriage showed me a beautiful
example of true love rooted in kindness and friendship.
It's that kind of steady, healthy love that this book explores.

CHAPTER ONE

The morning I first see him is the morning I need it most.

I guess that's sometimes how the universe works.

It ignores your requests time and time again until finally, when you're about to throw in the towel and just give up, it delivers you that One Thing that keeps you hanging on. That One Thing that replaces your seething scowl with a spellbound smile. That One Thing that makes you absolutely certain that magic is more than a myth and that your Hogwarts acceptance letter will be arriving after all, just a couple decades late.

That One Thing that makes you twirl in your fuzziest bathrobe to old Taylor Swift songs, physically bursting with that giddy feeling you thought you'd outgrown years ago. That One Thing that shows you that despite all the angry, jaded words you've been spewing, love actually isn't dead after all. It's more alive than ever, and it's been reborn just for you.

Maybe that One Thing is the dream job you land after being laid off. Maybe it's the pregnancy after years of trying. Or the new friend who appears out of thin air when you need her most.

Or in my case, maybe it's an English prince riding a white steed past your window.

Well, not a white steed, technically speaking. He's riding a red double-decker bus that has an organic food delivery advertisement plastered across it—"NudeFoodMood.com." (Symbolically seductive foreshadowing, perhaps?)

But it's close enough to my fairy-tale fantasy and just about as enchanting an entrance as I could ask for in modern-day London.

The morning started out particularly poorly. I woke up with a backache from the droopy mattress and then stubbed my toe on the characterful bed frame of the North London flat that I'm renting. *Characterful* is just the British way of saying "extremely old and probably broken." I've learned this much since moving across the pond.

Rather than letting my stubbed toe simply be a stubbed toe, I naturally spiraled into a place where it's a gigantic metaphor for my complete incompetence as an adult. What chance do I have of becoming a Fortune 500 CEO or shattering the glass ceiling if I can't even roll off my mattress without maiming myself?

The negative self-talk gained steam when my crumpet got stuck in the toaster. I've taken a liking to crumpets as they seem more sophisticated, more *cultured*, than waffles even though they're basically the same thing. I pried the crumpet out with a fork and shoved the mangled thing into my mouth while standing over the sink, full of unwashed dishes. More evidence of my utter incompetence.

Then a bulgy-eyed fly snuck into the flat, buzzing all around, nipping at my tea. I chased the fly around for a solid ten minutes, swatting it with unopened bank statements that trigger my stress levels, as all physical mail does. In the end, I won the war but at the cost of insect guts on my carpet and no motivation to vacuum.

So when I sat down at my clunky baroque desk and began sifting through "high-importance" emails on my work computer, I was questioning my entire life path with disappointingly cliched existential angst.

Maybe I shouldn't have said yes to a six-month project in London and spontaneously moved to a new country by myself, even if it was an opportunity to fast-track my promotion and put an entire ocean between my ex and me. Maybe I should've stayed with Mateo and let him buy me that ring even though I didn't *just know*. Maybe I should give up on the idea that life or love will ever take my breath away again. Maybe I'm just a delusional thirty-one-year-old stuck in my millennial Neverland.

Maybe *not too bad* is what adulthood is, and I'd better grow up and face the synthetic pop music, or I'll wind up dying alone in this very flat, and no one will find my body until another tenant finally pieces together that the stench is more than the fishmonger next door.

I turned on my daily BBC news podcast, then promptly turned it off again as the host rattled off the headlines of unprecedented political discord and gang violence. Procrastinating reading my emails, I stared blankly out the window onto Upper Street, the bustling high street that emanates the little-village-in-a-big-city energy of Islington.

Upper Street is lined with bohemian boutiques, plant-filled cafés, and red telephone boxes repurposed into street artists' studios. Narrow Tudor homes are cobbled together next to pitch-roofed

Victorian properties and simple Georgian terraces, with silver birch trees and grassy squares providing some consistency of greenery. Weathered brick, slanted gables, and trash bags piled high on the stone sidewalks add a dose of authenticity to the cityscape. It feels like a movie set, which is precisely why I chose to live here.

But rather than scooping me into its romantic folds, Islington's charm has exacerbated my isolation, reminding me that I don't have someone to go with me to the single-screen cinema or help carry my groceries as I trudge back from Chapel Market, three tote bags full of produce, pastries, and peanut butter (to my immense relief, peanut butter hasn't been nearly as difficult to find in the UK as I'd been warned).

Today's sky is blotted with low clouds that look like they might lift soon. That's how it goes here. The sun never seems too far away, keeping you believing it might show its face soon, but it can rarely be bothered.

My mood was as drab as the weather, and I needed something good to appear. Or someone.

And suddenly he's there. Right there out my grilled window, seated on the top deck of a close-topped bus that's waiting outside my flat at the St. Mary's Church stop.

I live on the second floor—the first floor, according to the Brits—so the bus's upper deck is just below my eye level, and I peer down at the gorgeous man. *My* gorgeous man, as my mind immediately lays claim to him.

It's like he chose his seat because he knew it would be directly in my line of sight. You can't deny the subliminal tugs of fate.

Everything stops and starts and somersaults in simultaneous bliss. My calloused toes wiggle in anticipation, and the thrill works its way up into my crumpet-filled belly, and up again into my black-and-blue heart that suddenly feels brand-new again. My fingers start dancing too, like they're playing a perfectly tuned piano to my life's soundtrack, which I haven't heard until now but somehow already have memorized.

The bus is crowded with commuters, but I can only see one person. Everyone else fades away as extras.

He's everything I hoped he'd be. So good looking that it actually hurts, and carrying himself with such a manly sort of grace. Dark and handsome, he looks to be tall too, dressed in a wool pea-coat with a maroon scarf that exudes European sophistication. He has clean-cut, olive skin, his hair is slightly coiffed, and he's reading a magazine that must be the *Economist*, because he has that worldly look about him.

His profile could slice open the hardest heart—an aristocratic nose and a confident jawline with a slight softness in his chin that indicates he has a brilliant sense of humor and will laugh at all my jokes, even the ones that are ever so rarely not that great. Chemistry is coursing between us like electromagnetic waves. Only fifteen feet away, and I can basically hear his voice murmuring into my ear in his posh accent as we canoodle in bed while I snooze the alarm: *"Morning, darling. Shall I fix us some brekkie whilst you draw a bath?"*

He's the ideal blend of Mr. Darcy and Cedric Diggory, and I start berating myself for ever dating anyone who fell short of this exquisite standard.

I'd guess he's about my age but looks a bit older given how put together he is. Quite a contrast to my mismatched outfit of joggers and a shapeless blouse featuring a chocolate stain just beneath where the computer camera hits (I've really mastered the Zoom life).

He certainly seems to have the means for a private car, but chooses to take the bus anyway. This says a lot about how he views himself and the world.

We'll be Britain's next power couple, rivaling the royal family, or perhaps even joining them. His uncle is likely a duke, or at least an earl. I'm not fussy about needing a title myself, but I wouldn't say no if they offered it up, that's all.

Let's not get too carried away now, Kat, I tell myself, and then swiftly proceed to analyze what our future children will look like. My prince has very defined bone structure, which is a blessing for our offspring due to the fact that my cheeks have yet to shed their toddler fat.

And then it happens. The most extraordinary thing in the world—and yet somehow also the most natural. His neck swivels, and he looks out the bus window and up into my flat. Directly at me, like he could feel my gaze undressing him and wanted more of it.

I've been people-watching from my window for the full two months I've lived here, staring out at Upper Street as the world whizzes by in red buses and black cabs, lorries and electric scooters, bicycles and baby carriages. And never before has anyone spotted me spying. Bus passengers mostly just look at their phones, and occasionally down at the white Veja shoes and rubber wellies scurrying along the sidewalk; at the young parents queueing up for morning loaves and sultana scones at Gail's Bakery; at the terriers and corgis yapping from the ever-blooming churchyard.

But no one ever looks up. No one ever notices me. Until now.

My eyes lock with my mystery man's for one glorious, terrifying second as my heartstrings unravel and my insides spill all of their messy contents into a puddle on the insect-stained carpet.

Objectively speaking, I'm an eye contact expert. I should really add it to my résumé under the "Special Skills" section. Perhaps my talent is in some way correlated with my disproportionately large marble-gray eyes. I had a perpetually bug-eyed expression as a kid, and my eye contact acumen became apparent back in fourth grade, when I could tell that Joey Rice wanted me to sit by him on the haunted hayride, and then he passed me a note with those exact sentiments. Though I had a massive crush on him, I obviously said no and avoided him like the plague until high school graduation. But the point is that I've always been fluent in reading eye contact like a second language.

Even to this day, I maintain that eye contact can be the highest form of intimacy, above sex. It transports you through time and space, down into one another's eternal souls that have been burned down and burned out but are now suddenly set on fire once more. Eye contact innocently unleashes all the sealed-shut valves in your heart and affirms that someone can see into you, through your well-constructed walls, and beyond your bodily veneer. And that you can see into them too.

This eye contact from my suitor on the bus is no common or cursory glance. It's as meaningful as it comes, laced with questions and answers and oaths. So I do what any poised adult would do in this divinely crafted meet-cute.

I let out a strangled yelp and tumble out of my chair so he won't see me. There I stay, cowering beneath my desk like a puppy who's just heard thunder for the first time.

By the time I collect myself and peep out the window again, the bus is leaving. It's barreling south at an insensitively fast speed, oblivious to my need to stare at this man for the rest of the day, the rest of my life.

CHAPTER TWO

There's a wiggling of a door handle, and my first reaction is that my prince is also a wizard who has apparated up the stairs and come to assure me that my love is requited with equal passion. I've worked myself into such a tizzy that I'm genuinely crushed when he does not in fact materialize.

It's just my neighbor Jules, barging in like she does best, a hand-rolled cigarette in one hand, a coffee mug in the other—whiskey-filled, no doubt. She works late shifts as a bartender at the King's Head pub across the street, and her circadian rhythm is off. Or at least that's how she explains drinking before noon.

Jules is not my flat mate. I live alone, thank goodness, and Jules is next door with her fiancée, Nina. Our little building is called Marlow House. Most buildings over here have names, dating back many centuries. My apartment and Jules's are attached via a door that is simply too characterful to have a functioning lock. Jules makes my place an extension of her own and tells me to do the same with hers, but I have a thing about respecting other people's space (a quaint concept, apparently).

I'm saying all this like I'm annoyed by her, but the truth is that Jules has been something of a godsend, the social lifeline I didn't want but definitely needed.

A full head taller than I am, with the sturdy build of someone who proudly rejects society's dieting culture, she takes up a lot of space in the best sort of way, leaning into her power to make everyone around her bigger too. Jules's corkscrew red hair signals from miles off that she's a firecracker, and her Irish ancestry is on full display, with fair skin, seafoam-green eyes, and a thick smattering of freckles. But she was born and raised in East London, and her plain-speaking cockney accent is entirely irresistible, even to an introvert like me.

"Everything okay, babes?" Jules asks. "Thought I heard you give a shout." Navigating around the clothes drying rack that I've set up as an intended blockade, she saunters into the sitting room, donning a "Woman Up" T-shirt and zebra leggings that she executes with aplomb.

Jules takes tremendous pride in defying the reserved British stereotype. The day I moved in, she delivered a welcome basket of Pimm's, sausage and mash pie, and velvety Cadbury chocolates.

Taking a slow drag of her cigarette, she chases it with the contents in her coffee mug. Ordinarily, I'd pounce with my most vehement "How can you possibly still smoke when you know it gives you cancer?" tirade, but today I just grin back and heave open the blessed window to help the wisps of nicotine and tar escape.

"What a jolly good world it is," I say—*sing*, more like it, not caring how off-key I am.

Jules looks suspicious, wrinkling her studded nose as she tries to sniff out my motive. An ordinary nose stud would blend into her freckles, but not this one—it's a purple rhinestone flower that spans half her button nose. "What's got you buzzing?" she asks.

"Blimey, mate," I say, trying out an accent of my own, given my future role as an English heiress, "is it a crime to be chuffed to bits on a ravishing autumn morn?"

A rain shower has unleashed outside, and the passersby are all but gouging each other's eyes out with umbrella spokes. Car horns and squeaky brakes fill the damp September air, but it all sounds like an angelic orchestra to me.

Jules peels off the false eyelashes she's still wearing from last night, as if she thinks they're blurring her vision. "Bloody 'ell, what's gotten into you, Kat?" Her accent drops "h's" at the beginning of words, and middle "t's" are usually chucked out too.

"Let's don't be so dramatic, Jules," I say, practicing my curtsey with ballerina-like grace, or so it feels. "I'm the same optimistic Kat as always."

"Rubbish," Jules rebuffs. "Pure rubbish."

I can understand her reaction. To put it mildly, I've been more Scrooge than sunshine since she's known me, having to face the facts that London isn't the enchanted kingdom that *Love Actually* and *Harry Potter* led me to believe.

Beyond my Islington sanctuary, tacky McDonald's and Pizza Express storefronts squeeze out mom-and-pop shops; jackhammers drill incessantly; and the Tube is every bit as grimy and screechy as the New York subway. Big Ben is shrouded in scaffolding, and even high tea has turned out to be little more than a tourist trap.

And the dating scene—don't get me started. I'd expected elegant dinners at private members clubs with refined gentlemen, but England is infested with as many Peter Pan boys as America. Since it's been impossible to meet anyone IRL (the Brits have this thing where they think it's hugely impolite to strike up a conversation with strangers), I've re-downloaded the apps, regressing to a depressing phase of life I thought I'd left behind many years ago. The boys—definitely *not* men—I match with misspell my name as they message me last-minute *Hiya Cat, u keen for a cheeky pint?* and then show up late to divey pubs, boasting sleeve tattoos and smoker's breath.

So far, I've bailed on every date after half an hour. It's only taken two minutes to know it wasn't going to work out. I've endured the remaining twenty-eight minutes out of sheer courtesy.

But that's all in the past now because here it is, the proof that I was right to hold onto my high standards. "I've found him," I tell Jules.

"Found who?" she wants to know.

"*Him,*" I say, rather annoyed that she isn't able to read my mind, but also overjoyed to have an excuse to retell the whole story. "My prince."

I've shared the SparkNotes version of my dates with Jules, and she's declared that I'm being far too choosy. "What're you on about?" she asks expectantly, arching one wispy eyebrow, then the other. "What's the punch line?"

"No punch line. I've fallen in love." Prancing around the flat, I fan out my joggers. The pilled cotton feels like a proper ballgown.

"You're 'igh on summat," Jules says, eyeing me closely for signs of drugs.

"And never coming down," I agree, grinning up at the vintage wood beams on the ceiling. "I'm serious, Jules. He was right there." I point out the window and know I must look like a lunatic, but I relish it, the feeling of being crazy. For so long now, everything has been muted and monochrome, and now it's loud and vibrant again, and I'm going to keep shouting about it until Jules can hear the songs and see the starlight too. "He was sitting on the top deck of the 4 bus and giving off incontrovertible 'future husband' vibes."

Something switches in Jules's eyes where she goes from being exasperated to amused. She plops down on the undersized sofa that came with my "fully furnished" flat, along with a droopy mattress and five flimsy clothes hangers. In an attempt at salvation, I've covered the couch in a plush slipcover and adorned it with tasseled throw pillows that appeared as the top result of my "cultured home decor that can be machine washed" Google search. The off-white walls have been left bare to honor my lazy style that I pass off as minimalist chic. There's really no point investing in art when I'm only here for a short time.

"Righ'o, babes," Jules says with her endearingly crooked-toothed grin. She takes a hearty swig from her mug as she cozies up for a good story. "Back up and start at the beginning."

"The beginning." The phrase moisturizes my chapped lips with all its untainted potential. "It goes like this: I fell in love this morning." My tone is matter-of-fact, even as everything else feels the opposite of logical, twisting and turning and reshaping all my jagged fragments into joyous fantasies.

Recounting the events, I expand the one and a half seconds of eye contact into a fifteen-minute tale. (I leave out the detail of disappearing beneath my desk, as it's not central to the plot and doesn't do justice to the composed heroine that I identify as.)

"This is full-on," Jules says, once I start talking in circles. "Should've known you would deliver a quin'essential 'ollywood rom-com."

"It's not a Hollywood rom-com," I say, my chin jutting out in defiance. "It's a real-life rom-com. I'm going to marry him, Jules. Just watch."

A chortle catches in Jules's throat as if she's trying hard not to let it escape all the way. "What if the bloke's already got a partner?"

"Impossible," I snap, grievously offended at the very suggestion. "There's no way such an upstanding gentleman would cheat with the kind of intimate eye contact that he shared with me."

"'Course not," Jules recovers, mouth twitching as she takes another drag of her cig. "But 'ow are you going to track 'im down? This city has got nine million bloody people. The odds aren't exactly in your favor, babes."

"Yes, well the odds of us being born weren't in our favor either, were they?" I retort. "But here we are."

"Can you actually prove we're alive, though?" Jules poses, taking on a philosophical posture as she stretches out on the sofa, tube-socked feet dangling off the edge. "We could be in a simulation." This is her second-favorite rant, behind moaning about the classist discrimination of cigarette taxes.

"I don't really care if it's a simulation or not, so long as my prince and I are in it together," I reply, with a splash of self-righteous sass. "He'll be back on that same bus tomorrow, I'm sure of it."

"And then what? You'll 'old up a sign in your window that says 'MARRY ME, ROMEO'?"

"Don't be ridiculous. That would be over the top."

"But falling in love at first sight from your window is proper chilled," Jules deadpans.

"You can laugh all you want," I tell her. "But I'm going to end up with that man. In fact, I'm deleting my dating apps right now. No need for them anymore!" Giddy with relief, I find my phone and delete them on the spot, feeling a weight lifted as I watch them vanish from my home screen, clearing out literal and metaphorical space.

"You had the exclusive talk with your eye contact, I reckon?" Jules says.

"Indeed we did."

Eye contact is how Mateo and I began too. Five years ago, I was out at The Spaniard in the West Village with one of my roommates, and Mateo caught my eye from across the bar. Immediately, I declared that he was going to be my next boyfriend. My roommate laughed it off, but I proved to be correct. Mateo had a bottle of champagne delivered to our table and then sauntered up to ask me out. I hadn't imagined the attraction, and the memory gives me confidence that I'm not imagining it now either.

And this is different too. Mateo had more of an ego right from the start, flexing with grand gestures that I should've known he couldn't sustain. My double-decker bus prince gives off more genuine energy that bodes well for our future trajectory.

I ended things with Mateo back in January, eight months ago now, after he told me to send him a link to the engagement ring I wanted. Perhaps he genuinely thought he was being nice to let me pick it out, but it felt like he wasn't willing to put in the time and effort to choose something special. The Mateo I'd fallen for would've spent months custom designing a ring with sentimental significance. But somewhere along the way, he'd stopped trying and started taking me for granted. It felt like our relationship was on autopilot, and he was content with the coasting but I was not.

I wasn't exactly a saint either, flying all over the country for my job and only making time for him on weekends. All the cracks showed through when he decided things were good enough to get married, and I decided that good enough just wasn't good enough.

It was downright petrifying to walk away after four years with him, after picturing a future together and thinking everything was following the life plan. And then having to face being single and alone again, in my thirties no less. But it was still less frightening than it would've been to walk down the aisle with that gut feeling that it wasn't right, that I was settling for someone who didn't cherish me.

My bus beau will cherish me. The proposal will be swoon worthy, and after a heartfelt speech on a Santorini beach, or perhaps a Parisian balcony, he'll offer me his grandmother's diamond, fitted on a modern band engraved with our initials and an ellipsis to symbolize the blending of past, present, and future.

"Bonkers," Jules mutters now, cutting through my trance. "Well, I'm gassed for you, babes, I am." She recovers, tossing a throw pillow affectionately my way. "But just in case it doesn't work out—"

"Which it will," I say, catching the pillow and rocking it against my chest. "He and I are on the same page."

"Deffo. 'Appy days."

Her skeptical inflection doesn't faze me. Nothing can touch me up here. Nothing except the ping of an email. It's my boss asking if

I'm joining the weekly status meeting, which is the passive aggressive way of scolding me for being one minute late.

I wish I were above caring about such earthly things as work meetings, but alas, I'm gunning for that promotion and need to be on my A game until decisions are made in December. Just three months from now, I could be the youngest female partner in the history of Leo & Sons Consulting Group. I won't be derailed now, not even by a prince.

Shooing Jules out of the flat, I hastily dial in on my computer, trying to compose myself. My face is still flushed, and my heartbeat hasn't gotten back on track and now never wants to.

The faces of four white men, all different stages of balding, fill the squares on my screen. It's my boss, plus the executive team for our client, Turpi Oil. They're one of Europe's biggest oil and gas companies, and they've hired us to improve their profitability as fossil fuels go out of style and new environmental regulations threaten their preeminence.

"Good of you to join us, Kitten," the CEO says. The others snigger, as if this demeaning pet name is very clever.

Toxic masculinity runs as deep in the office as the wells where Turpi drills for oil in the North Sea. I abstain from apologizing for being late because I know it will come back to haunt me. It will ring in my boss's ears when he's thinking about promotion candidates— the girly *Sorry* that he'll associate with weakness, with subservience. Not with leadership.

"Shall I kick it off?" I ask, deepening my voice an octave or two to hit the pitch that they'll equate with credibility.

The clones nod curtly in unison, so I start running through the agenda items, fielding questions seamlessly, as if on autopilot.

The whole time, though, I'm not really there. I'm snuggled up in the memory of those dark brown eyes flashing at mine—*into* mine—like they were taking a picture so we could frame it above our fireplace mantel someday and slow dance in front of it each night, forever paying homage to how it all began.

CHAPTER THREE

I hardly sleep that night and not even because of the sagging mattress. All night I'm wired, my mind filling in the blanks about him and us, stringing together story lines out of shimmering thread. And my heart sewing those stories into its lining, patching up holes and transforming the frayed fabric into a soft quilt of possibility.

By the time my alarm goes off, it feels like I've known him all my life.

He's an Oxford man, born into West London wealth and connections. Though he doesn't have to work, he chooses to anyway, determined to carve his own path. He's launching a campaign to be a Member of Parliament so he can use his platform for good and improve socioeconomic equality throughout Britain and beyond.

Our work schedules might present a challenge, but we'll make it work. Perhaps I'll request more UK-based cases, or he'll travel with me and postpone his campaign for a couple years until we're ready to settle down in a South Kensington mansion, with a summer chateau in the Lake District and a beach villa in Mallorca for romantic getaways.

His name is something stately like Alexander, never shortened to Alex except by cricket coaches and calculus tutors. The oldest of three children, he played somewhat of a parental role to his siblings growing up, as his parents were absorbed in, and addicted to, the ceaseless see-and-be-seen circuit of upper-crust English society. Having every opportunity to be spoiled, he's escaped unscathed—winningly humble, with the quiet confidence that comes from knowing that nothing is out of reach.

The smaller details of which boarding school he went to, or if he's a tea or coffee person, are second to the soul-level connection we've established. That said, I get the feeling it was Eton and that he takes an oat flat white with just a dash of cinnamon.

It's not like I believe the factual truth of everything I've conjured up, but I certainly believe the intuitive truth of it, which is what matters.

If I were still in my twenties, I'd text the seventeen best friends in my group chat: Getting ready to see bus crush again, wish me luck!!! And nanoseconds later, my phone would be blowing up with all-caps replies of AAH YOU'VE GOT THIS!! and DIBS ON MOH AT THE WEDDING!!!

But thirties life isn't like that. My friends from the post-college Manhattan years are married now, settled in the sleepy Connecticut suburbs. They've all gotten on the same marriage train that I hadn't realized had pulled up to the station until it was already gone. I'd gotten my chance to jump aboard with Mateo, but it had felt like I'd be following other people's happiness rather than finding it myself. My best friend Blake does a good job of checking in pretty often, but she just doesn't have that much time, what with a baby, husband, and an investment banking job. And now the five-hour time difference between us.

I'm not bitter about how we've drifted apart, though I do sometimes miss the feeling of being swaddled by so much sisterly love, staying up late rehashing the hellish dates (humorous in hindsight), when I'd cling to their zealous assurances of *"That man-child is not worthy of you!!!"* And the next night, I'd comfort them with the very same words, meaning every one.

But there's no space for nostalgia right now, not with the fresh memory of Alexander lighting the way like the Narnia lamppost.

I wonder if he's been thinking about me this much. Men don't usually get *quite* so carried away with these things, but he seems to be more in touch with his feelings than the average guy, so there's a better than even chance.

Out of necessity, I take a bath because the shower nozzle has the weakest water pressure I've ever seen. It's a freestanding ceramic tub with characterful legs that make the whole thing wobble precariously when I sit up or recline.

I even shave, which has become quite the rarity. No, Alexander won't see my legs up close (yet), but it still makes me feel a bit more like a velvety vixen.

My body isn't nearly the spindly thing it used to be, as the carbs have caught up to me over the years, and I now disdain the curves that I spent my teen years desiring. I guess that's just how we're wired as women—to always want to look different from the way we do right now.

I've gotten better, though, at hiding and disguising the parts I don't like through spandex shapewear and tailored suits. Keratin treatments have smoothed and straightened my naturally frizzy hair, and I've dyed it a rich chocolatey shade to cover up the lackluster mousy brown. My bushy brows have been laminated, so they're sleek and shapely, and expensive foundation covers up the acne scars from old breakouts, and some new ones too because apparently I haven't yet outgrown the pimple-popping life stage.

In hopes of emanating a more sensual aura through the window, I spritz myself with my best Burberry perfume, which promptly makes me sneeze and coat my floral-scented wrists in snot.

I decide to blow dry my shoulder-length hair, something I haven't actually done since moving here. Once I'm a CEO, I'll have twice-a-week blowouts and a personal stylist, but for now, ponytails and dry shampoo get me through. Plugging my blow dryer into the adapter and then the outlet, I flip my head upside down. There's a dramatic zapping sound, and a burning plastic odor fills the bathroom. Too late, I recall what I've heard about US blow dryers not taking kindly to UK adapters. The voltage is wacky, and a section of my hair is caught in back of the blow dryer, and I have to snip the charred strands free with scissors.

Doing my best not to extrapolate this as an omen for what's to come, I spend a few minutes attempting to style my wet bangs before giving up and just pinning them back. (Note to self: Never ever let a hairdresser talk you into getting bangs again, no matter how inviting "just a wee fringe" sounds in her accent. You simply do not have the face shape to make it work or the patience for the maintenance. End of story.) The only benefit of the bangs is that they cover the forehead lines that are deepening every day, accelerated by work-related stress. I've always felt too young for Botox, but that's starting to change. On the plus side, I don't yet have crow's feet around my eyes, though perhaps that's just a sign that I don't laugh enough.

I clean up my desk a bit, hiding the Shreddies so Alexander won't suspect that I'm one of those uncivilized people who reaches her hand straight into the box and shovels down cereal between meetings. He'll find my little quirks adorable later on, but in these delicate early stages, it's important to present a more polished image.

In the spirit of decorum, I eat my crumpet with a fork and knife and slowly sip chamomile tea, taking deep breaths to trick myself into believing that I'm calm as can be. My nervous system is too smart for those games, though, all keyed up as if I've been hooked up to a caffeine IV.

Yesterday, Alexander came by a few minutes before eight, so today I'm superglued to the window by seven forty-five.

Outside, the world is going about its business as if there's nothing special whatsoever, completely oblivious to the emotional earthquake that broke the Richter scale. The queue is still winding out of Gail's, the cyclists are still maniacally zigzagging through the cars, the church bell is still tolling from the limestone spire on the quarter hour. I want to give everyone a good shake, tip the snow globe and, watch the flakes flutter and fall in new places.

But the monotony reassures me as much as it riles me. It means Alexander, too, will be following his same routine as yesterday.

A number 4 bus rolls up to the St. Mary's stop, halting to a standstill to let passengers on and off. My breath goes on strike as I scan and rescan the top deck for Alexander. He's going to be there. He's got to be.

But he's not.

The same pattern persists for the next two 4 buses that pass by. My stomach jolts up to my pinched throat and plummets back down again like an amusement park ride, sans the amusement.

Eight o'clock comes and goes. The work emails surge in, one after another. I log onto my computer and jiggle the cursor so the "available" green dot appears by my name. It's a useful hack to make my boss feel like I'm right there at his beck and call, even if my spirit is far, far away, floating through the heavens that aren't seeming quite as lucky as they did yesterday.

As I keep staring out the window, my eyes become dry and itchy, and my faith starts to shake from Alexander's sustained absence.

I do my best to formulate a reasonable explanation. Maybe Alexander doesn't actually commute on the 4 bus at all—perhaps he had a special meeting yesterday that brought him this way. And he wanted to take the same route today so he could see me again, but he had to attend a ribbon-cutting ceremony for a charity event in Notting Hill and didn't feel right prioritizing his romantic pursuits over his philanthropic commitments.

I can respect that chain of events, even if I don't agree with his decision.

But then the darker theories start clawing at me. Maybe he actually *was* on one of the buses that passed by, but he was seated on the far side, or the bottom deck, so I couldn't see him. Maybe he didn't care enough to try to find me again.

This scenario scrapes as I try to swallow it. It would mean that he didn't feel the same connection as I did. And one-sided connection isn't really connection at all. It's just obsession.

Maybe Jules was right to be a skeptic. Maybe I read our eye contact wrong. Maybe it was nothing but a one-time gift to help me feel less alone in this overcrowded, isolated world. Something to help me believe that I wouldn't always be numb. That I could and would feel again.

I try to make peace with it, the poetic arc of all that might have been. But turmoil churns inside of me, that frenzied longing to fill the blank pages, to scribble calligraphy love notes all over them with Alexander's fountain pen.

Is there anything crueler than having such tantalizing beauty snatched away before having a fair chance to explore it? I wish I'd never gotten a glimpse at all.

Mateo's accusations ring in my ears, the words he left me with when I left him: "You have such unrealistic expectations. Good fucking luck finding someone who lives up."

Alexander was going to prove Mateo wrong. He was going to show that I *could* find someone who lived up to my ideal. That I could have a fairy-tale beginning that also became a fairy-tale ending. That initial attraction could grow and strengthen over time, rather than just fade and fracture.

Losing Alexander before I ever even had him feels like a vortex of gravity yanking me back to the stone-cold earth, telling me to wake up and smell the urban dumpsters because I'll never marry a prince or be a duchess. I'll always just be Kat, a type-A overachiever who never fails to fail when it comes to true love.

CHAPTER FOUR

I invested so much time—*wasted* so much time, it feels like—in a relationship with Mateo that didn't work out. I can't get those good years of my life back, and now I have to start all over again with someone new. Someone who isn't Alexander after all.

The prospect of being spit back out into the dismal dating pool and having to re-download the apps to keep swiping soullessly for my soulmate makes me physically nauseous.

By eight thirty AM, I'm forced to accept defeat and join a Zoom catch-up with my boss to discuss phase one of our project, which we're presenting to Turpi next week.

Turpi has refused to enter the twenty-first century, so they're being left in the polluted dust by all their competitors who started investing in clean energy years ago. New environmental regulations across Europe are setting caps on emissions, and Turpi's business model is under attack from policy makers and socially conscious investors alike. But rather than pivot or wake up to the inconvenient truth that they're part of a melting iceberg (and are quite literally melting the icebergs themselves with their contribution to global warming), Turpi has doubled down on fossil fuels. They've hired Leo & Sons to assess how they can "improve operational efficiency" (i.e., strip out costs through some combination of automating processes and firing people).

As the case leader, I'm managing the project and am responsible for the deliverables as well as the two junior consultants on our team. My boss, Oliver, is the partner on the case, which means he doesn't do any of the actual work. Somewhere north of fifty, Oliver has a one-expression-fits-all stoicism and wears unvarying charcoal pinstripe suits, whose double-breasted blazers he always buttons over his monochrome ties and portly belly. His hobbies include micromanaging to convince himself he's not losing relevance and leaving the office at one PM to play golf, in that order. As far as I can tell, he's simply there to provide the stature and gravity that I apparently lack.

"I really think we need to include the data that show that expanding into renewable energy is Turpi's best bet," I tell Oliver through the screen. "Even without government subsidies, solar and wind have become cheaper than oil and gas in many markets. Sure, there'll be an initial hit to profits as Turpi invests in the infrastructure, but it's the best long-term option. The *only* long-term option, really." I've made this point about a dozen times, and each time Oliver says the same thing.

"I'm not arguing with your numbers, Kat," he replies. His crisp English accent has the infuriating effect of making insane things sound quite sensible. "But we need to take our direction from the client. Harold has made it very clear that he's opposed to renewables, so that's that."

Harold is Turpi's CEO, the one who called me *Kitten* on yesterday's call. His great-great-grandfather founded the business, so Harold now sits in his predestined throne as king of the dynasty. He quite literally wears his arrogance on his sleeve with monogramed cuff links and gold pinky rings on each hand, and he has a bad habit of dropping his eyes to my chest when I'm talking, like he thinks he's above modern rules of appropriate workplace behavior. He's part of the reason I prefer working from home. And also part of the reason I need to become a CEO someday, to kick his generation right out of the corner offices with my pointy-toed pumps.

Neither of my parents are in the business world. Dad's a social worker and Mom's always stayed home. But ever since I can remember, they told me I could be whatever I wanted when I grew up, even president or a Fortune 500 CEO. When I asked what a CEO was, Dad said it was the person who got to tell everyone else what to do. "And they never have to wash their own dishes," I remember Mom adding. I thought that sounded pretty great—the no dishes part especially—and as I got older, the allure only grew.

It's why I worked so hard to get into the University of Michigan and then to land a coveted Wall Street job after graduation, subsisting on cold brew and four hours of sleep per night before taking the Leo & Sons job to work with global CEOs.

Generations of women have fought hard for equality, and now it's my turn to stand on their shoulders and help finish the work, or at least take it one notch farther. I'll swing a sledgehammer through the frat house roof and throw a party as it falls to the ground and we women dance on broken glass, admiring our limitless reflections in the shards that once caged us.

My ambition hasn't come without fallout. Friendships have fizzled, my family have been hurt by how little I see them, and Mateo probably blames my travel schedule for our relationship faltering, though I know deep down it was something bigger.

"But aren't we ethically compelled to tell the truth about their failing business model?" I ask Oliver now, trying to keep from sounding argumentative while also standing my ground. "Investing in renewable energy is the right thing to do from both an economic and an environmental perspective."

I'm not someone who goes to climate rallies or anything, but I'd like to be on the right side of history and not feel like I'm contributing to Earth's destruction by condoning—even empowering—Turpi's flagrant carbon emissions. And the financial models are on the same side as my morals. "The future is green, no matter which way you look at it."

"I hear you," Oliver says, "but let's not forget that Turpi is paying us ten million pounds for this project. Our job is to make them happy."

"I thought our job was to make them money."

My stony-faced boss nearly smiles at that, like my naivete is darling indeed. "How about this," he proposes. "No clean energy slides in the PowerPoint, but you can voice over that side of things during the meeting and gauge Harold's reaction. Fair play?"

I want to push back, but Oliver is in charge of my promotion, which basically feels like he's in charge of my entire future. So I grit my teeth and repeat, "Fair play."

It's probably good that I have the presentation to focus on for the rest of the day so I don't obsess about Alexander and how he let me down. If I'm being self-aware about it, I *am* still obsessing, but it's layered beneath the work stuff, shoved under the stress and deadlines of corporate life.

Did you see him again?! Jules texts in the afternoon.

Nope, I reply without explanation. I'm not in the mood to talk about it.

Aww shite babes. But there's always tomorrow! Xxx

Her optimism annoys me as much as her pessimism did yesterday. I've just about accepted that nothing is going to happen with Alexander, and her cheeriness feels like it's rubbing salt in my open wound.

Yup! I text back because I don't want Jules thinking I'm mad at her when I'm really just mad at myself and the world, and this love lottery that seems to have voided my winning ticket. There's always tomorrow.

*　　*　　*

It turns out that I haven't successfully given up on Alexander after all. All night, I'm back conjuring up dreamlike scenarios where he meets my eyes and silently pledges his unfailing attachment until the grave and beyond.

It's not that he's not interested in me, I conclude when I groggily get out of bed the next morning. I must have just jinxed it by trying too hard.

So, back to my most authentic self, I scarf down my crumpet with one hand while scooping Shreddies from the box with the other. Logging onto my computer, I scroll through my emails. There's an updated presentation in my inbox, sent across at 3:48 AM by one of the junior consultants on my team. The twinge of guilt I feel that she stayed up so late working on it quickly fades away as I recall all the years I grinded through all-nighters too. Everyone has to put in their time to make it to the top.

Unless you're like Harold and born into privilege. Or Alexander, but that's different—he still takes the bus and probably even does his own Waitrose grocery shopping.

Apparently I haven't successfully stopped thinking about him. I glance out the window every now and then (okay, every ten seconds) but my eyes aren't stuck to the street the way they were yesterday.

A 4 bus rolls up to St. Mary's, humming to a stop right in front of me. Allowing myself one quick glance, I brace for the letdown. But there isn't one.

He's there again, back in the exact same spot, reading his magazine and looking just as jaw-droppingly gorgeous as I'd made him out to be in my memory.

He's wearing the same peacoat and maroon scarf as last time, which I find perfectly endearing. What a wonderful quality that he isn't one of those overly showy princes who refuses to be caught in the same outfit twice. It fits with what I've already suspected about him—that he's a man of the people who wants to understand the plights we commoners face, even though he's clearly the least common human in the history of humanity.

Amid my delight, there's devastation. He's so casually staring down at his magazine, seemingly oblivious to my presence. With all my lost and refound hopes, I channel my most alluring energy, willing him to look up at me as new passengers board the bus. But he doesn't shift his gaze, not even an inch.

Wild with desperation—but with the competing need to appear cool as a cucumber—I stand up and fiddle with my linen drapes in hopes that Alexander's peripheral vision will snag on the movement and compel him to look at me. It's ever so slightly more subtle than the alternative of pounding on the window and bellowing, *"HEL-LOOOO, MY LOVE . . . LOOK HITHER!"*

But somehow, despite all rhyme or reason, Alexander remains immune to my bewitching powers and keeps staring down at the magazine as if it's the most riveting thing on the planet.

And then the bus is gone, rolling away and flattening my dreams as it goes.

I'm alone again with my disappointment. It's a different flavor this time. There's the sweetness of having seen him again mixed with new sourness at having been so completely snubbed.

It's a heavy blow, to feel invisible to someone I was so sure had seen me. Did he not feel the spark? Did he forget where my flat was? Is he already in a relationship and trying his very best to resist the monumental temptation I present?

Or, the other voice in my head—the kinder contrarian—interjects, *maybe he's simply too much of a gentleman to be caught staring up at a lady in her home.*

It's a fair point, and one I grip with both hands and feet. Could what I perceived as indifference actually have been self-restraint?

I don't want to make excuses for him, but he was no doubt raised in a traditional household with prim and proper manners. And given how cautious the Brits are not to intrude upon other people's space, it's quite possible that Alexander was hoping I was looking at him—burning to know if I was—as he passed my flat just now, but was too respectful to verify it.

As my emotions tangle, relief rises to the surface. The one thing I know is that he consistently rides a 4 bus. It wasn't just a one-off. He'll be back again.

It's Friday, and though I would usually welcome that fact, it now fills me with agony at having to wait until *next week* to see Alexander again. For as down-to-earth as he is, he certainly spends his weekends in limos and private jets, not buses, and I can't fault him for that.

Around six PM, Harold sends me a WhatsApp message. Kitten! Come to Annabel's tonight, we're getting a table. Just mention my name at the door and you're golden.

Since it's the job of consultants to be on call 24/7 for our clients, I've had to provide Harold with my cell number. He doesn't hesitate using it.

Annabel's is one of London's most glamorous members clubs, and if it were another occasion, I'd be all for tossing back espresso martinis and rubbing shoulders with A-listers. But the idea of having to be "on" for work snuffs all the fun out of the situation. I can't have more than one drink without risking being deemed an airheaded party girl. And it's not like Harold and his gang would be pleasant company. Far from it.

My name is Kat, I reply, more fearless over text than in person. And thanks for the invite, but I'm actually heading out of town for the weekend.

It's not a lie—just an exaggeration. I'm off to Bath on a solo trip, but not until tomorrow morning. Tonight, I just sprawl out on the couch with a pint of brownie macchiato gelato, bingeing *Married at First Sight*, a popular UK reality show that's sort of the British equivalent to *The Bachelor*. Strangers are matched in a social experiment, and the first time they meet is at their wedding. Some of the couples from prior seasons are still married and have kids together. I've become somewhat addicted to the show and the way it offers up evidence that fairy tales don't have to be fictional.

I restrain myself from looking up spoilers for the current season, but there are two couples that I'm convinced will make it even after the filming ends. They have the most tender eye contact, and they're definitely going to go the distance.

Just like Alexander and me.

CHAPTER FIVE

It's in Bath where I really start to bond with Alexander on a deeper level. We have no shortage of things to talk about as I picture him walking beside me, arm in arm, through the postcard-perfect streets.

It's a stunning sandstone town set down in a valley and named after the ancient Roman baths that were built around natural hot springs. When I get off the train and start past the grand colonnades, archways, and cathedrals, I expect the usual loneliness to seep in. The harsh juxtaposition of the external splendor to the internal emptiness. But the loneliness doesn't arrive. Instead, I'm buoyed by a comforting sense of companionship. It's so easy to imagine Alexander here with me, and the make-believe conversations we've been having feel more real than anything has in quite some time.

I ask his opinion on the art gallery I stroll through (he much prefers Romanticism to Modernism), hear him recount the details of his cousin's wedding ceremony in Bath's Assembly Rooms (the queen couldn't attend but sent a handwritten card), and, after much persuasion, get him to divulge the story of the first time he was drunk (he was twelve, at the kids' table, and the nanny accidentally put a pitcher of wine, instead of Ribena, at their table).

And as we rest on a bench in the abbey courtyard, listening to a busker strum along on the guitar, Alexander deftly turns the attention onto me. *"And how about you, my lovely lady?"* he asks. *"Tell me your story. Is Kat short for Katherine?"*

"Actually no, it's just Kat, I say," reveling in how delicately he says my name, like he wants to treat it with care. My dad says it's because he can't spell words that have more than one syllable.

I'm worried Alexander will think I'm from a total hillbilly family, but he just laughs quietly, in even increments that have a soothing effect. *"What part of The States did you grow up in?"* he wants to know.

"In the Midwest. Kalamazoo, Michigan, to be exact. Funny name, I know. Lots of cows and cornfields."

"Is that quite near the Great Lakes?" he asks, contemplative expression ever so attractive.

"Impressive geography knowledge." I applaud and show him a photo on my phone. *"This is Lake Michigan. We'd go to the beach in the summer, or else just hang out on the little lake behind my parents' house."*

"Stunning," he says, but he's staring more at me than at the photo. *"Looks like the seaside in Cornwall where I learned to ride horses."*

"Michigan winters are freezing though. We had to walk two miles to school through feet of snow because the superintendent didn't believe in snow days, even if the buses got stuck. And wow, I sound like my grandparents right now."

"I reckon that's a rather charming life," Alexander says with his refined smile. *"I quite fancy the idea of being off the grid. Escaping the rat race."*

"Well, you're very welcome to come visit at Christmas," I say. *"My parents would simply adore you."*

I'm aware that this kind of thing is way too bold for me to actually speak aloud, but that's the best thing about imaginary conversations. You can give yourself lines that are much more eloquent and daring than the inarticulate fragments you'd stutter in real life.

"You reckon they'd approve?" Alexander says, frowning with a flattering sort of fret.

"No doubt. Mom will love you right away, making you say all these words in your accent while putting you to work peeling potatoes. And Dad and my brothers will start out skeptical of a foreigner, but they'll come around when you go snowshoe rabbit hunting with them and don't wince in the hypothermia-inducing air."

"Snowshoe rabbit hunting? That sounds capital!"

"We'll see what you think when you return with blue lips."

"Well, perhaps you could be so kind as to help me warm them up?"

"I think I could do that."

"My apologies, that was rather cheeky of me . . ."

Raindrops land on my lips, which are split into a blithe smile. I'm brought back to the scene before me, where the busker is now playing The Beatles' "Here Comes the Sun" as the clouds drizzle with that dry English humor.

I find myself thinking about how Mateo never visited Kalamazoo. We'd spend vacations in Florida, or with his family in California. *"Why would we go to that place? It's a right-wing echo chamber in the Arctic, like you're always saying,"* he'd shoot down whenever I'd broach the idea of paying Michigan a visit. *"Let's just fly your folks to Miami."*

While dating Mateo, I'd actually liked how his veto gave me an excuse not to return to my hometown, not to have to relive those cringeworthy years before I found my footing. But looking back, I see it differently.

Mateo's version of me was someone who'd always been a confident city slicker who could afford Ritz-Carlton weekend trips. He had no interest in seeing the shy country girl who'd clipped Meijer grocery coupons at the kitchen table and built forts in the woods, making friends with the voices in her head because she hadn't been invited to the sleepover.

In a way, I think this has actually been one of the things that's helped me get over Mateo. I can only miss him with the parts of me that he really saw. And it turns out he didn't see that much of me after all. He just wasn't that curious.

"I'm curious," Alexander murmurs in my ear. *"I want to see all of you."*

I'm perfectly aware of my insanity, but the benefit of being alone all weekend is that I don't have to rationalize it for anyone. I can just bask in its glow and follow it to the ethereal ends of the earth.

Still half in the dazzle of my daze, I seek shelter from the rain at The Bath Bun, a traditional, floral-patterned tea shop tucked away in a sycamore-tree square. A waiter greets me, dressed in a lace apron and old-fashioned bonnet. "Is it just you today?" she asks with a pitying smile.

"Yes," I say, self-aware enough of my crazed state to abstain from explaining the whole story about how I'm actually accompanied by the living phantom of a prince who's working up the courage to make a move after we've made eye contact exactly once while he was passing by on public transportation. "Just me today."

CHAPTER SIX

Back in London, I scamper out of bed on Monday like a little kid on Christmas morning. It feels like it's been ages since I've seen Alexander in the flesh, and I'm frothing over with the anticipation of seeing my prince again, of catching his eye and holding on for dear life.

I start to temper my expectations in case he's not there. But then I say to hell with it. I'd rather crash from a great height than never have seen the view at all.

Perched on the edge of my ergonomic chair, I sip my tea with my pinky gracefully outstretched, sitting up straight and elongating my torso to give the appearance that I'm taller than the puny five foot two that I am. I practice my most effortlessly charming oh-hello-love-of-my-life-didn't-see-you-there smile. My teeth are bright and straight from years of braces and annual whitening sessions, but my lips are on the thin side, so I keep them coated in liner, which leaves them dry and chapped. I'm always dabbing on new brands of lip balm, each as ineffective as the last.

My eyes flit between my computer screen and the window. Then, at seven forty-five on the dot, he's there. And not just that, but he's looking out the bus window, gazing up at me with that chiseled countenance and pensive passion. His deep brown eyes intertwine with mine in one fell swoop, and my body freezes and breaks out in sweat at the same time.

It's all the corroboration I need to confirm that he feels it too. That he's equally aware of, and enthralled by, our otherworldly connection. That his dreams and desires align with my own.

I try to wave or smile or stand up, but I stay stiff as a scarecrow, having as little control over my appendages as I do over my emotions. Our eye contact breaks with a terrible clatter as he looks down at his lap, like he's embarrassed to have been caught spying.

Damn the English and their propriety.

But even amid the agony of our truncated ocular conversation, I can't help but admire his manners, his restraint. He's clearly a gentleman who doesn't want to come on too strong. Anyone with lesser breeding would be crawling through my window by now, hoping for a quickie before work. This proves he's looking for something serious, not just a casual fling.

The bus leaves the stop, and Alexander is out of sight, but certainly not out of mind or out of heart.

I feel lighter all day, like there are springs beneath the warped hardwood floor of my flat, sending me upward into the reverie that just might become my reality after all. While on mute during Zoom meetings, I flip-flop between gleefully humming Disney tunes and furiously chiding myself for not being more flirtatious while he was looking my way.

"You need to give boys some encouragement." I hear my mom's advice, back from my high school days. It feels equally relevant now since I've basically become a bashful, besotted teenager once more. *"They're intimidated by you."*

That was always the reason my mom would use to justify why I was single for every school dance. It couldn't have had anything to do with my acne or ACT books or overall awkwardness. I was simply too beautiful and brilliant for my own good. And the best thing was that she genuinely believed it.

Next time, I decide. Next time I see Alexander, I'll give him some encouragement. Smile his way and maybe even bare a few teeth if I'm feeling bold.

"What're you smiling about, Kat?" one of the junior consultants asks as I daydream about it during one of the Zoom meetings.

"Just excited for the presentation tomorrow," I lie smoothly, accustomed to masking my feelings at work before anyone gets a good look. "I think the management team will be pleased with our analysis."

The junior looks unconvinced but doesn't probe. He has too many things on his to-do list to waste time investigating how his boss might possibly have the bandwidth to be happy.

*   *   *

I go into the office the next day for the presentation. Having to head out early, I know I'll miss Alexander. It sends a pang through me, enduring another twenty-four hours of estrangement. I hope he won't read my absence as a sign of my disinterest, or worry that he scared me off with the intensity of his eye contact. The thought of making him doubt my feelings is excruciating, but he'll have to wait until tomorrow to have his questions answered.

It's important that I'm face-to-face for the presentation since Turpi's management team is old school and places a "high value on the intangibles of in-person interactions." Which means the men get a power trip from seeing how many bodies are physically strapped into their seats all day, carrying out orders like the dutiful cogs they are.

I don't like the rules of the game, but I still have to play by them to get to the next level. Alexander appreciates that I'm a career-driven woman, finds it refreshing after the coddled finishing school girls he's mingled with all his life. He's told me as much in our conversations already.

I take the tube from Angel Station over to Canary Wharf, where Turpi's headquarters are located. Canary Wharf is the charmless, soulless business district east of Central London, located on the Isle of the Dogs, a very apt name. Full of half-empty skyscrapers and half-used yachts, it's pretty much another Wall Street, perched on the Thames instead of the Hudson.

Drained before the day has begun, I traipse into Turpi's opulent lobby. As a consultant, I work on-site at the client's office while I'm staffed on the case. My commuter trainers, squeaking on the porcelain tiles, are soggy from the morning rain shower. In the loo that's almost always empty due to the lack of women who work here, I whiz through my two-minute makeup routine and take the lifts to the thirty-second floor.

Consultants are notoriously assigned the worst of the seating at clients' offices, and Turpi has relegated me to one of the scrunched desks in the open floor plan, a sitting duck to be roped into another request that I have to say yes to because the client comes first, and pushing back would lose me points if it got back to Oliver, jeopardizing my promotion.

I swap out my trainers for a pair of tall pumps I keep under my desk. All the research shows that taller people are favored when it comes to pay and promotions. It's one of the factors that holds women back. So for a decade now, I've been wearing toe-pinching heels as an equalizing tactic. My feet have become numb to the pain, and I take this as proof of my progress.

After firing off a few emails at my desk and ensuring that the juniors have printed out the presentations to the higher-ups' liking (single-sided, size 11.5 font, 1.25-inch margins), I make my way over to the conference room.

A long, sleek table is fitted with twelve beige leather chairs. The floor-to-ceiling windows are speckled with raindrops, and the melancholy Thames is just barely visible through layers of haze. It feels like we're suspended in clouds, but with none of the fluffy lightness you'd hope for.

Harold is sitting at the head of the table. He has the build of a former rugby player who refuses to accept that his prime is decades behind him. His sagging skin, always spray-tanned, is inflated with all sorts of fillers as he wages a war on wrinkles. Going bald is something else he's fighting, as his thinning hair—longish, stringy, and dyed butter blonde—is always fluffed up in an elaborate effort to hide his scalp. Perhaps it's the ridiculous hair or the extravagant pocket squares in his suits or the fact that he's newly divorced (for the third time), but he reminds me of a parading peacock.

Turpi's CFO and COO are seated on either side of Harold like drooling yes-men. From Leo & Sons, it's just Oliver and me. The juniors aren't invited to the meeting—they just circulate the meeting requests and prepare the materials.

Sitting down next to Oliver, I adjust my chair to its full height and lean in with my elbows propped confidently on the table so the men will be more inclined to take my words seriously. The only other woman in the room is Harold's assistant, who's scurrying in and out, delivering tea and biscuits as if we're invalids who can't get out of our chairs and help ourselves. It makes me cringe, and I'm comforted only by knowing that when I'm CEO, that kind of thing will never happen.

"Good to see you again in person, Kitten," Harold says, eyeing me up and down like it's part of his job description. "That turtleneck is as high as the Eiffel Tower." He pounds his hands on the table, pinky rings rattling hollowly as he tosses his head back and roars with laughter.

A furnace burns under my flustered cheeks. The black turtleneck I'm wearing under my blazer is indeed quite high. The intent in dressing like a nun was to increase the professionalism of the meeting, but apparently that was very idealistic of me.

"Let's get started, shall we?" Oliver says, perhaps trying to deflect the crass comment, or just in a rush to get through all forty-two slides in our deck.

Harold's assistant fiddles with the projector, and the first slide of our PowerPoint deck shows up, large and illuminated, on the wall, complete with the riveting title: *Phase One Recommendation to Increase Turpi's Profit Margins and Return on Equity.*

More than happy to take credit for the work he hasn't done, Oliver walks through the recommendations to reduce global headcount by twenty-five percent.

Stats like this used to devastate me. *Cut one quarter of all employees? Are you kidding?* Behind that single number are thousands of names and stories, individual people who will have to find another way to put food on the table for their families and pay for their kids' education.

But today I just hear it as another amorphous statistic, an eye-catching figure to please the client who's funding our salaries and bonuses. My skin has hardened, but I'm not sorry for it. The only way to move up is by dialing down sentimentality and mimicking the unruffled approach that men have mastered for so long.

Still, I'm not going to turn into a total doormat. At the end of the presentation, I voice my argument for expanding into clean energy. "I'd like to bring up the elephant in the room," I say, meeting the eyes of my audience to help the words sink in. "In order to stay competitive, it's time for Turpi to start playing offense, not just defense. And yes, that means renewables. Solar and wind would result in a short-term hit to profits as you invest in the infrastructure, but in year three and beyond, it's highly accretive. You'll plug your losses from the bottom up and see double-digit growth in both revenue and profits."

Harold's orangey face twists into a smile, like he's in on some joke that's too vulgar for my womanly ears. "Retirement sounds pretty good in about three years," he says. "What d'you reckon, lads?"

His compadres chortle in agreement, and the implication is clear. These three "leaders" don't care how the company does after they're gone—or even if it survives at all. They just want to coast along with the status quo, stripping out as many costs as possible to increase the value of their stock options before cashing out and leaving their successors to deal with the consequences.

"Green energy is just a fad anyway," Harold goes on. "Mark my words."

I want to point out all the flaws in his argument, but Oliver shoots me a look across the table—a look that says *"Let it rest, Kat. Remember your place."*

And so that's what I do. Bite my tongue and stay silent during the bullshit Harold is spewing, repeating to myself that I can fix this kind of thing later, once I'm calling the shots at the top of the ladder. For now, I need to stay focused on getting to the next rung. Sometimes the end justifies the means.

After we wrap up, the men file out of the room. I follow them out, but Harold pauses in the doorway, blocking my exit. "I've got to say, Kitten, it was hard for me to disagree with you," he says. "The way you were batting those eyelashes."

"No eyelash batting," I say, jaw clenched. "I was just presenting the facts."

Harold pats my shoulder, a gesture of condolence that makes my skin crawl. "You want to know what the real problem is here?" he goes on.

"What's that?" I ask, knowing I won't like the answer.

"You're too pretty for this kind of work," he says. "You're wasting your prime grubbing away when you should be out having a bloody good time."

I feel like I've been slapped on the skin beneath my turtleneck. "Looks don't have anything to do with it," I reply, trying to think of a more assertive retort to put him in his place, but too caught off guard by his unabashed ambush.

"Looks always have something to do with it, luv," Harold says. And he waves his hand to let me go in front of him through the doorway, as if he's the most chivalrous man of them all.

CHAPTER SEVEN

I swing by the King's Head after work, in need of a drink and a distraction. Tucked into the ground floor of a Victorian townhouse, the pub is quaint and cozy, heavy on mahogany and musk. In the window, a sign boasts "Oldest theatre pub since Shakespearean times," a rather common claim in these parts. A coal fireplace burns in the corner, and an eclectic mix of antique mirrors, sepia-tone portraits, and health and safety certifications dot the forest-green wallpaper.

It's Thursday, London's rowdiest night of the week, and the tables and high-tops are packed with cigar-puffing men who give off the impression they've been coming here for thirty years, juxtaposed with younger creative types who had likely intended to soak up some culture in the backroom theatre but were so wrapped up in their groundbreaking arguments about the meaning of life that they decided to skip the show for another round of pints and pickled eggs.

I'm hoping Jules will be there. And sure enough, she is, working behind the horseshoe-shaped bar, pouring liquid gold from the everlasting tap. Her curly red hair is slung into a top knot, and she's wearing frayed jeans and a King's Head polo that she's cut the collar off of, pushing the dress code as far toward casual as it can go. "Y'right?" she says when she sees me. "Bloody 'ell, look at your costume."

Having come straight from the office, I'm still in my pantsuit. "It's not a costume," I say, though I wonder if it might be—if maybe I'm just playing dress-up to try to get people to see me as someone they never will.

Claiming the last open stool, I keep my leather tote bag on my lap so it won't have to touch the dusty floorboards. "Long day at work," I say with a grimace.

"A tumble down the sink should 'elp," Jules declares with confidence.

"What?" I scowl. "How on earth would tumbling down the sink help?"

"It means a drink," she says, setting a foamy pint of Young's ale in front of me. "Keep up with the cockney rhyming slang, what'd I tell you?"

In East London where Jules grew up, it's tradition to randomly replace the word you actually mean with a rhyming phrase. The coded language evidently started centuries ago as a traveling salesmen's tactic to confuse buyers, and some of it has stuck around, likely for the sole purpose of confusing outsiders like me.

"Oh," I say, sipping gratefully and feeling the ale seep down into my stiff bones like oil. "Wipe the tears."

"What's that? You gutted 'bout something?"

"No," I say. "'Wipe the tears' fits the cockney rhyming scheme for 'cheers,' doesn't it?"

47

"Ah no, you can't just make it up as you go, I'm afraid. There are specific phrases you've got to choose from."

"No fun." I pout.

"So 'ow's the prince hunt going?" Jules asks, leaning her elbows on the counter and flashing her wrist tattoo. She's told me that she and Nina got matching designs—overlapping circles—the night of their engagement, to symbolize two wholes joining together, not two halves. "Give me all the goss."

Bubbles fizz in my stomach. "I saw him yesterday," I say. It feels achingly long ago. "He looked at me again. Straight in the eye."

Jules lets out a whistle. "Why aren't you more chuffed about this?"

She's understandably thrown off by my low-key demeanor after I've been high-key obsessing about him.

"Just frustrated with work stuff." I want to be daydreaming about Alexander, but Harold's self-righteous face is taking up all the real estate in my mind, poisoning my bliss.

"We work to live, not live to work. Don't forget that," Jules says. "Now I've got ter get your nosh." She heads back to the kitchen and returns a moment later with a plate of food that she puts in front of me. "Salt beef bagel," she presents proudly. "Best in town."

A toasted bagel is overflowing with meat, mustard, coleslaw, and pickles. I take a bite, mostly to be polite, and I'm surprised at how good it is, filling a craving I didn't know I had.

"Lush, innit?" Jules says, looking pleased. "So when's the engagement 'appening?"

I can tell she's trying to boost my spirits, but I'm not in the mood for it. "Don't mock me. You said so yourself, I'm wasting my time with the bus lad."

"C'mon, I was only taking the piss," Jules says. "Just go talk to 'im, what d'you have to lose?"

"Only the very last scraps of my heart," I answer, pouring on the melodrama.

Because here's the thing: I'd forgotten how magnificent it was to have a crush. That swelling of boundless promise, all the immaculate imaginings of what might be and could be and will be.

Part of me is convinced that Alexander and I really are going to work out. But the other part, the spiky logic lurking beneath the cotton covers, is aware that there's a *slight* chance that I may have overhyped this whole thing, and that as soon as I touch it, the crush will pop in my face and leave my eyes stinging with residue. And that I'll be slung straight back to the drawing board.

"What if he's not like what I pictured?" I say to Jules. "Or what if *I'm* not like he's pictured?" My voice is small but the fear is big.

"Then we'll find another bloke for you to shag," Jules says, ever the pragmatist. "Not exactly a difficult task."

"That would make me feel worse," I say, sulking.

"China plate," Jules says, helping herself to a couple of my thick-cut chips and drowning them in mayo. "That means 'mate,' by the way. Reckon we're getting ahead of ourselves. Maybe 'e'll turn out to be exactly the man you think he is."

I perk up a bit. "I think he might."

"So tomorrow you'll find out."

"Tomorrow?" I screech, like a baby bird whose mother has just left the nest. "I can't. It's too soon—we need to build a stronger foundation."

"Meaning you need to make more eye contact from afar?" Jules clarifies.

"Correct. It's a slow burn, and I like it like that."

"Quit faffing around, babes," Jules says. "You're not Rapunzel waiting in the tower for 'er bloody prince to come and save 'er."

"I know that," I say, bristling. "I'm a future CEO."

It sounds harsher than I intend, like I'm putting down the fact that Jules doesn't have grand career aspirations, that she's happy bartending for as few hours a week as it takes to cover her living costs.

"What I mean," I clarify, "is I'm not ready to talk to him. Not yet."

I just can't take that kind of disappointment right now. For a little while longer, I want to stay curled up in the cocoon of my unblemished fantasy. Preserve this symbol of hope without having it exposed as faux.

I know it sounds absurd, that I could be wrecked by a complete stranger not turning out to be who I thought he was, but that's how it feels. Alexander has helped me feel vindicated for breaking up with Mateo, helped show me what I want and deserve in a partner. And he now represents so much more about my beliefs in love and serendipity and happy endings. It's probably not fair to him to have to carry all this on his broad shoulders, but it really can't be helped anymore.

The story is there, and I add to it each morning I see him. It's brightened up my whole life, and I don't want to risk losing the light. Not yet.

Perhaps Jules picks up on my unspoken thoughts. "Righ'o, babes," she says. "I'm giving you one more fortnight to pine from afar, and then you're getting on the bus and talking to the bloke. Or I'll get on myself and tell 'im you fancy 'im."

"You wouldn't."

"Wouldn't I?" Jules challenges, and I know she would, in a heartbeat. "After one Jägerbomb, I've got no shame."

"Doesn't even take one," I mutter under my breath.

Customers are flagging Jules down from high-tops, but she neglects them to keep talking to me. "Just remember," Jules says, reaching over the counter to ruffle my hair in a maternal sort of way, "you're one fit baked bean."

"Is that supposed to be a compliment?"

"Means 'sexy queen,'" Jules translates. "But no matter what 'appens, me and Nina are always 'ere for a bevvy and a cuddle. Don't go forgetting that."

I'm old enough to know that Jules and I won't be close friends forever. I'll move away after my case ends, and staying in touch won't extend much past the occasional Instagram "like." But I can still appreciate that we're intersecting now, at this London juncture that's felt too sharp all by myself.

"Alright, I'll do it," I say, nodding with resolve as I wash down the beef bagel with beer. "I'll get on the bus and talk to him. Within two weeks."

"Pint-y promise?" Jules says, holding up her ale for a toast.

Praying I won't regret this, I raise my glass and clink it against hers. "Pint-y promise."

CHAPTER EIGHT

The deadline Jules has given me is Friday, the fifth of October. I'm not sticking to that deadline just because of Jules. I'm too old to let other people run my life. It's more that she's given me the kick in the shins that I need to honor the whisper inside me that's telling me to take this chance. The whisper that's telling me it *will* work out, despite all the rational stats stacked against us. And that even if it doesn't, I'll be glad I tried and took fate into my own hands rather than sitting by and being a passive protagonist in my own life story.

Still, I soak up the next couple weeks from the window, procrastinating getting on the bus for as long as I can.

It's a wild thing, knowing that within a matter of days I'll either be living out my highest hopes with the man of my dreams or crying alone on a sofa with gelato that's salted with my own tears. I'm anxious to know which of those two conclusions awaits, but in no rush to force an outcome in case it's not the one I want.

Alexander and I settle into a rhythm of sorts, as you do when you start to get intimate with someone. I go into the office on Tuesdays and Wednesdays, and Alexander is never there on Thursdays, so I only see him Mondays and Fridays—the most beautiful bookends to the week. Usually on one of those days, he'll be looking out the window, and our gazes will graze with celestial grace. It's clear that he's worried that looking at me *every* time might be overpowering and fall in the stalker category, not that I would mind, of course.

I don't want to leave it to the Friday deadline, in case something goes amiss, as in if I chicken out and refuse to board the bus. So I decide to build in a couple days of buffer and make my move on Wednesday. I'll take Alexander's bus to Blackfriars and then transfer to the tube to finish my journey to Canary Wharf. It'll double my commuting time, but that hardly matters. I don't have any meetings until later in the day anyway.

I'm a wreck getting dressed that morning, changing my outfit three times, even though I'd laid it out the night before. It brings back shades of the first day of school as a kid, those untamed butterflies flapping in my stomach as I skipped around the house, hoping with my whole heart that Davis Dean would be in my homeroom and that *this would be the year* that he'd wake up to the fact that I'd be a way better girlfriend than Alison Wells with her silky blonde hair and Abercrombie skirts. (For clarification, I have no lingering bitterness. I honestly hardly even remember their names. This is simply an illustrative example.)

In the end, I decide on a professional black jumpsuit with a bold red trench coat, hoping it strikes the right vibe of *corporate exec who's ready for a cocktail at Soho House if the situation should present itself.*

The sky is spewing that Londonesque mix of mist and rain, and I should wear my wellies, but my legs are too short for flats, so I opt for heeled booties instead. An occasion like today's is well worth scuffing up my shoes for.

I've bought a UK blow dryer that doesn't sizzle my hair, so I give myself a decent blowout and even spruce up my makeup routine with some contouring. Or rather, attempted contouring. The end result resembles nothing of the sculpted look in the YouTube video I've followed. My face just looks like it's been smeared in dirt, and my pointy cleft chin looks even more prominent than usual, making me wish I could pad it with some of the fat from my cheeks. Irritating my rosacea as I scrub myself clean in defeat, I revert to my minimalist routine to make it out the door in time.

The gales hit me straight away, and though I try to block the elements with my wooden-handled umbrella, my carefully styled hair is thrown into a state of complete disarray within thirty seconds. If my windswept look doesn't charm the argyle socks off Alexander, I'll have to rely on some good ole American charm to do the trick.

In another stroke of bad luck, the fishmonger stench is extra strong this morning, and I'm doubtful that my perfume is potent enough to withstand the raw haddock and salmon aromas seeping out from Moxton's, the small but mighty storefront wedged beside the King's Head.

Huddling under the bus stop shelter, I repeat to myself all the reasons that I'm more than capable of the task before me.

You're an independent, thirty-one-year-old woman. You're climbing the corporate ladder at lightning speed and making it on your own in a foreign country. You can board a damn bus and talk to a guy.

A 4 bus pulls up. My heart thumps in uneven increments, and my breath comes in fits and starts. It's ridiculous that I'm having such a severe physical reaction, but I'm also enthralled by it, the way my body is still so susceptible to my emotions.

He's not there.

I'm torn between disappointment and relief. I don't have too much time to recover, as the next bus comes a minute later.

And he's on this one, in his usual spot.

He's glancing out the window but of course doesn't know that he should be looking for me down on the street. I'm glad he doesn't spot me, though—I'd rather surprise him with a graceful appearance.

It feels disorienting, looking up at him from the street after weeks of peering down at him from the window. The proportions are off, and it makes me a bit dizzy. Or maybe that's just thinking about what's coming next.

Here it is, the moment I've been waiting for over the past month—and probably my whole life, for those of us (me, myself, and I) who are being dramatic about this.

You can board a damn bus. You can board a damn bus.

I repeat the mantra while trying to follow the other commuters through the open doors. But I'm stuck in place.

With anticlimactic haste, the doors squeak shut, and the bus starts down Upper Street again, sweeping Alexander away.

I regain control of my body a little too late.

Refusing to accept defeat, I start off after the bus, sprinting down the sidewalk, skidding on the damp cement in the impractical shoes that I very much regret wearing. I can't see where I'm going, as I'm still holding my umbrella like a battle shield to avoid getting completely soaked, lest I forfeit the last shred of elegance. A deranged Mary Poppins without the benefit of flight, I'm bumping into people left, right, and center, poking them with my umbrella spokes and spewing crazed apologies as I bolt onward, consumed by one thought only.

I've got to reach the Islington Green stop in time to board the bus there and redeem my cowardice. I've got to.

Panting, I pause to peek out from under my brolly to see how much farther I have left to go. The bus stop is still a ways off, and the bus is already pulling away.

I'm furious with myself. *How cowardly can you be, Kat? No wonder you're single.*

But after the initial anger, and then embarrassment, subsides, I decide it's probably a blessing in disguise that it didn't work out today. My soaked, wheezing state isn't exactly ideal for making a first impression with a prince.

Starting off toward the underground, I take my usual trains to Canary Wharf. Alexander won't be on the bus tomorrow since it's Thursday, but Friday will be the day. No excuses this time.

CHAPTER NINE

Friday starts out better right from the start. The sun is shining, and soft October rays cast a hopeful glow over my flat as I make my tea and go through a similar primping routine as before, sans the contouring. I opt for a charcoal-gray pantsuit this time, with the same red trench coat. Though I'm tempted to wear trainers based on the prior debacle, I make myself stick with heels so I'll be more likely to actually board the bus rather than run after it while an onlooker records a video and turns me into a cautionary meme.

Turning on Taylor Swift's "Love Story," I cling to its optimism as I walk down the stairs of my building and out the door into the crisp autumn air. The weather and the melody seem to be reassuring me that it's perfectly right and reasonable that I should live happily ever after with someone I fell in love with at first sight.

As I wait at the bus stop, I text Jules, just to make it that much harder for me to back out. About to introduce myself—wish me luck!

I expect that she'll still be sleeping, but she replies a moment later. Yass babes, going to the window to watch.

Don't you dare.

I look back at Marlow House. Red terracotta with cream molding, it's three stories high, plus a squished fourth floor with tiny dormers popping out from the black slate roof. The top level used to be servants' quarters, apparently, back when this entire townhome would have been owned by a single well-to-do London family, rather than spliced into six parts to renters just passing through. The aqua door was hardly wide enough for me to yank my suitcases through, but the novelty of the little mail slit and brass lion knocker makes up for the impracticality.

Triangular trims border the tall, narrow windows, and Jules's face appears in the one adjacent to my own. She blows kisses and makes some raunchy gestures, and I want to hate her for it, but it just makes me love her that much more.

A 4 bus comes into view, cruising closer, too quickly but also not fast enough. Slowing down, it huffs to a stop right in front of me.

Alexander is there, in his spot. And this time, my body is prepared.

Nerves quivering but feet staying firm, I walk onto the bus. Tapping the contactless payment on my phone, I soldier on, up the stairs. I'm out of breath by the time I get to the top, and not from the incline.

My eyes know exactly where to go to locate Alexander, and he's centered in my view as I start walking down the aisle. More than a phantom, more than a daydream. Here he is, in luminescent 3-D, right before me. Tall, dark, and as handsome as ever.

There's just one problem. The seat next to him—*my* seat—is already occupied.

Another woman is sitting there, and though she and Alexander aren't talking, or even brushing shoulders, I immediately suspect her of ulterior motives. She's clearly trying to steal him from me.

Perhaps *steal* isn't quite the right verb since I'm not technically with Alexander yet, but try telling that to my bleeding heart. It feels like betrayal, and it throws a wrench in my plan of oh-so-casually sitting next to him and watching his lips split into a demure and dreamy smile as he recognizes me as the elusive love of his life, here at last.

Alexander is looking out the window, which restores my confidence. He's obviously hoping to find me sitting at my desk. He must be feeling dejected by my absence, wondering how he'll possibly cope the rest of the day without our eye contact to get him through.

I like the notion that I'll be able to cure his sadness, and I've come too far now to be derailed. So, still unnoticed by Alexander, I take a seat a couple rows behind him and bide my time.

The back of his head has a very nice shape, and his chestnut-colored hair, which has just a slight wave to it, promises to be fantastic to run my hands through. But I can't help but notice that his scarf doesn't look to be the sophisticated Italian thread I expected. It appears to be a hand-knit thing, reminiscent of the sweaters my mom still insists on making my brothers and me every Christmas.

No matter, though. It's just a sign he doesn't want to show off his privilege. And even a shabby scarf takes on a cultured quality when wrapped around the neck of a noble.

The daggers I'm shooting at The Other Woman must work because she alights a couple minutes later at the Angel tube station. Before anyone else can beat me to it, I hurry in to take her spot.

Pausing before I sit down beside Alexander, I soak in the sight. It's surreal to be so close to him, to have my fantasies so close to being fulfilled. My heart physically palpitates as my stomach scrunches up, and I pause just slightly to revel in the fullness of it all. There simply can't be anything more exhilarating in the universe than readying yourself to plunge into an epic romance.

Alexander is back to reading his magazine, somehow still oblivious to the fact that I'm right beside him. Or perhaps he's already spotted me out of the corner of his eye but is too tactful to put me on the spot.

Either way, it's clear I need to be the one to make the first move.

What I'd like to say is, *"There you are, my love!"* or *"Darling! It's me! After all this time!"*

Those would be my lines in a movie. But what I end up squeaking out in a strangled, high-pitched voice is, "Excuse me, can I sit here?"

Some of the words stick together and others are spaced too far apart, but Alexander seems to understand me just fine. He looks up, and I wait for the recognition to dawn on him, for the relief to seep across his face that after weeks of eye contact, I've finally appeared. That his hopes and prayers have been answered. That he hasn't been waiting in vain and now won't have to stand outside Marlow House with a guitar and speakers, serenading me with love songs to win my attention, as no doubt he'd been contemplating.

But there's nothing there in his eyes. Nothing except a blank, courteous stare.

And then he speaks. "Oh yeah, of course," he says. "My bad—lemme get this backpack out of your way." He lifts an old Jansport from the floor, stashing it on his lap. There's actual duct tape around the frayed straps, with a "Respect Your Mother Earth" keychain dangling from the zipper.

I stand there, disoriented, and not just because he carts around a grungy backpack rather than a sleek leather briefcase. His voice isn't the crisp English accent I expected. It's earthy and coarse and all too familiar.

CHAPTER TEN

"You're *American*?" I ask, falling clumsily into the seat beside him as the bus lurches forward.

It sounds like an accusation, and it is. Of all the scenarios I dreamed up, never once did I entertain the idea that my English prince might turn out to be an American imposter.

I'm praying I might've misheard him, might've wrongly detected the accent. As if to balance out my oversized eyes, my ears are extra small, and I'm far more perceptive with sight than with sound.

But my vision starts to betray me too.

Alexander smiles again—a big, flappy thing that feels offensively friendly. His mouth stretches so wide that his gums show through. It's so different from the subtle and sophisticated mannerisms I'd imagined. The longer I look at Alexander, the more things are visibly off.

His features aren't nearly as refined as they'd appeared to be from afar. His nose, though well shaped in profile form, is wide and sprawling from the front, and his hair isn't coiffed after all. He simply has a cowlick he hasn't outgrown. His skin is pastier than I'd thought—sand-colored rather than olive—and spidery blue veins show through around his temples. The clean-cut look I'd adored strikes me as too boyish close up, and I doubt he could grow a beard even if he wanted to. He's probably at least a couple years younger than I am, and smaller framed than I'd thought too—still decently tall but in a gangly sort of way. More honey toned than brown, his wide-set eyes lack that deep, broody resonance I'd loved so much.

I want to look away so the scene will cease to crumble, but it's impossible to stop staring.

"Guilty as charged," Alexander says. Only it's becoming all too clear that he's not Alexander at all. Not in voice or demeanor or name or anything else. "You're American too?"

I nod, too overcome by the letdown to formulate actual words. But then I persevere onward, determined to at least get the answers I came here for. "Have we met before?" I ask.

I want him to be the one to say it. To admit that he recognizes me. That he's been staring at me through the window, imagining our life together too.

He seems to be racking his brain, wiggling his mouth from side to side in a goofy posture of contemplation. There's a pronounced dimple in his cleft chin that adds a look of softness to his whole face. "Hmm, don't think so?" he says. "Have we?"

The worst part is that I get the unshakable sense he's being genuine. There's none of the intimacy I felt through the window. None of the chemistry that hints at all the history we have together.

Could he have just been absentmindedly looking outside all those mornings, and I was so desperate for someone to see me that

I convinced myself he did? Why did I ever think it was a good idea to get on this bus? How could I have ever actually believed all that nonsense about him and us?

It's my fault, but I'm in no mood to carry the blame, so I push the brunt of it onto him. Why would he give such misleading signals? And why is he even in London at all? Why couldn't he have stayed back in America and cleared a space for an actual Englishman to sweep me off my feet?

It's one big faff, as Jules would say. I want to whine and pout and curl back under my duvet in bed. I wish I could dial back time and cradle the innocent crush against my chest and keep it there forever without ever subjecting it to the cruelty of Real Life.

"Yeah, guess we haven't met," I falter, feeling like I'm stuck in a bad dream. It's too mundane of an interaction to qualify as a nightmare, and somehow that makes it more difficult to bear. The normalcy of it all.

From a purely objective perspective, his looks are still above average, but combined with his laid back, overly affable mannerisms, his attractiveness score has plummeted.

Giving me his full attention, he closes his magazine, and the cover sends another jolt of displeasure my way. It is not, in fact, *The Economist*, but rather a comic book, featuring cartoon foxes in capes and goggles.

"Ah yup," he says, following my gaze to the dreadful magazine. "I'm kind of a nerd. More than 'kind of,' actually." He lets out an easy laugh. It's light and breezy, without any of the gravitas I'd yearned for. "I'm a teacher, and this is what all the seven-year-old British kids are reading, so I'm trying to be quasi-relevant."

I have the deflated sensation of sinking even farther down into my seat. It's almost like I'm having an out-of-body experience, looking down from above, watching my painstakingly preened self physically shrink on the spot. The man who once melted me in the most romantic of ways is now making me dissolve into a polluted pool of disillusion.

He's a school teacher who likes comics? Could he be any farther from a well-heeled political figure who spends his commute reading up on world events?

The juxtaposition slaps me, and I can almost hear a cold voice cackling up in the clouds as Cupid's adversaries rejoice in my misery.

"How 'bout you?" he asks. "Where're you from, and what're you up to in London?"

His accent reminds me of my family. I'm not sure if it's just that I haven't spoken to another American for a little while, so all the dialects sound the same, or if he's from the Midwest too. To be honest, I'm not at all curious to find out. I'm too busy feeling sorry for myself and sorry about how this whole fiasco is unfolding.

"Moved here for work," I answer curtly. "Was in Boston and New York before this, and a bunch of other places."

"Ah, so you're used to city life?" he says, not seeming to pick up on my icy tone, or perhaps just bulldozing through, convinced he can crack my shell. "I moved from small-town Michigan, so it's been a bit of a shock."

I wait for the punch line. It doesn't come. This is it, the final blow. My aristocrat from Oxford is actually a school teacher from Michigan.

It would be a small consolation to find some amusement in all this, but I simply don't have the stomach for it. Still, I can't just sit here and not say anything. It was basically instilled in me from the cradle that you can't run into someone else from Michigan and not make the connection.

"What part of Michigan?" I ask aloofly.

I wait for him to hold up his hand and point to where in the "mitten" he's from. Locals call it that because the state is shaped like a mitten—the thumb on the east side by Detroit, and the Great Lakes bordering the land from all sides.

Sure enough, he raises his veiny palm. "Do you know the hand thing?" he asks.

"Indeed," I say dryly. "I'm from Michigan too."

"Holy cow," he says, bubbling over with chummy energy that's so far from the poised and polished man I'd imagined. "What a small world!" His amber eyes get wide, and he looks way too excited by the coincidence. "What part?"

"Southwest," I answer, trying to keep it vague. (It now seems completely out of line that I should divulge the hundred-mile radius wherein my parents live, when yesterday I would've happily invited this man into my bedroom without ever having exchanged two words.)

"No way—I'm from Kalamazoo!" he says, as if this just keeps getting better and better. "Well, a super small town outside K-Zoo, but that's the closest big city." He taps his forefinger to his palm, right over the spot where I grew up.

I can barely keep my eyes from rolling out of their sockets at hearing Kalamazoo described as a big city. With its blink-and-you-miss-it "downtown" that you can walk across in five minutes, it's hardly a booming metropolis. I don't weigh in with my opinion, though. I'm too busy feeling sorry for myself.

"Oh no," I mutter under my breath, but not as quietly as I mean to. Though I don't find any of this funny, I can't deny the comedic elements here, at least to an outsider. Perhaps I wasn't specific enough with the universe—I asked that my life be a romantic comedy, not an *un*romantic comedy. Maybe something got lost in translation as I was manifesting, and two abominable little letters were tacked on to thwart my happiness.

The non-prince, the anti-prince, keeps yabbering on in that too-friendly way that Michiganders do. "Yeah, so I grew up in Vicksburg and now teach at Three Rivers Elementary, and I'm doing a student-exchange program in London for this year," he says. "Where did you go to school? Is your family still there?"

A pinched sound catches in my throat—the result of what happens when you try to laugh but can only cry. I went to Schoolcraft from K through twelve, the district right next to Vicksburg.

This can't be happening. I'm almost expecting him to say "April Fools!" even though it's October, or my alarm clock to go off and wake me to a day that is still unspoiled.

But this isn't a joke, and it's not a dream. It's real life, doling out debris in as casually cruel a form as it comes.

"I went to Schoolcraft," I grit out, resolved to get the bitter truth out of the way so I can come to terms with it and then forget this whole thing once I get off the bus in a few minutes.

"Holy cow," he says again. Perhaps it's his favorite phrase due to the fact that the cow-to-human ration in West Michigan is a solid four to one, or at least that's how it feels driving through the country roads and vast open farmland. "You're not kidding?"

Unfortunately not, I think to myself, but don't say that aloud. I just shake my head. I'm not trying to cement any kind of connection between us, not when the bond I'd wanted has been so brutally broken.

"Maybe we *have* met before? This is crazy," he says, delightfully oblivious to any signs that I might not be equally thrilled to discover our commonalities.

From a great and gloomy distance, I observe the irony in how fully invested he is in this conversation and how absent I am from it. Whereas just a little bit ago I would've given my right leg—potentially both legs—for him to be so fascinated by me. The depressing difference that ten minutes can make in the course of a life.

"Crazy," I agree.

"I'm Rory, by the way," he says. His Michigan accent makes the "r's" so hard and twangy that it gives me bad flashbacks to that place I had to leave because all the dirt roads led to dead ends.

"Kat," I say shortly. "I'm Kat."

"Ah dang it, don't think we can be friends then," Rory says. "I'm a dog person, not a cat person."

"Mmm," is all I manage to say, unable to muster up a courtesy chuckle or even crack the semblance of a smile. It's a terrible joke, and what's even more terrible is that although I obviously have zero interest in Rory—negative interest, actually—I'm still offended by how he so quickly relegates me to the friend zone.

"Sorry," he says. "Bad dad joke. Can I still blame it on jet lag? I moved here a few weeks ago, and it's my first time out of the country, so I'm having some major culture shock. I know it's technically the same language, but"—he lowers his voice and looks around sheepishly—"I can't understand half of what English people say."

I don't even try to keep up an interested expression as he's talking. My face falls into the sunken pits of despair, where my heart and hopes also now reside.

The bus screeches to a standstill, and I seize my chance to evacuate this situation before it spirals any farther. "This is my stop," I announce, though it's not. "Great to meet you, Rory," I say as I abruptly stand up.

"Hey, Kat?" Rory asks, before I can make a clean getaway. "Would you be up for coffee sometime? Would be great to have a friend from back home."

There it is, that offensive "f" word again. Prickling up, I reply, "I don't really consider Michigan home anymore."

He looks a bit dejected at that, and his face is much softer, much less chiseled, than I thought it was from my window sleuthing. He reminds me of my little brother for a second, and I have an absurd urge to reach over and wrap him in a bear hug, the kind my family still greets me with when I (sometimes) go home for the holidays. I don't give him a hug, but I do say in a noncommittal tone, "Coffee sounds good, though."

Rory grins that wide-faced grin and passes me his phone to enter my contact info. Blame it on my honest Midwest upbringing, but I enter my real number rather than a fake.

"See ya soon!" he says, as if this is jolly news indeed. As if we weren't supposed to be Britain's next royal couple snogging at black-tie galas, and now our best hope is being two cornfield-bred pals catching up over coffee.

I should've known better. I'm too old to believe in fairy tales, let alone fairy tales that feature me as the heroine. How could I have suspended my judgment for the sake of such a nonsensical story? It was all just one giant lapse in judgment, a childish tactic to distract me from having to actually grow up and face the razor-blade reality that I'm single and so alone, with absolutely no promising prospects on the horizon.

"Watch it," a woman on the bus grumbles as I only half accidentally elbow her out of my way, to get off this dream-crushing vessel before the closing doors trap me in. "Who do you think you are?"

No clue, I think to myself as I shoot her my dirtiest scowl and step out onto the sidewalk strewn with lifeless cigarette butts and broken glass that appropriately fit my current emotional state. *But evidently not a future duchess.*

CHAPTER ELEVEN

Something in me hardens after the encounter with Alexander. *Rory*, I mean. My brain is taking a little while to adjust to the ugly truth, though my heart has caught on all too quickly.

As quickly as the world transformed into a mystical sphere of wonder when I first spied Alexander, it now devolves back. All the round and reflective edges are sharp and serrated again. The bold, splatter-paint colors of yesterday are muted by a thick coat of grays and blues, everything washed out through the grainy filter of the heartbroken.

Perhaps it sounds a bit dramatic to declare myself heartbroken by a man whose real name I didn't know until this morning, but it doesn't *feel* dramatic. And so here we are, back in that inconsolable emotional state where I just want to curl up on the couch and binge-watch rom-coms for as long as it takes to physically transport myself into the movie, away from this unscripted mess of a life.

Slouching at my desk in Turpi's office, I do my best to avoid conversation with anyone and everyone, keeping my headset on so it looks like I'm on calls even when I'm not.

I would go back to Marlow House to work, or rather, jiggle my mouse while placing a bulk order of cookie dough from Deliveroo, but I have my quarterly performance review this afternoon, so I have to stick it out.

The meeting is one on one and takes place in Oliver's office, a glass-walled cube that Turpi has allocated him while the case is ongoing. Since he's only working there temporarily, he hasn't decorated the office at all, though he's still brought along a few tacky work trophies displayed proudly, as if they were Super Bowl laurels he couldn't bear to be separated from.

Leo & Sons Partner 2022. Leo & Sons Partner 2021. And so on . . .

I sit down in an empty chair across from him, rolling my shoulders back and trying to give off as much confident-but-not-cocky energy as I can, to demonstrate that I'm ready to be made partner.

The first fifteen minutes of our meeting are an unhelpful combination of small talk about how I'm finding London, plus the typical, fortune-cookie platitudes that managers use when they're being lazy or deliberately ambiguous: "You've hit the ground running since this case started." "You're a valued member of the team." "Keep putting in the work, and good things are in store for you."

There would have been a time when I would've lapped up this sort of praise, but I know better now. I know that words mean nothing without action to back them up. And maybe it's because I'm so bummed out by this morning's events, or just because I've been in the business world for too long to trust the system with my career, but I tackle head-on the question that I used to dance around.

"So," I say, clenching my jaw in the masculine posture I've learned over the years, "am I going to make partner?" I'm determined to get answers about where my career at Leo & Sons is going—or not going.

Oliver's unemotive face doesn't change, but he tugs uncomfortably on his pinstripe blazer, and I get the feeling he's not used to such a direct question, or at least not from a woman. "You're doing brilliantly, like I said," he declares. "Can't argue with your performance. I'll be doing what I can for you come December."

It's more fluff, and I'm not having it. As partner, my boss has the clout to get me promoted if he pushes for it. The insinuation that it's not within his power is as infuriating as it is insulting. "What can I do to improve my chances?" I ask.

It's October now, and promotions will be announced early December, but the decisions will be made in the next couple weeks. It's crunch time.

"Well now," he says, fumbling around for the words, as if it wasn't his job to have thought about this beforehand and to deliver helpful feedback in this meeting.

"Yes?" I press, trying to disguise my impatience as eagerness. Every boss I've ever had (all of them male) has resisted giving me constructive criticism, as if afraid I'm going to burst into tears and file a complaint to HR if he dares to injure my delicate feelings. My bosses have never, however, seemed to hesitate passing along honest feedback to other men, one of the reasons men continue climbing up into the C-suite while the women peter out in middle management.

"I reckon you could focus on your client relationship skills a bit more," Oliver stammers. "At the partner level, that's most of the job."

"Does Harold not like me?" I ask, because this seems to be the implication.

"No, he quite likes you, he does. Think he just wishes he saw you around a bit more—join us for drinks, that kind of thing. The out-of-office activities become more important the higher you climb."

I sit there, taking the words head-on. More than being upset with Oliver, I'm upset with myself. I'd been thinking that as long as my boss and the Leo & Sons higher-ups saw I was a top performer, that would be enough. But I've overlooked Harold's importance in the equation. As CEO of the firm we're hired to serve, he arguably holds even more weight than anyone at Leo & Sons. I can't get there without him.

It's a foolish oversight and one whose implications make me queasy. If cozying up to Harold is my ticket to the top, I'm not sure what to do.

I consider bringing up the inappropriate comments Harold makes and how he never seems to take what I say seriously. How he looks at me like a piece of meat, not a professional. But Harold hasn't done anything conspicuous enough to warrant a formal complaint, and the last thing I want is to have my name attached to a sexual harassment scandal.

"Thanks for the feedback," I say, staying composed so Oliver will be inclined to share more with me in the future. "Really appreciate it."

"I'm saying this as your pal as much as your boss," he goes on. "Just know your strengths with Harold, and don't be afraid to use them." Breaking from his stoical expression, he gives the smallest of winks, like we're in on a private joke. Like my promotion is just a game that I have to play the right way to get. Like he's giving me the green light to flirt with Harold to boost my client service score.

The insinuation makes my skin crawl. But before I have time to figure out how to reply, Oliver is dashing out the door to another meeting.

Back at my desk, I stare at the email I'm drafting to Harold and the management team with an update on our implementation plan. It takes me an excessively long time to type the right words. Maybe because I've gotten the feeling that my words don't mean much, not compared to the outfit I wear when I deliver them.

Just yesterday, I thought I'd land the promotion and the prince. Today, it looks like I'm not getting either one.

CHAPTER TWELVE

"This is bonkers, babes," Jules says that night as I swivel miserably on a barstool at the King's Head, gulping down my second pint of Young's. "Your prince charming is a bloke from your 'ometown? How bloody perfect is this?"

"It's not perfect in the least, Jules," I snap, patience gone along with everything good. "It's the opposite of perfect."

I've spent the past half hour filling her in on the day's events, and she seems to be missing the moral to the story—that the universe is plotting against me, punishing me for some crime I've never committed.

"I can't believe I got it so wrong," I lament for the hundredth or so time, brushing the flyaway fringe out of my face. It quickly flops back into my eyes, and I take it as a symbolic attack that I'm unable to see anything clearly these days. "And I can't believe I let myself believe all that BS I invented. Why'd you let me carry on like a complete and utter lunatic?"

I try to turn it on Jules to deflect some of the blame, even though I know deep down that finding a scapegoat won't ease the scraping sensation inside.

"Don't say I didn't try to bring you back to Earth," Jules retorts, her green, lash-adorned eyes handing back the blame. "But you weren't 'aving it. I'm coming 'round to agreeing with you, though."

"Agreeing with me on what?"

"That fate has brought you and Bus Lad together."

I exhale an exasperated sigh. "It's not fate," I say. "I've just told you. It's the *opposite* of fate. Some cruel joke to amuse the charlatans up in the sky, that's all."

"Oh c'mon, babes, you're both from the same bloody corn-field," Jules says. This is her (not too inaccurate) interpretation of Michigan, thanks to the Google photos she's looked up. "It's got to be a sign, innit?"

"If it's any kind of sign, it's just a sign that you should never ever let your emotions carry you away down a rom-com rabbit hole," I say, "lest you discover that it's actually a black hole that takes plea-sure in crushing you to smithereens."

"Look on the bright side, hey?" Jules says. "Imagine if 'e'd actu-ally been an Oxford prat. Would've been insufferable—trust me on this. D'you want my lump of ice?"

"Why?" I growl. "An ice pack isn't going to fix this headache."

"Lump of ice means advice," Jules says, and then prattles on before I can tell her no thank you, I don't actually want it at all. "My advice is just get to know this Rory bloke. Even if you're just regular mates, not soul mates, that wouldn't be the worst thing, would it?"

"I don't need another friend," I say, though I know that's not true. I shouldn't rely on Jules to provide one hundred percent of my emotional support this side of the Atlantic. "And anyway, I need to focus on my promotion," I go on. "Which seems to mean buying low-cut dresses and asking Harold if there's anything I can possibly do for him, *anything at all?*" I pinch my face at the outrageousness of it, the demeaning and archaic structure I thought had been toppled years ago but apparently is still going strong.

"'Arold sounds like a proper wanker," Jules says, disgustedly scrunching up her nose—adorned with a crescent moon stud today. "Invite 'im 'ere for a pint, and I'll serve the ale straight over his shiny little 'ead." She holds up the nozzle that's hooked up to the tap and pretends to spray.

Though I'm rather fond of this picture, I don't allow a smile to sneak out. I'm fully committed to being utterly despondent.

The pub is getting too crowded and rowdy, everyone gathering around to watch a soccer game that's just starting on the TVs. It strikes me as terribly insensitive that they care so much about something that means so little when all the big things in life are going to shambles. I need to leave, need to be alone, but I'm not done with my pint yet. "Can I take this with me?" I ask Jules, feeling highly attached to the half-empty glass in my hand. "I'll wash it and bring it back tomorrow."

"Don't you want to stick around for the footy?" she asks. She's donning a maroon West Ham jersey instead of her collarless polo uniform, and I'll be surprised if, within a few minutes, she's not leading the pub in those obnoxious soccer chants that the English love so much.

My scowl says it all.

"Righ'o, then," Jules says. "Let's top you up before you're off." She refills my pint under the tap.

I try to slide a couple tenners across the counter, but Jules pushes them back. "On the 'ouse tonight," she insists. "And bartenders actually make a living wage in this country, so I don't need your sympathy tips." She wags her tongue good-naturedly.

"Alright," I reply, scooping the money back into my wallet. "After all, it's *your* fault that my romantic life has turned to shite, as you Brits say."

"How d'you reckon?" Jules asks, hands on her hips.

"You're the one who convinced me to introduce myself to Alexander-slash-Rory," I slur. "Brilliant plan, that was."

"It's a bloody good thing," Jules defends. "Now you've got your eyes wide open."

"I preferred it when they were shut, thank you very much."

With that witty one-liner, I show myself out, teetering alone back to Marlow House. Forgetting how cars drive on the left, I look the wrong way as I'm crossing Upper Street, and a moped whizzes by, too close for comfort.

Marlow House looks haunted tonight, all dark and shadowy, secondhand light from lampposts flickering across the old-fashioned window panes in eerie patterns, like ghosts. Rather than scaring me, it almost comforts me in a pity-party sort of way. Sharing my place with spirits would mean I'm not so alone.

Back inside my flat, I strip down to my underwear. I'd donned my sexiest lace thong for the big moment of Meeting My True Love, but now I swap it out for my baggiest briefs and pull on my sweatpants that I call pajamas.

Wrapping a tartan blanket around me, I slouch on the sitting room sofa with a sleeve of McVitie's dark chocolate biscuits in one hand and my pint in the other. I text my friend Blake, saying we need to catch up, though I know she's fast asleep back in New York. With my computer connected to the TV, I turn on *Married at First Sight* so I can sink even deeper into my sulk.

The whole premise of the show now seems glaringly flawed and vapidly commercial, a ridiculously insincere profit-seeking scheme that manufactures fake love for money.

Willpower gone, I look up spoilers and read the gossip columns on my phone. The two couples I'd been so sure were going to live happily ever after have both broken up, and within three weeks of the show's finale. One of those couples had apparently staged the whole thing to boost their social media followings, and the husband in the other couple was caught cheating with a teenage girl half his age, then tried to defend himself by saying it wasn't his fault, that humans just aren't genetically wired for monogamy.

For a moment, this all makes me feel a bit better, like I'm not alone in my woes. But then the full weight of the other couples' breakups presses into me, and I become entirely inconsolable, convinced that love is officially dead forever and ever. If Hollie and George from the show can't survive, despite how lovingly they stared into each other's eyes at the altar and cried like babies on each other's shoulders when they opened up about their parents' divorces, what hope do I possibly have at finding love and actually making it last?

I might as well just give up now. Adopt a few cats and embrace the spinster life. Have *Love Loser* tattooed on my forehead and monetize my misery by going viral on TikTok as "that comically sad cat lady." Then I'll use the profits to buy a vacation home on some tropical island where no one can find me, except tanned and toned gardeners I'll admire as I lounge by the pool but will never actually speak to lest I break the illusion once more.

These are the highly rational thoughts looping through my brain as I hastily brush my teeth, then plop into bed. I pull the duvet up to my chin and seal myself in, safe in an envelope of a love letter that Alexander will never read because Alexander doesn't exist.

Wiggling around from one side to the other and back again, I'm unable to get comfortable. I feel lonely because I'm tipsy, or maybe I'm just tipsy enough to admit that I feel lonely, that I have for a while now.

I miss Mateo. Or at least I miss having *someone*. Someone whose arms I can fall into at the end of a long day. Someone who holds me close and tells me that he's right there, that everything is going to be okay, no matter what work drama or deadline I'm stressed about.

This didn't actually happen all that often, even when I *was* with Mateo, because I was always traveling and networking and *grinding my way up*, but hindsight makes our relationship look a bit warmer, a bit cozier, and in this moment I'm nostalgic for something that may or may not have ever existed in the first place.

I guess I never really confronted the breakup head-on. I distracted myself with work and then the move to London and the new case and the full pipeline of dating app suitors. And then when those guys let me down, I latched onto my double-decker prince, convinced that he was the panacea that would save me. Now, in the wake of the collapse, I'm flailing around in the vacuum that's been left behind, oppressed by all the extra space.

I turn my phone off so I won't fall into the trap of re-downloading the dating apps and binge-matching with fifty-two new people to make me feel wanted, all of whom I'll promptly ghost tomorrow. And also so I won't drunkenly reach back out to Mateo.

But even as the loneliness presses in and presses out, I don't have any real desire to contact Mateo. I don't consider asking for another chance. He wasn't the right person for me. He never loved me deeply enough for me to feel confident building an entire life with him.

Maybe that's because you never loved yourself deeply enough, the little voice in my head whispers.

I try to shut it out but can't help but wonder if there's some truth in it. If maybe someone can only love you as much as you love yourself. If maybe the reason I felt like Mateo didn't know me was because I actually didn't know myself. If maybe I've been trying so hard to *become* someone that I've lost touch with who I *am*. And who I used to be and who I've always been.

The bedroom walls shift around me, mocking me with their movement when everything inside me feels so stuck. Aching to be held and aching to hold, I wrap my arms around my spare pillow and suffocate it with all the love that I have nowhere else to spill.

CHAPTER THIRTEEN

Maybe yesterday hadn't really happened. Maybe it was one elaborate trick of the mind, a side effect of too much cumulative caffeine. It might've just been a bad practical joke played by the neurons in my brain, which have a very unfortunate sense of humor.

Sprawled in my Marlow House bathtub, I try to soothe myself, though I feel the truth in my brittle bones and burning muscles.

Without ever having done more than a few down dogs in my life, I decided to attend a two-hour yoga class to bring some calm and clarity. After the first few treacherous sequences, I sought refuge in child's pose and stayed there until shavasana. "I salute your courage for showing up for yourself," was what the impossibly lithe instructor said on the way out, bowing in a prayerful posture, probably just giving thanks that I didn't kill myself and subject him to a lawsuit.

Now I'm nursing myself back to life from underneath the bathwater, which I periodically have to drain and refill to keep it hot.

My fingers and toes have shriveled up, and my stomach growls ominously, unamused with the measly green juice I've been feeding it after my ill-fated yoga adventure.

Rain is pattering on the skylight of the bathroom. It's not a cathartic downpour. The white-gray sky is just spitting haphazard droplets, like it can't be bothered to put in much effort.

My breath is even shallower and choppier than it was before yoga. I reach for a cucumber tonic juice on the floor beside me—nearly capsizing the tub in the process—and put on a moisturizing face mask from Boots pharmacy because these are the things that are supposed to make you feel better.

While waiting for my forehead lines to be miraculously erased within fifteen minutes, as per the claims on the pastel packaging, I turn on my phone for the first time since yesterday, resigned to face the world again. The work emails flood in, along with only two measly WhatsApp messages. One is from Blake, saying, yes, we should definitely catch up soon, with an excess of exclamation points, but no suggestion of when. And then the second message is from a +44 UK number I don't have saved.

Hi Kat! Rory here. Great meeting you yesterday! Fancy a coffee soon? (Practicing my British lingo!) Let me know what your calendar (oops, I mean "diary") looks like. Weekends are pretty wide open for me. ☺

The brightness of the message makes everything inside feel painfully dim, painfully dull. I sink farther down into the wobbly tub as the message confirms the ugly truth that all my grand Alexander hopes have gone up in the wispy smoke of a Michigan bonfire.

Finally extricating myself from the bath, I wrap myself in a towel and walk into the kitchen to stress eat some Shreddies. Then I screenshot Rory's text and send it to Jules, with the emoji that looks to be in the most agony.

The lad is keen, Jules replies, after I've removed my face mask to find absolutely zero improvement. If anything, I'm now more wrinkled because I'm frowning about the false marketing promises and the way my pores feel clogged with slime.

He's not keen, he's just being friendly, I text back. It's a highly annoying Midwestern trait.

Go on then, what do you have to lose?

A perfectly good hour of my life in which I could be meeting an actual prince.

Listen to yourself . . .

What?

Love you babes but your expectations are way too high.

No they're not, I fling back bitterly. It's good to have high standards.

They'll make you bloody unhappy.

If I'm being honest with myself, I probably do have something of an addiction to the poetic arc of disappointment. I'm self-aware enough to admit that I may possibly have the *slight* tendency to build things up a little too much and then feel sorry for myself as they come crashing down around me.

Not just with Alexander. I did it with Mateo too. Idolized him as The One. After our magical eye contact moment at The Spaniard, we exchanged "I love you's" within two weeks. And the next four years were a steady downward slope from the summit where we'd begun, a far cry from the carriage ride into the sunset that I'd pictured.

I refuse to settle for a mediocre relationship, or a mediocre career, and I'm usually proud of myself for this. It means I know my worth and my potential. But today I wonder if it just makes me a juvenile fool. If my perfectionism destines me for nothing but perpetual misery.

A wave of inspiration hits to clean the flat, and I act on it before it passes. Wielding the vacuum like a weapon, I suck up the cereal bits and crusty peanut butter globs that have flattened into the floorboards. I wash all the dishes in the sink, and though I don't bother to dry them (why waste the effort when the air will do that for me?), I line them up on the drying mat. Fanatically dusting the window, I try to brush away all memories of Alexander.

In the end, I decide to text Rory back. Technically speaking, it's not his fault that he's not an English prince, and I suppose I don't really have any grounds to punish him for that, as much as I'd like to.

Still, I keep my reply noncommittal so I won't feel so bad if I bail, which I most likely will. Hey Rory! Yeah coffee could be good— maybe next weekend?

He replies within sixty seconds, which feels aggressively eager. Works for me! Do you have a favorite coffee shop?

I, too, reply right away because there's zero point trying to appear more desirable to someone I don't actually desire. Gail's on Upper Street? I suggest, trying to minimize the effort that I have to put into this.

Yeah that's great! What day/time is best for you?

I'm not thrilled that he's pinning down specifics, but I can always use the "So sorry, had to work this weekend!" excuse. Maybe 11 am next Saturday?

Brill! (Just learned that expression!) Can't wait!! ☺ ☺ ☺

His enthusiasm is really getting under my skin, as if it wasn't already. I know he just moved here and doesn't know many people, but still, there must be something wrong with a guy who so happily arranges his schedule around me. Someone who seems so excited about the prospect of spending his Saturday morning with me at a coffee shop.

I add the event in my phone calendar, scheduling it for thirty minutes, then draw shut the sitting room curtains so I don't have to see the buses go by. I don't need any more rude, red reminders about how far yesterday's events diverged from my dreams.

CHAPTER FOURTEEN

I start going into the office every day. Mostly so I can see Harold and the Turpi team more, given the feedback from my performance review. But commuting also helps because I can't bear to think about the alternative—working from the desk in my flat, watching the 4 bus stop right outside. I know I wouldn't be able to keep from checking for Alexander, and seeing Rory would just crush me all over again.

One afternoon the next week, Harold sends an email around to a few of us. There's nothing in the body of the email, just the subject line: Annabel's tonight. Meet at the lifts at half five.

I'm used to ignoring these kinds of notes, since socializing with work people is much more of a chore than a treat, but today I reply, determined to play the game. *Win* the game. Thanks, Harold— looking forward to it.

Outside the office, we flag down a couple of cabs. Harold beckons me into one with him and the CFO and COO, while Oliver and the juniors get in the other one.

London cabs have two benches of seats in the back, facing each other. I take a backward-facing seat so I only have to look at Harold, rather than sit next to him.

It's a long drive from Canary Wharf to The West End, especially at rush hour. The narrow streets twist and turn in that classic English way that make you lose your sense of direction within five minutes, if you'd managed to have one at the start.

"Mad traffic," Harold grumbles as the cab crawls through the queue of cars. "Reckon we can do pre-drinks in here, hey?" He pops a bottle of Dom Perignon that seems to appear out of thin air. The CFO passes around champagne flutes as casually as if they were red Solo cups.

"What's the occasion?" I ask, taking a champagne glass.

"The occasion is that you're finally coming out with us, Kitten," he says.

They all laugh, the same gritty octaves, and I do my best to disguise my sneer and smile along. *Just play the game,* I remind myself.

Even though I've made up my mind that I will only tolerate the evening—*not* enjoy it—I've got to admit that there's a certain novelty to sipping a three-hundred-pound bottle of champagne in the back of a London cab. Especially en route to the city's most glamorous hangout . . . even if I am with Harold and his sidekicks.

By the time the cabby announces we've arrived, I'm feeling slightly dizzy from some combination of the bendy streets and two glasses of bubbly.

From the outside, Annabel's doesn't look nearly as majestic as I might have thought, given its reputation, though perhaps that's just because everything in its Mayfair neighborhood drips with money, so it's hard to stand out. If I didn't know better, it might just be another three-level sandstone townhome with a massive, pristinely painted black front door.

A doorman stands outside, dressed in a tuxedo and a top hat. "Mr. Turpi," he says, tipping his hat. "Lovely to see you, as always." He opens the huge door for us, and I step inside.

Immediately, I feel like I've been catapulted into a different realm—a spell-cast version of London plucked straight from a magazine or a high-budget Netflix series.

Opulent chandeliers dangle from the coffered ceiling, their ornamental crystals winking with a wicked sort of merriment. Velvet maroon wallpaper rims the foyer, and a golden-tasseled spiral staircase twists up and out of sight. Tropical ferns and dyed pink ostrich feathers poke out of giant porcelain vases.

The competing styles of riches are pushed together so confidently that the place seems entirely unconcerned with anyone's conclusion that it might all might be a bit outlandish, a bit *too much*.

Annabel's interior has all the drama that the outside does not. And for better or for worse, it feels more impressive, more special this way. Reserving the fancy trappings for only those charmed individuals who are on the list, rather than making them freely available to be glimpsed by squibs on the street.

I want to despise the club for its flashiness, its elitism, but I find myself falling in love with it instead. An unexpected liberation fills me as I spin my neck around every which way, trying to sponge it all up. I get the feeling that I can be anyone here. That this is some kind of delightful suspension from reality. Almost like a less trashy slice of Las Vegas.

What happens at Annabel's . . . The phrase pops into my head like a promise.

Someone offers to take our coats, and I feel Harold's eyes on me as I shed my trench and reveal the black sheath dress underneath, sans the blazer I was wearing at the office. There's nothing scandalous about the dress, but it's not exactly my most conservative option either, hugging my curves more than my typical work outfits, cutting slightly lower at the front.

One hand resting on the small of my back, Harold escorts me into the next room—a restaurant with swooping green drapes, a gargoyle-guarded fireplace, and elephant landscapes painted onto the yellow walls. Impeccably dressed diners pick at aubergine and oysters while carrying on hushed conversations, perhaps because they don't want to be overheard, or are just scared that showing any emotion will undo the Botox.

We keep going, back into another room with darker lighting, no windows, and a salacious sort of energy wiggling its way along the electro-jazz currents of the music. A long marble bar stretches the length of the room, and the only lights come from the wild walls, which are piped with glowing jungle patterns. The ceiling, lined with reflective metal strips, looks like it's out of a sci-fi movie.

A waiter appears (everyone and everything seems to just *appear* here) and leads us to a corner booth. Cheetah-print plush seating wraps around a rectangular glass table with multiple crystal ash trays.

"Your usual spot, Mr. Turpi," he says fawningly. "A round of old-fashioneds to start?"

"And let's add in a Manhattan, shall we?" he says. "For our American guest of honor." He pats my shoulder as we sit down, like I'm something to show off.

I don't flick his hand away or tell him that I don't like Manhattans. I just thank him and scooch over to make room for the others from our group who are piling in too.

The first round arrives quickly, followed by tequila shots with pineapple juice—called Craig Davids, as I know from Jules. I try one of everything, just for something different. And it's easier to sit back and sip than actively contribute to the conversation with Harold.

The people-watching scene is incredible. I don't recognize anyone, but I get the feeling I *should* recognize some of them from the way they're carrying themselves, like they're used to posing for the cameras or running from them, depending on their mood.

The juniors are whispering excitedly, pointing to the next table over. The group of mannequin-shaped women are alarmingly gorgeous with mile-long limbs and stone-cut faces.

"That's Emory!" one of the juniors tells me when I ask what's going on. At my blank expression, she adds, "Only Britain's top model!" She whips out her phone camera.

"No photos allowed in here, I'm afraid," Harold says, craning his way into the conversation. "Annabel's is our one reprieve from the paparazzi." He says this with the air of someone who is compelled to frequently evade the press with tiresome disguises. "But I reckon I could get you a cheeky picture with Emory. We're quite close, we are."

I figure he's just talking a big game, but he stands up and swaggers over to Emory's table, resting a hand on her bare shoulder. I wait for her to shoo him away, but she flashes him a warm smile, rising to embrace him. She towers over him, all legs and bones, and next thing, she's coming over to our table and taking duck-faced selfies with the starstruck juniors. On her way back to her group, she kisses Harold's cheek, making his whole chest puff out, as if the mark of her red lipstick is the highest status symbol a mortal man might hope for. "What'd I tell you?" he says once she's left, as the juniors coo with awe.

After another cocktail—some peach-colored slushie with cotton candy on the rim—the room starts to sway in an artistic sort of way. The tropical walls slope up to the sci-fi ceiling, and I picture myself joining a colony of aliens in the rainforest, swinging freely from the treetops.

Oliver heads out, says it's his anniversary so he's got to get home to take his wife out to dinner. He announces this like it's a chore, like he'd much rather stay here and get pissed all night. As he leaves, he nods to me as if to say that he's glad that I'm taking his feedback to heart.

The music has slid into 2000s pop. "Oldies are my favorite!" the juniors exclaim, making me feel ancient. Bouncing up on the couch, they dance and holler to Mr. Brightside. I reach out a hand to help them down so they won't hurt themselves or cause a scene, but Harold warns me off. "Let them at it," he says. "They're just having a good time—can't fault them for that." He looks very pleased to be associated with the young, lively table.

Something takes hold of me, or lets go of me. I should be able to break out of my corporate image a bit and have some fun. Everyone else does it, and people like them better for it.

To symbolize my newfound spirit, I take the clip out of my bun and let my hair fall to my shoulders. I get up and join the juniors on the couch, working to stay upright as my heels wobble on the cushion as we dance.

I try to remember the last time I really let loose. Definitely not on any of my thirty-minute dates. Probably last New Year's Eve in Miami with Mateo, except even then I was worried about having to get up early the next day for work. Ugh, Mateo. Why couldn't that have been *it*? Or why couldn't Alexander have been? Why am I just as far from finding my person at thirty-one as I was at twenty-one?

Trying to shake it off, I dance and lip-synch. It reminds me of being back at my very first frat party, but with better alcohol and a far more sophisticated backdrop than a U of M frat basement where my feet physically stuck to the Keystone Lite–coated floor.

Jumping down from my plush-bench stage, I hurry to the bathroom to relieve my bladder, which I've only just now realized is about to burst.

The women's loo is sensory overload—all pinks and pastels with ribbons of lace wrapping here and there and everywhere just because they can. The marble toilets feel almost too beautiful to urinate in (not that it stops me), and the ceiling is entirely covered in fresh pink roses. I want to touch the velvety petals to confirm they're real, but I can't reach.

As I wash my hands under the golden swan faucets, I notice a tube of red lipstick abandoned on the counter. It's a bright, blazing red—too daring for me, but I want to try it on. No one else is around to claim it, so I take the red wand out of its tube and smack my lips with its fiery stain, liking how it plumps them up in look and feel.

Looking into the bathroom's gilded mirror, I see someone different staring back at me. An alien goddess who lives for the moment and stars in intergalactic films. Someone who just wants to have a good time and look divine as she waltzes from world to world.

Feeling very light in my body, as if I might escape it altogether, I rejoin the others. The juniors are bolting off, one to go to a flat mate's birthday, and the other to put himself to bed after too many shots.

Harold's sidekicks have dissolved away too, perhaps roaming the room for romantic targets. "Your spirits are much improved this week, Kitten," Harold says, handing me another Craig David. "Good shagging, I hope?"

I nearly spit the tequila out of my mouth but swallow it in one gulp instead, chasing quickly with pineapple juice. "No comment," I say coyly, feeling newly bold under the coating of the red lipstick, like I can explore my fictional character a bit further.

"Well, you could bag any guy in this place," Harold goes on, "so let's hope you're putting that to good use, hey?" He casually rests his hand on my knee, over my black tights, and keeps it there, as if it's perfectly appropriate.

My first instinct is to yank my leg free of his grip, but I don't. Maybe because I don't want to upset him or maybe because there's a small, shameful part of me that doesn't mind the sensation of his hand resting on my leg. It doesn't make me shudder or cringe like I expect it to.

I'm so deprived of physical contact these days. The only touch I get is the accidental kind—people shoving me out of the way on the tube or accidentally brushing my shoulder at Waitrose as we contend for last cheese twist in the bakery.

He starts tracing casual circles on my kneecap, as if he's testing out whether I'm going to stop him or not. I don't.

I tell myself to knock it off, that Harold is vile and despicable and everything that's wrong with the world. But it's harder to recall all that right now, with all the shapes spinning and somersaulting as the last shot starts to kick in.

And it's not that big of a deal. It's only my knee.

CHAPTER FIFTEEN

Except it isn't only my knee.

Harold starts to fiddle his way up my thigh, then back down to the knee, then up again a little higher, like he's testing to see how far he can go. His touch doesn't feel good, but it doesn't feel bad either. It's neutral, with the sense that it could get better if I let it.

I'm not Kat anymore. I'm the extraterrestrial being who's tired of being the good girl. Tired of following the rules and doing it the right way. The right way has led me right into a dead end.

Know your strengths. Oliver's voice reverberate in my thoughts, and it makes me wonder if letting Harold carry on might be the thing that helps me make partner. I'm not proud of it, but I can't scrounge up any repentance either.

Harold's hand is at my groin now, fingers tap dancing over my tights, poking lightly at the fabric. I should swat him away, stand up and walk away, but there's a certain curiosity to see what comes next, almost like I'm watching myself star in a movie where my character knows how to play the game. She struts confidently across the screen, glad to be single because she's not betraying anyone. Except maybe herself, but that's not so bad.

The room is turning on its head, and I like it better upside down. Right and wrong seem like very subjective, very snobbish things that we'd all be better off without.

Harold's face is closer to mine. "Shame you have these on, luv," he murmurs, plucking at my tights. "How about a quick change in the loo?"

I find myself thinking about it. Contemplating what would happen if I went into the bathroom and returned without tights. If I let Harold's hands go where they wanted.

His fingers are tapping against my tights again. There's a pulse of heat between my legs, and beneath the numbness of my outer shield, my lonely body wants him to keep going.

My phone buzzes from the table. Instinctively, I reach for it and check the text that's lighting up the screen. It's Rory.

Hi Kat! Hope your week has been brill (my new favorite word). Still on for 11 a.m. at Gail's tomorrow?

The text's grounding effect is immediate.

I picture Rory—not as Alexander but actually as Rory. His wholesome smile. His candid honeycomb eyes and twangy Michigan accent. The shock on his face if he saw—*if my family saw*—where I was right now. What I was doing and what I was letting someone do to me.

And just like that, Annabel's spell is broken. The heavenly mirage is exposed as a devil's den. My body burns, but not in the hot, hormone-charged way. It burns cold with regret and repulsion. Stomach clenching, I feel like I'm about to be sick.

I look over at Harold. He's a slimy pig again, sitting there with his collar unbuttoned and gray chest hair poking through. Looking at me so smugly, like he's certain that we'll be shagging within the hour.

The self-disgust starts to swell and suffocate. How could I have been so reckless?

The room is still spinning. It's impossible to tell what's moving and what's not. The trees on the wall make me think of the woods I grew up in, the way the delicate ice crystals cling to the bare maple branches on a cold winter morning, so pure and innocent and untouched by humans.

It makes me want to cry, but I'm not able to. It's like everything has been stuffed with shallowness. And all that's left is the shell of me.

I want to be better than this. I'm not sure if I am, but Rory's text makes me want to try.

Freeing myself from Harold, I stand up to locate my bag. "I've got to head out," I tell Harold. I'm still drunk, but the sober part is quickly reclaiming space, like it's realized the urgency.

"What's the problem, luv?" he asks. "You're not trying to dash away from me, are you?" He says it lightly but there's a darkness in his eyes that warns of trouble if I were.

"'Course not," I lie. "Just late for a friend."

Harold hugs me goodbye, his hands cupping that place that he now seems to think he owns. I want to slap him. But more than that, I want to slap myself. I don't do either of those things—I just dash out the door.

In no mood to wait for an Uber, I keep shuffling in the dark the full three miles home, heeled booties clanking desperately against the sidewalk. Panting off what just happened feels good, or at least it feels less bad. I don't stop until I reach the graffiti-streaked telephone boxes of Upper Street, when I finally slow to a walk.

It's only nine thirty by the time I get back to Marlow House, but it feels like three AM. I throw up in the toilet and then stay crouching over it for a while, dry heaving and spitting. I'm not sure if it's from drunkenness or just self-disgust.

What if Rory hadn't texted me? Where would I be now? Thank God I don't have to find out.

After chugging two glasses of water, I take a makeshift shower, standing up in the rickety tub and spraying myself down with the nozzle. Though the water pressure is weak, I'm too restless to sit down. Lathering on the bodywash, I try to make myself clean, and stay in there until the hot water runs out.

I reply to Rory's text as I limp into bed. I have to concentrate very hard on making sure there aren't typos so he won't think I'm wasted.

Yes, still on. See you then!

CHAPTER SIXTEEN

In the morning, I still feel dirty. The kind of dirty that can't be slept off or washed off or peeled off. The kind that grips you and sticks to you and gives you no escape from your mistakes.

Rain is smacking against the grilled windows, and the events of last night rush back with alarming clarity. Daylight shines an ugly spotlight, making everything look even more wrong and feel even more raw. I just want to bury my face under the pillow and never come out.

As I lie there, the hangover hits. One of those throbbing things that makes me aggravated at the world and everyone who has the audacity to exist in it. Myself, most of all.

I know that it was Harold's fault more than mine. I know that if something like this happened to one of my friends, I'd be furious with her if she didn't report him straightaway.

Still, I find myself wondering what would happen if I didn't say anything. If I just let it be.

The thoughts rise to the surface, amid the sinking sensation. Maybe last night was enough for Harold to want to put in a good word for me to get me promoted. What's done is done anyway. Even if I make Harold pay for it, I can't make him un-touch me.

The shame settles in my groin, a limp and self-loathing sensation. Picking up my phone, I'm confronted with two unread texts.

First, there's Harold, at 1:37 AM. Thanks for opening up tonight, Kitten . . . to be continued. Xx

The double entendre drenches me in sweat all over again. I think about how I just sat there, egging him on.

My hypocrisy makes me want to gag. Here I am, trying so hard to rise up as a woman in business and give little girls someone to look up to in the C-suite . And yet I'm resorting to slimy tactics to help me get there.

The next text is from Rory, about half an hour ago. Heading out now. See you soon! ☺

Weirdly, Rory's message makes me feel worse than Harold's. It reminds me of innocence and kindness and all the things I don't deserve.

We're due to meet at Gail's in ten minutes.

I want to bail for multiple reasons. First, because I don't think I can physically lift myself from this bed, let alone dress myself in actual clothes. Second, because I don't want to see his chipper smile and be reminded of what a complete moral failure I am. And third, because I still won't be able to stop wishing he were Alexander instead, and I don't need any more proof that there's no happily ever after in store for me.

But he's already on his way. He's probably already arrived. Gail's is literally right below my flat and across the street. It would be rude to cancel now. And I really do need a coffee. Make that three.

Yanking myself up, groaning as I go, I pull on my oldest jeans and an oversized sweater, hoping to hide under the fabric and put as much space between my skin and the world as possible. I apply a quick coat of makeup, finishing with an excessive amount of lip balm to help the dry, cracked feeling in my body.

Pulling on my hooded raincoat, I hobble down the stairs and out the door. To overcome my conditioning to American traffic patterns, I look both ways before crossing Upper Street.

Rory is there, standing outside under Gail's red awning. He's wearing a raincoat and wellies today. There's a half second where I still see him as the dreamy and dapper Oxford man I was once enraptured by. But then he gives a goofy wave from under the touristy Union Jack umbrella he's holding, and the posh picture is punctured. He's bouncing on his toes in a jittery, ungraceful way, and he looks even scrawnier than I'd remembered, just about swimming in his oversized raincoat.

"Kat!" he says, flagging me down as if I haven't seen him or remembered what he looked like. "It's me, Rory!" His face springs into that boyish smile, and I have a strong urge to clamp his mouth shut so he looks more like the refined picture I'd had of him.

"Hi there," I say, hoping he can't see or smell my hangover. "Good to see you again."

"Great day, isn't it?" he says, with no trace of irony. "The London rain reminds me of the spray coming up when you're out wakeboarding on a lake." His gold-flecked eyes stretch wide with excitement.

"That's one way to look at it," I grumble, already regretting coming. His positivity is too much to bear, especially right now.

He holds the door for me, bells jingling as we walk inside. Yeasty aromas and cinnamon roll scents twirl through the bakery, and a pang of hunger shoots through me. My last proper meal was lunch yesterday.

Rory orders hot chocolate with whipped cream—a disappointingly fitting diversion from the oat flat white I'd imagined for Alexander. I ask for an almond croissant and a double-shot latte, and I pay for it all before Rory can get out his wallet.

"You didn't need to do that," Rory says, looking a bit out of sorts, like it's an insult to his masculinity to be treated by a woman.

I nearly make a comment about antiquated gender norms, but I'm too tired to go there. "No big deal," I say. It comes out short and spiky.

Gail's is a long, skinny café, with a seating area in the back. We scout for a table, but they're all packed full of young families. Parents cling to coffee mugs like medicine bottles as toddlers paw at pain au chocolates and coloring books, shrieking for attention with "Mummy, look!" and "Daddy, noooo!" Through the bowed skylight, the spire of St. Mary's church rises up like an anchor in the air, pigeons and seagulls vying for real estate atop the cross summit.

"How do you feel about a walk in the rain?" Rory asks when it's clear there's no space for us in Gail's. "I haven't spent much time in Islington—just passing through on the bus. I'm up in Finsbury. More affordable."

He doesn't say it like he's self-conscious at all, but I can't help but feel embarrassed for him anyway. "A walk sounds fine," I say, which is true. Being outside feels less oppressive, less stifling.

"Cool beans," Rory says, because apparently "cool beans" is an expression that still exists in the modern age. Pulling out that flimsy Union Jack brolly, he holds it over us as we walk outside.

In the rom-coms, this is where the man keeps the woman perfectly dry and murmurs sweet nothings in her ear as they cozy up under the spacious umbrella. In real life, this is where a nasty gale hits us head-on, and the runty thing turns inside out and snaps, leaving us standing there, damp and platonic under the spitting skies.

"Dang it," Rory says, fiddling with the spokes to try and fix them, though it's clear they're mangled beyond repair. "I paid twenty pounds for this." He doesn't look upset, just dejected.

Rory seems like exactly the kind of person who'd get swindled by merchants. I want to feel sorry for him, but I'm too busy feeling sorry for myself now that I'm cold and soaked straight through to the bones.

"I could get my umbrella from my flat," I offer, because that seems like the most expedient solution (other than saying, "Ah well, looks like this coffee chat just isn't in the cards. Hope you have a great day—see you never!" which is what the hungover, short-tempered part of me is inclined to do).

"Do you live near here?" Rory asks.

"Right there, actually." Without thinking, I point up to my sitting room window. Too late, I realize I've just made it uncomfortably clear that I've had him commute to my literal doorstep.

He doesn't seem to be put off by my lack of thoughtfulness. "Oh awesome," he says, gazing up at Marlow House. "I've actually noticed that window before."

Curiosity surfaces, pricking through the Annabel's-related ignominy that's still coating me in crusty dirt. I look at Rory, wondering if this is it, if he actually *was* aware of our eye contact all this time. And if now he's finally going to admit to it.

"You have?" I ask, doing my best to sound very blasé about this development. Though the situation can't be rectified in that Rory still won't be anything like I'd hoped, my own judgment and eye-contact fluency can still be redeemed. It would be a small consolation, but a consolation, nonetheless.

"Yeah," Rory says. "I have this quirk where it bothers me if things are crooked. And um"—his raindrop-splotched face flushes, and he pauses awkwardly, as if he's wishing he hadn't brough this up but is now too far along to abort the topic—"I saw that your curtains are a little off center."

I stand there, blinking at him through the drizzle, waiting for the punch line. "What's that?" I say, because there's got to be more to the story. My pride needs there to be.

"Your curtains aren't symmetrical," he says, now looking down at his wellies. "Just a little off-center, that's all."

He says it in that down-home way that makes it impossible to question that he's telling the truth. I still do question it because I can't bear to think that *that* was the reason he was looking up at my flat—not because he was transfixed by my breathtaking beauty, but simply because he was irked by the lack of symmetry of my curtains.

It's preposterously insulting, and insultingly preposterous. I keep thinking this situation can't devolve any further, and yet here we are, sinking lower once more.

CHAPTER SEVENTEEN

Whatever miniscule patience I'd started the day with has quickly evaporated into the soggy air. "It's rude to look in people's windows," I snap at Rory, not bothering to try to sound polite any longer.

"I know. I'm sorry," he says, looking genuinely disappointed in himself. "It's an OCD thing. Not a good excuse, just a flaw of mine . . ." He trails off uncomfortably. "It's not like I ever saw you or anything, I swear."

This only makes things worse. How could he *not* have seen me? All those days when I was there sitting at my desk, positioned squarely in the middle of the window, pouring my entire soul and then some into his eyes?

I don't accost him with these questions, or with my perspective on the matter. Nothing productive can come from it, not when it's been revealed that he's completely opposite to any love interest of mine anyway. "It's fine," is all I say. "Let's just start walking. We don't need a brolly."

But Rory insists on holding the broken umbrella over our heads, propping it up with two hands, refusing to see that it's doing absolutely no good. If anything, it's making us more wet with how the raindrops are splashing off of the battered spokes, down onto our faces.

We start south on Upper Street, following the route of the 4 bus down toward Islington Green, the triangular town square where dogs scamper around in the matted-down grass, no one seeming to mind the "Dogs Must Be on Leads" signs. For as rule abiding as the Brits are, dogs seem to have a free pass and are shown far more empathy and affection than humans.

All the dogs seem to be drawn to Rory—they come over and nip affectionately at his legs, and he bends down and scratches their ears and their bellies, like they've been lifelong friends. I don't join in, not keen to smell like wet dog or have my expensive coat ruined by claw marks. But it does make me miss Murray, my family's black lab that my brothers and I got one Christmas. He died a few years ago, and I never got to say goodbye.

As if I don't have enough negative feelings in my body, regret and longing pile on. Whenever I'm stuck in a down mood, all the bad emotions have a way of amplifying all at once. It feels like my heart is expanding, but not in a good way. In a crippling and over-whelming way that just makes everything ache.

I check my watch discreetly while Rory's wrapped up with an Australian shepherd. Or at least, I think I'm being discreet, but apparently not.

"Do you have to go?" Rory asks. "I don't want to hold you up."

"Not yet," I say, though we're nearly at the thirty-minute mark. "But I do have a hard stop at noon for a work call." I hate how cruel and corporate the lie sounds aloud, but I don't have the energy for anything else. Especially not the truth about how I actually just have to climb back into bed and bury my head in a pillow and try to forget how I let a creepy client touch me like a trophy last night.

After he's done petting the dogs, Rory resumes attempting to hold the umbrella over us, and we walk past Tesco and Barclays into Camden Passage, a narrow, no-cars-allowed cobblestone street, packed tightly with speckled-brick shops and high-end hairdressers. It's my favorite street in London, but it feels too crowded today, like there's no space to breathe. Weekend market vendors have squeezed in to set up pop-up stalls selling antiques and jewelry, costume hats and watercolor canvases, vinyl CDs and gourmet cheese.

"Holy cow," Rory says, soaking up the sights like a kid at Disney World. "My mom would love this."

Abruptly, the rain shifts from drizzle to full-on downpour. Rory finally seems to admit that his broken brolly isn't up to the challenge, so we seek shelter under the awning of a bridal shop that's displaying a sequined princess ballgown in the window. It's exactly the sort of once-in-a-lifetime dress I've always dreamed of walking down the aisle in. The gap between where I thought I'd be in my early thirties (married with a couple kids) and where I actually am (completely and utterly single, resorting to falling in love with imaginary men because the real ones are no good) makes me feel even worse about everything.

Everything in me feels antsy to get back home and take another shower. "I should probably start heading back soon," I say. "For my work call."

Rory looks like he believes me, which hurts in an unexpected sort of way, though maybe that's just because everything hurts right now. "No worries," he says. "Consulting life is a grind, huh?"

"Yeah," I say with a grimace. "You could say that."

"That's one thing I miss about Michigan," Rory says wistfully. "The culture is more laid back."

I snort, then try to disguise it as a sneeze. Michiganders are certainly laid back, which is code for *unmotivated*.

"So what's your family think of you living in a different country?" Rory asks, as if he didn't catch the part about me being up against an (imaginary) time crunch.

"They're fine with it," I say before I really have to think about an alternative answer. "I haven't lived near them in years, so London's not that much different from New York or California."

"Do you think you'll move back closer to them someday?" he asks, getting nosy in that way that Kalamazoo people do.

"Highly unlikely," I say. "I feel like an outsider when I go back. Like my life is on a different track."

"And you like your track?" He doesn't say it in a charged way at all, but I clench up into a defensive stance.

"Of course," I say, slicing the words with an air of superiority. "I want to reach my potential."

Rory seems to chew on the words before digesting them. "In what way?"

"Rise up at work. Lead a company and have the influence to create large-scale change in the world." I've said this phrase to other people and myself so many times that it comes out smooth and polished.

"So your *career* potential," Rory clarifies.

"Correct," I say, annoyed at him for not catching on faster. "What other potential is there?"

"I like to think there's lots," Rory says, in a soft-voiced sort of way, like it's something he thinks about before falling asleep.

"For me, my potential as a friend or a son. Or as a husband or a dad."

It catches me off guard. "You're married?" I ask. I realize his relationship status hasn't come up yet—I'd just assumed he was single because Alexander was single. I check Rory's hand for a ring. There's not one.

"Nah," he says as rain thumps against the awning and streams down onto the cobbled street, filling the mortar crevices between the stones. "But hopefully, someday soon. I'm turning the big three-oh next year, so I'm getting up there."

I grunt in a grumpy sort of way because this stings, that I'm already over thirty and have a biological clock to worry about, unlike him. "Are you seeing anyone?" I ask.

"Technically, no," he says, but his expression says there's more to it than that. His eyes cloud over, and he seems to swallow heavily, his Adam's apple protruding from his skinny neck.

"What's the story?" I'm more curious than I want to be, but it's probably better to keep talking with him than be alone back in my flat, replaying last night's events on repeat.

Rory stashes his hands in his raincoat pockets and stares out at the market, as if deciding whether to tell me about it. "Things were serious with my girlfriend back home," he starts, forehead furrowed. "We'd been together a couple years, talked about marriage and all that. And then one day she wanted out. Said we'd fallen into too much of a routine. That I never pushed myself out of my comfort zone. And that my teacher's salary wasn't good enough to support the four kids and big house that she wanted."

He says it very matter-of-factly, but I can sense the hurt that hasn't healed yet. I only intended to feel sorry for myself today, but now I'm extending that sympathy to him as well. Instinctively, I can't help but trust Rory—maybe because we grew up in the same place or because there's just a candor about him that makes it impossible to doubt his character. Most adults, myself included, have gotten good at putting up walls and selectively showing different veneers in different settings while keeping the rest of us stashed away in some vaulted safe. I get the feeling Rory isn't like that. That he wouldn't know how to pretend to be somebody else, even if he tried.

"She said all that?" I ask.

"Indeed," Rory says with a brave-face grimace. "I mean, she phrased it nicer, but that was the gist of it."

I'm torn because, on the one hand, I can understand why she'd think Rory was boring and get freaked out picturing a ho-hum life together. Personally, I'd have the same issues with him. But she knew who Rory was when she started dating him, and she shouldn't be changing her mind and stringing him along. Besides, this is the twenty-first century, and there's no need for her to rely on a man to provide for her.

"Bonkers," I say, trying to make Rory feel better with some British lingo. "She's bonkers, mate."

"I don't know—I think she may have a point," he says, still looking downtrodden. "I do like my routine a lot. So I took the job in London to show her—to show *us*—that I could stretch out of my comfort zone and take chances." He makes a face to show that he's acutely aware of what a crazy decision it was. "And because I needed space. Perspective."

"Perspective," I echo. I have that feeling again that he might be my little brother, and I want to assure him that the right person will appreciate him just as he is. I'm in no mood to get sentimental, though, so I just pry a bit more. "So how's it going with her now?" I ask. "Do you still talk?"

"Every Sunday," Rory says. "But she wants to stay on an official break until Christmas. And then we'll 'reevaluate' as she says."

"Well, it sounds like there's a good chance then," I say. "I'm sure she'll come to her senses." I'm actually not sure of this at all, but I find myself wanting it to be true so that Rory will get the future he's planned out. There's an unexpected comfort in picturing someone else's life sticking to a small, cozy track, even though that's not what mine is—nor what I want it to be.

"Does she have a job?" I ask in what I hope sounds like a purely inquisitive tone, even as I privately judge the Midwest's prehistoric mentality that men should be the breadwinners.

"Emily doesn't want to work," he says, her name slipping off his tongue like it's his favorite and most frequently used word. "Which is fine—I want her to be able to stay home if she wants. But I wouldn't exactly be able to afford a mansion. Anyway, sorry I'm venting to you. I haven't actually told anyone all of this; it just kind of spilled out. I don't really have any friends here yet," he adds lamely.

This makes me feel both very bad and very good, honored that he's confided in me. "You're not venting," I say as we stay huddled under the bridal shop awning. "I asked you to tell me the story."

We trip into a lengthy silence that should be awkward but isn't. Trying to think of something that might cheer him up, I spy Badiani, a bright pink brick gelato shop two stores down. It's already decorated with Christmas lights, though it's not even November yet. "Very serious question for you," I pose. "Do you think it's too cold for gelato?"

Rory beams, and his huge, gummy smile seems to fit his face a bit more than before. "It's never too cold for anything that resembles ice cream," he declares.

"Spoken like a true Michigander." My pounding headache is starting to ease, and I'm almost enjoying myself, even if I am missing the more sophisticated and romantic conversations I could be having with Alexander if he actually existed.

Rory and I make a dash from the awning and into the shop. I taste-test twelve flavors before deciding on tiramisu, salted caramel, and pistachio. Rory opts for two different types of vanilla—French and Madagascar.

"Don't overdo it with all that variety," I comment dryly.

He grins self-effacingly. "Go ahead and judge, but vanilla is just as exciting as any other flavor. More exciting, maybe, because it doesn't lean on fillers to make it interesting."

"Hmm," is all I say. I don't want to push it in case it reminds him of his ex's critiques that he was too stuck in his routine.

I let him buy both of ours since I can tell he wants to, and our hands brush as he hands me my cup. There's no spark or anything, just a splash of light. "Can't believe they call this an extra-large," Rory grumbles good-naturedly as we make our way upstairs into the seating area. "Back home, this would be a baby scoop."

"And we wonder why America has a diabetes problem," I say, though I'm also missing the generous portions of the dairy-farm ice-cream stands I grew up going to.

We're the only customers in the shop, so we settle into a table beside the crooked little window that peeks out onto Camden Passage.

The gelato seems to cure Rory of his melancholy thoughts, but it does the opposite for me. I take a couple of spoonfuls but find it hard to swallow. The sweetness reminds me of the sugary cocktails last night.

"Don't like your flavors?" Rory asks, eyeing me with concern. "Told you that pistachio one looked suspicious. We can swap if you want."

"It's not that," I say as my stomach ties itself in new knots. "I'm just . . . not feeling great."

"Dang it, that's my fault for having us out in the rain. My nana is always warning me against that." He looks disappointed in himself.

"It's not a cold," I say. My voice catches, nearly breaking, and it makes me feel very weak.

We sit there for a minute as Rory waits to see if I'll elaborate. When I don't, he leans in closer and talks in a very low voice, though there's no one else around. "You don't have to tell me anything," he says, "but I'm here if you want to. We're each other's people, Kat. I've got your back."

We're each other's people.

It's such a simple, soothing thing to say that it makes me want to burst into tears. I can't cry though—I'm too drained of emotions and too blocked by feelings.

I know I couldn't be persuaded to tell anyone else about what happened. Not Jules, not Blake, not anyone at work. Certainly not my family. But for some reason, maybe because I have nothing to lose or nothing to gain, I find myself telling Rory now.

"I had a bad night last night."

I keep my eyes on my gelato while I speak, so I won't have to see the way Rory's warm eyes widen in horror when he realizes the kind of person I am.

I don't tell him everything. But I tell him enough. About the feedback from Oliver in my annual review. About how I went along to Annabel's and intentionally had too many drinks. How Harold touched my leg and how I didn't push him away.

Rory doesn't say anything while I'm talking, doesn't make a sound. When I've finished, I steal a quick glance at him. He looks visibly upset, jaw and palms clenched. It feels deservingly awful to have his opinion of me ruined so swiftly. Why did I have to divulge all this to him? Why couldn't I have just kept my mouth, and my legs, shut?

"I was stupid," I say, meaning many things at once. "So damn stupid."

"Stop that," Rory says, and his voice sounds gritty and harsh, different than I've heard it before. It's no surprise he's upset with me. I'd be equally appalled if the roles were reversed. "Stop being mean to yourself," he continues.

This makes me whip my head back up to look at him again. Though his stance is rigid, there's a tenderness, a compassion on his face that I hadn't noticed before. "You have to press charges," he says.

"I don't know," I say, mentally listing all the reasons it's probably better not to report Harold. The most pressing one is that I don't want to be associated with a sexual assault scandal. That kind of notoriety would taint any future success, or rule me out from it altogether.

"Kat," he says, and I have new appreciation for the way he says my name, elongating the middle vowel with that Michigan warmth. "We can't let someone treat you like that. Okay?"

The *we* lifts a massive weight off my shoulders. I didn't even realize how alone I'd felt until this moment of not feeling it anymore.

He's right, even if I don't want him to be. "I know," I agree, feeling meek and small, so far from the strong and independent woman I want to be. But I'm also feeling like maybe it's okay if I lean on someone. Maybe it's safe.

I try another spoonful of gelato, and it goes down easier this time. Ravenous, I keep eating.

"How can I help?" Rory asks, like he can see that I'm at war with myself.

"You can't," I say, but what I mean is *You already are. You're already helping.*

He seems to sense that I don't want to talk about it anymore right now. That I've pushed myself to my limit, and I'll shut down with anything more. But I can also tell that he's not going to let this drop.

"Here," Rory says, pushing his gelato toward me. "Finish mine up. I'm full."

I know he's not actually full, that he's just trying to make me feel better. But I accept it anyway. "Alright," I mumble, gratefully scooping his vanilla with my spoon. The simplicity hits the spot, and there's more nuance than I would've guessed between the Madagascar and French flavors. My taste buds feel more acute without the distraction of chocolate and caramel, though I don't admit that to Rory.

"Look," Rory says, peering outside. "The sun's coming out!"

Sure enough, rays are poking through the clouds, and Camden Passage is streaked with golden light. The market is back to its bustling affair as shoppers and vendors lower their hoods and umbrellas. Mellow rays make their way through the gelato shop window, landing on Rory's clean-shaven cheek.

"Good," I say. "Now we can toss out that mangled umbrella."

Rory's kept it on his lap the whole time we've been eating. "I can fix it," he insists, and I can tell that he's the kind of guy who can't admit when something's irrevocably broken.

CHAPTER EIGHTEEN

I work from home on Monday, chugging tea by the kettle as I avoid reaching out to HR. Rationally, I know I should report what happened at Annabel's, and I told Rory I would on our walk back from gelato.

But I don't want to.

If the news got out, the story would be tangled up with my name for years to come. I've worked too hard to let one night tarnish my reputation. It could jeopardize my promotion—or even if it didn't, people would be quick to discredit the partner title as something I didn't actually earn.

And though the events have already happened, there's a feeling that I can negate them by staying quiet. That I can stay unsoiled in other people's eyes and be less blemished in my own.

My inner deliberation is stuck in a circular loop, moving more backward than forward, when a double-decker bus squeaks up to St. Mary's outside. I glance out the window, glad for the distraction.

I've told Rory to look for me on his commute to work. To avoid sounding like a creepy stalker lady, I've made it seem like this will be the very first time I'll be perched in his line of sight.

There he is, peering up from his usual seat on the bus.

It feels different from when we made eye contact before (or more accurately, when I *thought* we'd made eye contact). There's none of the scintillating drama, none of the goose bumps or heart palpitations.

I miss the butterfly rush that comes from having a crush, and there's still a substantial part of me that resents Rory for his role in ruining my royal future. But there's a slim silver lining in no longer feeling like I have to be graceful or sophisticated enough to earn his approval. Now that I know he's no knight in shining armor, there's no pressure to impress.

Mouth stuffed full of Shreddies, I wave at Rory. He waves back wildly, like spotting me is just the greatest thing in the world. It makes me roll my eyes, that his life is so uneventful that this is a big deal for him. But it wins me over too.

How are my curtains this morning? I text him, as the bus rolls out of view down Upper Street. Still crooked?

I've fiddled with them, trying to even out the sides so it won't trigger his OCD. I don't like the idea of making him stressed out, even over something small like that.

Nice and symmetrical! ☺ he replies. You sure know how to make a guy's day.

I catch myself smiling, although I'm not exactly feeling in a joyous mood. My phone buzzes again, and Rory's name is back on my screen, almost as if he could feel my nerves reverberating through the coiled London streets.

Have you reached out to HR yet? It'll all be okay!

The accountability makes it harder to give into the temptation to just stay quiet. I know he'll be checking in. He already is.

Ironically, what I like best about Rory is one of the things that bothered me initially. That he's not interested in dating me. That he doesn't see me as anything other than a strictly platonic buddy to talk to while he pines after his girl back home.

Though I'm still not sure I approve of his ex, the fact that he's in love with her simplifies everything. I don't have to worry about Rory falling for me and my oh-so-charming ways, only to have to break his heart because there's absolutely no way I could or would fall in love with such a plain and simple hometown guy.

Knowing that he has no ulterior motive helps me accept and appreciate his friendship. At least in the moments I'm not still moping about how he's an American neighbor and not an English noble.

*　　*　　*

After a dozen rewrites of the email to Leo & Son's HR team, I do end up sending it the following week, right before the self-imposed window closes when I'd end up talking myself out of it for good. The final version doesn't say much, just that I have a time-sensitive matter I'd like to discuss in person or on the phone.

It's impossible to focus on work as I await a reply. I keep my video off in the status meeting and try not to gag as I see Harold's face. His pompous demeanor is unchanged, like that night never happened. In some ways, I welcome this deletion. But more so, I resent it and his privileged pageantry to carry on as if all is well in the world.

A full four and a half hours later, Helena from HR replies with a curt one-liner: Will find time for us to connect. Thx. A calendar invite pops up—a fifteen-minute Zoom meeting two weeks from now.

She apparently missed—or just disregarded—the *time-sensitive* part of my message. I propose a new time for this afternoon. Not knowing if she'll show, I dial into the Zoom meeting and try to repeat the script in my head. I've written bullet points of what I want to say, and I keep them open on a Word doc on my computer to prop up my wobbly courage.

Helena's bird-shaped face pops onto the screen seven minutes late, which leaves exactly eight minutes for our conversation. She's multitasking on her phone—texting or replying to emails or maybe swiping through a dating app.

I spit it all out in one breath before I can change my mind..

Helena handles the news without the smallest change in her appearance, though perhaps that's due to the excessive Botox that seems to have frozen her face in a constipated expression. She seems shockingly unshocked, and it gives me the feeling that I'm not the first person who's reported something similar against Harold.

This injects me with a surge of boldness. I'm not just doing this for me; I'm doing it for the other women who've been on the wrong end of Harold's eyes and hands. And all the future women who might be if he doesn't face any ramifications for his actions.

Helena starts asking questions that sound like they're being read from a checklist. "Could you please confirm whether you've spoken about this with anyone else at the company?" she asks in a harsh European accent.

"No," I say. "I came to you first."

"And from your perspective, was there consent?"

"No," I say, wavering as that word crawls its way up and down my body. "There wasn't."

"So you told him to stop?" Helena asks in that same brusque tone.

I fumble around for the right reply. "Not exactly," I say, humiliation hitting me squarely in the chest, "but that's not the point."

"So you did *not* tell him to stop? Or that it was making you uncomfortable?"

I take a deep breath, trying to keep calm. "That's correct. But—"

"Please do refrain from interrupting," she says, voice clipping.

I'd hoped to find an ally, an advocate. A woman who might have some empathy for the situation. And who might be able to do something about it. But how wrong I was. It makes me wonder if a portion of the ten million pounds that Turpi is paying Leo & Sons for the project is making its way directly to Helena. Or maybe she's just been instructed by her boss not to do anything that would jeopardize client relationships. After all, the top value of Leo & Sons is "client-centricity," meaning that clients are at the center of everything they do. So employees at Leo & Sons come second to their clients.

"Look," I say, trying to sound respectful but firm. "There need to be repercussions for Harold. I'm prepared to escalate this."

This seems to change Helena's attitude, if only a little. "Please do be assured that we take allegations against clients very seriously and will investigate," she says, but I can tell her mind is elsewhere and that she's already dialing into her next meeting.

"And I trust you not to speak about this with anyone else," she says. "We do want to ensure rumors don't spread."

"It's not a rumor. It's what happened."

"Let's just let the investigation sort it, shall we? Thank you for reaching out." Abruptly, she leaves the call.

I'm left there, alone on the Zoom call, staring at my own filtered reflection, trying to process what just happened.

Everything feels murky and corrupt, and I don't know where to turn. I end the Zoom call so at least I don't have to look at myself anymore. Then I text Rory.

Just talked with HR.

I prepare myself that I won't hear back for a while since he's probably in the middle of class, but he calls me right away. It's more than a bit jarring to receive an actual phone call. I've inherited the Millennial phobia of talking on the phone, except when it's for work, but I pick up now, right before it goes to voicemail.

"Hey, how'd it go?" Rory asks quietly. In the background, I hear the liberated chatter of children, and it makes me unexpectedly nostalgic for a stage of life I can never get back.

"I'm not sure," I say. "The HR woman says they'll look into it. But she seems determined not to incriminate Harold."

"Well, you've done the right thing," Rory says, and his earthy voice is the grounding comfort I needed. "Proud of you. And if they don't hold Harold responsible, we can go from there. We have options."

Again, I feel like I'm part of a team. Like I have someone to help me through this, someone who has a very solid moral compass and can steer me straight when I veer off track. "Thanks," I say, hoping he can hear how much I mean it.

"Hey, Kat?" he says. "I wanted to ask you something."

"What's that?" For a split second, I worry he might ask me on a date. And then when he doesn't, there's this ridiculous one percent of me that feels disappointed.

"We're having Career Day for my class next week," he says. "Some of the kids' parents are coming in to talk about their jobs. We don't have any women in business on the panel, though. Any chance you'd do me a favor and join in?"

I feel entirely unworthy of the invitation. There's no way that someone who tries to flirt her way into the promotion should be allowed to give career advice to primary school students. I'd be a fraud up there. "I'm not sure that's a good idea," I say, almost annoyed with him that he hasn't figured this all out on his own.

"The kids are a good bunch," Rory goes on. "Year Two, they call it, instead of second grade. They're obsessed with all things American, so they'll love you right away."

On Rory's end of the phone, I hear one of the children pipe up in an adorable English accent. "America! Did you say America? Please will you take us there, Mr. Cooper?"

"Mr. Cooper," I repeat back. "That's you?"

"Indeed."

Rory Cooper. It's a simple, sturdy name. Nothing stately or exciting, but it feels secure.

I find myself wanting to help him out. "When's the Career Day?" I ask.

"Next Friday at one PM," Rory says. "No pressure either way, I know you're swamped at work. Just have a think about it, as they say over here."

"Alright," I agree cautiously. "I'll have a think."

After we hang up, I look out at Upper Street and the buses passing by, thinking about all those days I imagined my life with Alexander. He would've popped into primary schools for the occasional photo op, but there's no way he would've put in the time day in and day out to actually be a teacher. *There are people for that,* he would've thought to himself, even if he was too well bred to say such things aloud. And he'd probably be telling me to just let the incident with Harold blow over—to look out for my own career goals and not risk jeopardizing them.

Maybe it's just the kind of day I'm having, but I can't find it in me to be so terribly disappointed that my prince doesn't actually exist. Similar to how I felt when I was slurping down the last of Rory's gelato, not caring if it was dripping from my chin, I'm actually relieved that I've gotten Rory in place of Alexander.

Okay I'm in, I text him that evening, after his school day would have ended so I don't bother him while he's teaching. So long as I get snack time.

His name pops up on my phone, and it has that buoying effect. Deal! Setting aside some Kit Kats for you.

My parents used to call me Kit Kat, I reply.

Can I call you that??

Then he double-texts a moment later. My bad, I know you're not a fan of nicknames. Forget I said that!

I'd mentioned to him, one offhand comment during our conversation on Saturday, how I despise that Harold calls me Kitten. But Kit Kat is different. The name reminds me of family dinners crammed around that little kitchen table, fighting my brothers for seconds of our mom's famous bean-anza casserole (sharing the bunk bed wasn't exactly a treat those nights). Kit Kat makes me feel like maybe I could be innocent and carefree again, even though right now I just feel used and crumpled.

I actually like being called Kit Kat, I reply to Rory, because he has a way of making my secrets feel safe, even the little ones like this. So long as it's accompanied by the candy.

Brill! See you next week, Kit Kat. ☺

His text doesn't give me butterflies, and I again mourn the thrill of anticipation that comes from having a crush. But his words still make me feel a bit lighter. Not like I'm flying in an airborne chariot with my true love or anything romantic like that. Just like I'm ambling with an old friend through a dandelion-filled meadow, both of us barefoot in jeans and old T-shirts, with the summertime sun strumming against our skin like an old banjo tune.

It's way less exciting than love and gets me lamenting all the ways Rory is infinitely more boring than Alexander would have been. But when I'm not spiraling into my rom-com comparisons, there's something unexpectedly comforting about having him around. Especially right now, when I feel so far from home.

CHAPTER NINETEEN

Work carries on like usual, and the normalcy puts me on edge. It makes me doubt whether any kind of investigation is happening. Harold struts through the office as brashly as ever. He could just be posturing, but I don't think he'd have that much self-restraint to keep from fuming and gaslighting me if HR had actually questioned him about the incident.

Impatient for an update, I ping Helena at the end of the week. Days later, she gets back with a very helpful reply: *As mentioned, will circle back when I have an update. Please do respect our process.*

It leaves me feeling powerless, waiting on the system to judge whether I'm credible or crazy. I consider going straight to Oliver, but something stops me. Maybe pride or maybe shame. Probably both.

On the Friday of Career Day at Rory's school, I work from the office in the morning so I can be there for an org structure meeting (read: "a layoffs meeting"). Then at lunchtime—or more accurately, that hour of the day that *should* be lunchtime but is actually just shovel-down-cafeteria-food-at-your-desk-with-an-air-of-self-important-stress hour—I pack up to head over to Rory's school.

I haven't taken any time off since starting this case, so the prospect of escaping work for even a few hours is highly exciting. As I'm swapping out my pumps for trainers, Harold comes by and lingers at my desk, one hand resting on the back of the chair.

"Sneaking out for a cheeky long weekend?" he asks.

"Not sneaking," I say coolly. "I'm taking annual leave this afternoon to help a friend with something." Over here, annual leave is what they call paid time off.

I go to the lifts, Harold on my tail. "We're overdue for another Annabel's night," he says, as if he expects me to leap at the suggestion.

The grainy vibration of his voice gives me the feeling that I'm naked in a crowded room. I pull my blazer more tightly around me as I wait for the elevator, but the sensation doesn't go away.

"I'll put something in the diary for next week," Harold goes on, seeming to take my nauseated silence as a yes.

His mouth is curled upward into a satisfied smile, and he's eyeing me more audaciously than he ever has, like the challenge of landing me feels in reach now. He seems to think my rebuff is just an act that I'm putting on in the office, and that all the walls and clothes will fall away after he gets another few drinks in me.

Nothing I can say or do right now can set him straight, and it leaves me dizzy.

The elevator doors open. Harold doesn't follow me in, just watches the doors close and gives a salacious wink, as if we're in on some private joke.

It makes me more confident in my decision to report him. If calling him out on his misogynistic behavior costs me the promotion, then it's not a promotion I want.

Part of me still wavers and wonders if it I've shot myself in the foot, but I try not to give credence to those indecent doubts.

Heading out of the office, I make my way to the underground. Standing on the grubby platform, minding the gap as I wait for the train, I look over the talking points I've written for what I'm going to say to the kids. I don't trust myself to wing it. In fact, I can't remember the last time I winged anything. My corporate training has taught me that anything spontaneous reflects poorly as a lack of preparation. Unless you're a white man who went to some fancy prep school, in which case winging it is rewarded as endearingly off the cuff.

I get off the train in Clerkenwell, where Rory's school is located. Just one neighborhood south of Islington, it's an awkward blend of characterful taverns and corner shops, juxtaposed beside dodgy-looking apartment buildings jutting obtrusively into the sky to spoil the old-world illusion.

Hendrick Primary School is the name of the school, and it's a handsome building, or at least looks as if it might have been once. Multiple turrets twist up to the third story, giving the grounds an air of importance. But the brick is in need of a power wash, and the undersized windows are foggy and chipped. Something tells me this isn't where the royal family sends their offspring.

Making my way inside, I register in the front office, where I'm pointed in the direction of Mr. Cooper's classroom, one story up. The halls are narrow, with low ceilings and dim lights. Everything feels a bit sloped and scrunched. Still, there's a certain tidiness that's distinctly British, plus the universal optimism of an elementary school.

Rory's voice spills out into the hall from the classroom at the end of the hall. The door is ajar, and I stand outside watching him. He's at the front of the classroom, dressed in khaki pants and a checkered button-down, doing some odd kind of jig—bending his knees, then reaching up toward the ceiling, then fluttering his hands down like snowflakes.

There's a chant that goes along with it too. The kids are repeating the words back, mimicking the dance as they stand beside their chairs.

"Condensation, precipitation, runoff, evaporation," everyone says, the kids' British accents far overwhelming Rory's American one. And then it starts over once more. "Condensation, precipitation . . ."

They're acting out the rain cycle, and it's pretty adorable, especially with the English inflection and school uniforms—prim purple jumpers with collared blazers, and a mix of trousers and pleated skirts with knee-high argyle socks. The kids look like they're having the time of their lives.

Rory catches sight of me in the doorway. He doesn't look abashed to be caught doing a silly dance—he just grins that big Rory grin and waves me in.

"Look who it is," he says to the students. "Our first special guest!"

Lively applause ushers me into the classroom, reinforcing that sinking feeling that I don't deserve to be welcomed here.

The walls are painted robin's-egg blue, and they're covered with construction paper stars, large-print spelling words, and a projector screen. Rory's desk is at the front of the room, and then the students are gathered around a few long tables that are positioned in an inclusive U shape.

"What do you want the kids to call you?" Rory asks me.

"Um, Miss Kat, I guess?" I say.

In a louder voice, he addresses the students. "This is Miss Kat," he says. "She's one of our Career Day speakers."

The students pepper me with all sorts of questions: Did my parents think I was going to be a cat when I was born? And can I talk to animals or jump from tall places without getting hurt?

It makes me smile, how inquisitively their brains work and how freely they fling their questions out into the open.

Finally, Rory interjects to say they have to get back to the water cycle for a few more minutes.

One of the little girls trots right up to me. "Miss Kat?" she says, black-brown eyes wide and wonder filled. "My name is Mala, and cats are my favorite animal, if you must know." She tugs on her shiny black hair, tied into two long braids with mismatched bows. "Would you like to come stand by me? I can teach you the dance. It's rather tricky, but not to fret."

So I follow Mala back to her table, and with great earnestness, she shows me the exact technique of how I'm supposed to wiggle my hands for the rain and stomp my feet for the runoff part and make a swooshing motion for evaporation.

Following her lead, I join in with the class. Oddly enough, I'm having fun.

I say "oddly enough" because kids and I don't exactly mesh. I love my nephews, but they are exceptions to the rule. Friends' babies have never taken to me, and vice versa. It's made me wonder if maybe I'm not actually destined to be a mom. I like the idea of having kids, of being the badass CEO/supermom who *has it all*, but picturing the dirty-diaper-and-colicky reality makes me wonder if it's actually compatible with my career goals. I wouldn't want a nanny to raise my kids, but I can't picture giving up the time to be there myself.

The truth is that I'm terrified of losing myself to kids, of putting my ambitions on the back burner to care for other people. Maybe this makes me a horrible, selfish person. Or maybe it just means I'm a new-age woman who isn't content being a martyr to motherhood.

"You're meant to sing too, Miss Kat," Mala chides. "Don't be shy now."

No one seems to notice that I'm tone deaf, and it's unexpectedly liberating, the ability to completely butcher a melody without any kind of judgment.

But the best part is watching Rory. He lights up in action, bringing the shyer students out of their shell and keeping the boisterous ones in check without curbing their enthusiasm. It's so clear that this is where he's meant to be, and I feel a bout of anger toward his ex for pressuring him to take a higher-paying job just to fund her lifestyle.

The other adults on the panel start arriving. They all seem to be parents of kids in the class. Mala runs up to a woman in a custodial uniform, joyfully throwing her arms around her legs. "My mum is a caretaker at the British Library!" she proudly announces to the class. "She cleans the bookcases *every night*."

The students look enthralled, like this sounds like the coolest job ever. It gets me a little choked up as I think about how proud I used to be of Dad's social work job when I was little. "My daddy is saving the world!" I'd brag far and wide. But somewhere along the way, I became embarrassed by how little money he made and how Mom had never worked at all, unless you counted the jewelry parties she hosted, which I didn't. By the time I went off to college, I told people that both my parents worked in business and left it at that.

The Career Day lineup also includes a doctor, a chef, a construction manager, and an electrician. And me, the corporate sellout/consultant. Rory gives an introduction, and we all go around explaining what we do. When it's my turn, I tell the class that I'm a consultant, which means that I try to help businesses fix their problems. Looking down at the bullet points on my note card, I explain that I have different projects that each last a few months, and I explore ways for companies to grow bigger and get better.

"So you're like a doctor for companies?" one of the students pipes in.

"That's giving me too much credit," I say. "But I try to help."

Try to help. It's a phrase I've underlined in my notes. As I say it, though, it feels like one big lie. The truth is that I just do what the client wants and count down the days until I can get promoted and move on and up. If I was actually trying to help, I wouldn't be working as a sycophant for a big oil client that's polluting the very water cycle that the kids are learning about.

Perhaps Rory can tell I'm having a moment, because he tactfully moves on to the next speaker in the panel.

At the end of the session, Mala's mom turns to me with a smile and asks which one my child is. It startles me, realizing that I'm old enough that I could have a kid in this class. I have that cold-sweaty sensation that life is moving way too fast, that I've missed the boat.

"Oh no, I'm not a mom," I stammer. "I'm just friends with Rory—Mr. Cooper," I correct. "We're from the same place back in the States."

"Ah, bless him," the mom says. "Mr. Cooper is just lovely. Isn't he, Mala?"

"He's quite splendid," Mala agrees.

Her mom dashes out to collect Mala's younger siblings at playgroup. Mala asks if I'll stay, and I readily agree. I've already taken the rest of the day off, and I want to see more of Rory's teaching.

After a snack break (I collect my Kit Kats and Mars bars), Rory passes out construction paper and crayons and asks the class to write down their own dream job and draw a picture of it.

I'm certain that no one will choose consultant, but a few of the kids write it down, with various misspellings. It boosts my ego at first, almost like it's proof that I've chosen something noble. But then it dents my heart, picturing these free-form children having to dim their colors, clip their wings, and develop scaly exoskeletons to fit into the constrictive corporate box.

These kids seem so young, way too young to be thinking about careers. But when I was just about their age, I'd decided I wanted to be a CEO.

I watch Mala as she draws in every color crayon. "What do you want to be when you grow up?" I ask, trying to decipher the bright flowery shapes and squiggly lines.

"Happy," she answers through a gap-toothed smile. "I'd quite like to be happy. See here, this is the sky," she says, pointing to the shapes on the paper, which I now see are clouds and suns, not flowers. "I'm going to live up there and dance in the sunshine every day."

Another boy overhears her from down the table. "Don't be daft, Mala," he sneers. "*Happy* isn't a career."

Mala looks dejected, her little shoulders slumping as the grin slips from her face.

"Don't listen to him," I tell her. "Happy is a very good thing to want to be."

"You reckon so?" Mala says, perking up just a bit.

"Very much so," I affirm.

I feel Rory looking on. He says something quietly to the kid who made fun of Mala, making the boy wriggle sheepishly in his seat.

Then, pulling up a chair beside Mala, Rory picks up an orange crayon and starts drawing on his own sheet of yellow paper. "You know," he says, adding some smiley face suns. "I'd like to be happy when I grow up too. Is it okay if I steal your idea, Mala?"

Mala appears thoroughly cheered up by the idea that her beloved Mr. Cooper is taking her ambition seriously. "But Mr. Cooper," she says, with great solemnity, "you're already grown up!" Then she bursts out giggling, like this is just the funniest prospect in the world—Mr. Cooper trying to figure out what he wants to be when he grows up!

"I'm not so sure about that," Rory says as he continues to fill his blank canvas with color. "I don't think we're ever done growing up."

His gold-brown eyes catch mine, making me feel a little less lost. Or at least a little more okay with feeling lost. Because here we are, two people who were raised within a few miles of each other in small-town America, who are still growing up across the ocean here in the sprawling city of London.

Growing up together, perhaps.

CHAPTER TWENTY

The happiness thing stays in my mind for a while. The bright look on Mala's face when she'd said it—*"I'd quite like to be happy."*

It makes me wonder why I've never thought of my goals like that—as a feeling rather than a title. Why I've always been wired to *achieve* rather than simply *be*. I guess my logic has been that achievement will bring happiness. That one is a prerequisite for the other. But I'm not so sure of that as I used to be.

What if Mala's dancing-on-the-clouds drawing came true? What if you could fly through the sky without climbing a rigid ladder to get there?

I wonder how Rory would view it. It feels like he's always thinking about other people's happiness—his students', Emily's. But what about his own?

He called me after Career Day, but because of my acute phone phobia, I let it go to voicemail. The message he left had some really nice things about how great I was with the kids and how they're asking when I'm coming back next. I've taken to replaying it some evenings when I'm anxious to hear an update from HR or stressing about the promotion or wondering if I should re-download the dating apps. Hearing Rory's voice doesn't fix anything, but it calms me down so the breaths come from my belly rather than my throat.

One Friday evening, I'm walking along Upper Street on my way back from Sainsburys, carting two tote bags of groceries—mostly crumpets, peanut butter, and precooked roasts. I'd meant to go shopping last Sunday but haven't gotten around to it until now.

It's mid-November, and almost overnight, London has been draped in Christmas decorations, like someone has cast a snowglobe spell over the whole city. Since England doesn't have Thanksgiving as the line in the sand separating the holidays, the festive spirit seems to seep in earlier than in America.

Upper Street is in full fancy-dress attire, snowflake lights twinkling high above the cars, swooping the entirety of the two-lane road. Tinsel, miniature train sets, and Christmas crackers fill the shop windows. The old-fashioned lampposts are wrapped with garlands and bows, and the chalk menus outside the gastropubs boast of mulled wine and Yorkshire pudding.

The undeniably charming decor strikes me as insensitively cheerful. Like it's mocking the fact that I'm not in such a holly jolly mood. Laughing at the fact that Christmas is coming and I have no one to snog under the mistletoe. No one except the memory of a prince who never existed in the first place.

Back inside my flat, I set the bags down at my feet with a loud thump and shake out my tired arms. My plan is to get these unloaded, then take a hot bath and watch *Married at First Sight* while eating gelato straight from the pint. It's really not a bad Friday night so long as I don't compare it to the vibrant lives of everyone in Instagram, which I can't help but do.

"Well there you are," a voice says, making me jump.

My couch is occupied. Jules is there, sprawled out and smoking a cig, repurposing an empty beer can into an ashtray.

"What're you doing here?" I say, voice shrill as I recover from my scare.

"I was just sat 'ere checking in," Jules says. "Wanted ter make sure you 'adn't been slaughtered in your sleep—that sorta neighborly thing. Not much box and toys out of you recently."

"Box and toys?"

"Noise," Jules translates the cockney slang. "Been no noise 'round here, and you've been proper ghosting me."

"I haven't been ghosting you," I defend, though I know that I have left a few of her recent texts unanswered. "Just been slammed with work. Final countdown until the promotion decisions."

The night at Annabel's with Harold looms heavily in the air between us. I haven't told Jules about it yet and don't particularly want to. I'm trying to eject the events from my body and mind, and talking about them now feels like it would be giving them new life.

"Promotion sha-motion," Jules says, rolling her eyes with anti-corporate ardor. "Who cares what your bloody business card says? Those things belong in antique shops by now anyway."

"It's not about a business card," I tell her, lugging the groceries to the counter and unloading them into the fridge. "It's about what it represents . . ." With a heavy sigh, I feel the weight of everything that seems to be riding on the promotion. Proof that I'm living up to my potential. That I'm going places and getting there fast. That I'm not falling behind, at least not in my career.

"Take a bevvy," Jules says, magicking up a solution with a beer that she hands me from her stash.

I decline it. "As much as I appreciate the burglary gift," I deadpan, "I'm sticking to kombucha tonight."

Jules looks at me with an expression of utmost horror. "Not drinking on a Friday night? You're crackers."

I don't tell her about how I'm worried that the alcohol will trigger flashbacks of Harold. Or that it will make me unravel into a sad and self-critical place where I blame myself for the whole thing. "I'm trying to detox," I say. "Cleanse the body and all that."

It's as close to the truth as I feel comfortable sharing.

"Something's dodgy if you ask me," Jules says, wiggling her eyebrows one at a time, like they're doing an Irish jig. "I reckon I know what's going on 'ere."

I feel my face blanch. Could she have somehow found out about what happened at Annabel's?

"You've seen the bloke, 'aven't you?" Jules says with a confident lilt in her voice.

"What bloke?" Hoping she doesn't mean Harold, I open the window to let the smoke out.

"The English prince-slash-hometown farmer," Jules carries on.

Though I'm relieved she's talking about Rory, I feel my cheeks heat up despite the gust of cold air coming into the sitting room. "He's not a farmer," I say. "He's a schoolteacher."

"You 'ave seen him!" she says, freckled face lighting up in triumph. "Look at you, you're going proper pink in the cheeks."

"If there's anything off with my complexion, it's just because of all these carcinogens swirling around this room." I give her a lecture-like stare, which seems to have no effect.

"Spill the goss then, babes," Jules says, cozying up for a good story. "Have you shagged yet?"

I nearly spit my kombucha out. "Absolutely not. We've gotten *one* coffee, and I went to his school *one time* to speak for Career Day. That's it."

"Full on," Jules says. "You've already met 'is students? That's the equivalent of meeting someone's kids, innit? And you know what 'appens after the bell rings . . ." She makes a series of X-rated gyrating motions.

"False," I say. "There was none of that. There's zero sexual tension."

Jules isn't buying it. "Poppycock," she says. "Total rubbish. You were ready to shag before you even met 'im."

"Yes, *before* I got to know him as Rory, the ordinary American from my hometown. And if that's not enough of a turnoff, he's still pretty much with his ex-girlfriend back in Kalamazoo."

"Why isn't she 'ere then?" Jules wants to know.

"She broke up with Rory because she thought they were in too much of a routine," I explain, with the determined air of a disinterested third party. "And because he didn't make enough money, apparently."

"And what's keeping 'er from getting a job 'erself? This isn't the bloody eighteenth century, for fuck's sake."

"I don't know the details," I say, though I agree with her. "Just that he's still in love with her. Which is good," I add forcefully. "So he and I can be *friends*. No complications."

Jules makes a skeptical snorting sound, not bothering to try and muffle it. "Righ'o," she says. "So you're going on other dates then, are you?"

"Not right now," I say. "I'm focusing on myself for a while."

My preoccupation with finding a British beau is at an all-time low. The night at Annabel's seems to have turned me off dating altogether, puncturing any remaining illusions about finding an actual gentleman in this country.

Jules has a different take on the matter. "Meaning you're waiting for Rory to wake up and realize you're the one 'e wants?" she poses.

"How many times do I have to tell you?" I snap, patience wearing thin. "The very last thing I'd want is to be with someone from *Kalamazoo*. He represents everything I've worked so hard to escape."

"Alrigh', alrigh', don't get your knickers in a twist." And just like that, she cracks open a new beer and switches the subject. "So tell me, babes, what's the plan for our Thanksgiving do, hey?"

"What do you mean?" I ask, unable or perhaps just unwilling to shrug off my grumpy mood. "We don't get Thanksgiving off over here. I'm not doing anything, I have to work."

Jules looks more than a bit crestfallen. "But *babes*, I've been dreaming of a traditional American Thanksgiving feast fer *years*. Decades, really. It was one of the reasons I was so bloody keen to get on with you, if you must know . . ." She trails off wistfully, batting her stick-on eyelashes at me with a pathetically crushed expression that softens me more than I want it to.

To be honest, I'm not too excited about the idea of skipping Thanksgiving either. It always used to be my favorite holiday. As a kid, I loved being Mommy's little helper in the kitchen and then watching football on TV with my dad and brothers. Between the main course and dessert, we'd go for a family walk around the lake behind our house and then curl up with cinnamon apple cider and card games by the fire at night, our dog, Murray, snoring happily on the hearth, full from the bits of food we'd snuck him from under the table.

"I guess you and Nina could come over for dinner," I offer to Jules, as much for myself as for them. "Just something small after work."

Jules's grudge is instantly replaced with glee. "That's ace, babes," Jules proclaims, twirling her cigarette like a baton. "I've already saved a dozen pumpkin pie recipes I'm keen to bake. Never made a sweet pie before, only savory."

As she's prattling on about this recipe and that one, my thoughts drift toward Rory, wondering whether he has something to do on Thanksgiving.

"Reckon we should invite anyone else?" Jules says, as if tracking my thoughts. "Any other Americans who might be 'omesick?" She puts on an unconvincingly clueless expression, as if she can't possibly think of anyone who fits the bill.

Subtlety is not her strong suit. I scowl at her, though I do like the idea of Rory joining us. He was so great when I told him about Harold. And the more I think about it, the more I wonder if he invited me to Career Day more for me than for his students. As a way to help me get my confidence back and be reminded of the goodness in the world. He's definitely the kind of person who does favors for people under the guise of asking for their help.

"I'm sure Rory already has plans, if that's what you mean," I tell Jules, keeping my voice harsh so she won't guess at the softness beneath. "But I can ask him, I guess."

"Oh, *Rory!*" Jules says, all drama and delight. "I 'adn't even thought of 'im." She slaps her head lightly.

"Sure you hadn't," I grumble, but I text Rory right then, asking if he'd want to join a couple people at my place for Thanksgiving dinner. "And just for the record, if he does come, it will *not* be a double date," I tell Jules. "He's most likely officially getting back with his ex at Christmas, so he's off the market. Not that I'd be interested anyway," I clarify, flustered. "Just no scheming, that's all."

"No scheming," Jules insists, green eyes glimmering. "We'll just have some good food and bubble baths, we will."

"We're not taking bubble baths at Thanksgiving," I shoot down at once, feeling very bothered by the idea of being naked anywhere near Rory.

"'Bubble bath' just means laugh," Jules says. "It'll be a proper good time—that's all I meant. Now I'm sorry, I've got ter run," she apologizes, as if she had been invited over here in the first place. "Nina'll be home soon, and I was meant to fold the laundry on the rack. The things you do for love, I tell you . . ."

With that, Jules bounces off the couch, blowing me a lavish stream of kisses as she disappears through the door connecting our flats.

My phone buzzes, and Rory's name is back on my screen, along with his Thanksgiving answer.

Thanks so much for the invite! Would be chuffed to bits to join. ☺ What can I bring??

The response makes me smile, and my first inclination is to replace the grin with an expression of indifference or even annoyance so no one will misinterpret it as anything more than the purely platonic thing that it is.

But then I remember no one's around to witness the smile except the spiders lurking in the cobwebby corners of Marlow House. So

I let it stay for a moment, just until I draw a bath and lower myself into the tub, and the stress from work takes over again.

I add some suds until the bath water turns foggy and foamy, hiding my body underneath because I like it better when I don't have to see myself.

CHAPTER TWENTY-ONE

Working from home on Thanksgiving, I'm greeted with a slew of messages from my parents, brothers, and Blake, all wishing me Happy Thanksgiving and hoping I'm celebrating across the pond. Though I don't like missing people, I very much enjoy *being* missed, and I reassure them all that I'm hosting a dinner with some new friends.

Any British men in attendance?? Blake wants to know. Living vicariously through you!

No, I reply truthfully. I'm striking out in that department.

As I'm dialing into a meeting, Jules barges into my flat, balancing two pumpkin pies. One is sprinkled with sugared cranberries and the other has a veritable mountain of whipped cream.

"'Appy Thanksgiving, babes," she greets, cheerfully clanking the pies onto the kitchen counter. "'Ow do they look? I'll be back in just a mo' with the other nosh . . ." Disappearing through the door, she returns again with overflowing Tesco grocery bags and a massive frozen turkey that looks like it could feed half the British army.

"What's all this?" I ask, trying to sound appreciative but feeling more than a little stressed out at all the commotion. "I'm having everything delivered from Ottolenghi's—thought I mentioned that. No need for us to slave away in the kitchen and propagate societal gender norms."

Jules has a different take on it. "But I *like* to cook," she says, pre-heating the oven and dumping out no fewer than two dozen sweet potatoes from the bag. "Why should I keep from doing something I enjoy just because it fits a stereotype, hey? New-age feminism is being free to do whatever the 'ell we please, even if that's cooking in a frilly dress." As if to emphasize the point, she whips out a retro embroidered apron and ties it around her waist.

"Fair enough," I say, relenting, because it's impossible to disagree with Jules's confidence. "But would you perhaps want to use *your* kitchen as the headquarters for this progressive culinary revolution?"

"Can't do, I'm afraid," she says, pulling her corkscrew hair out of her face with a pink scrunchie that clashes horribly with her hair. "Nina's cream-crackered—*knackered*—from the night shift this week. That's nurse life for you, and I don't want ter be a bother. And anyway, reckon I'll need some help translating the American recipes. Everything's in Fahrenheit and cups, not Celsius and scales. It's mad."

"Isn't that what Google is for?" I grumble. But catching a whiff of her good mood, I relent. "Go ahead and stay—just keep out of view when I'm on my video calls."

"Will that pig 'Arold be on any of your Zooms?" Jules asks. "I'll walk in the background 'olding the sharpest knife so 'e knows what's coming for 'is town halls—*balls*—if 'e gives you trouble. 'Appy days." She cackles gleefully.

It tickles my heart, in a vengeful sort of way. If Jules only knew what really happened that night at Annabel's, she'd be poking the knife straight through the screen, into Harold's filler-injected face. Or making her way down to Canary Wharf to duel him in person.

As I carry on at the computer, Jules sets to work, slicing and dicing, basting and banging like she's auditioning to play percussion in a teenage rock band. I explain the background noise away to my colleagues as construction on my street.

"You know there are only four of us coming to dinner, right?" I hiss at Jules between meetings as she tries to jam additional casserole dishes into the oven beside the gargantuan turkey. "Not four hundred."

"Bugger off, crotchety corporate Kat. This is my first Thanksgiving, and I'm going to do it right."

Midway through my next call, Jules shrieks loudly. Hurriedly, I mute myself and switch my video off too. "What's wrong?" I ask springing up from my chair, expecting to see a missing finger and puddle of blood.

"It's all to pot!" Jules laments, just about yanking her hair out of her head. "I've forgotten the brown sugar in the bloody sweet potatoes."

"*That's* the big crisis? But you've already added three layers of marshmallows," I point out. "I'll go out on a limb and say they'll be sweet enough."

"'Ope so," Jules says, nervously sprinkling more sugar on top of the fluffy concoction. "Gonna run these back over to cook 'em in our oven since the turkey's 'ogging all the room."

The next time I look up from my screen, night has fallen. Jules is in the kitchen again, this time with Nina, who is the yin to Jules's yang. Small and svelte, with a delicate heart-shaped face and black hair that's cropped into a pixie cut, her mellow energy balances out Jules's rambunctious spirit. Quiet and soft-spoken, she looks genuinely delighted to let Jules be the star of the show.

"Hey, girl, can I, like, pour you some pomegranate punch?" Jules asks me in what I gather is her attempt at an American accent. She offers up a pitcher of a ruby-red drink ornamented with orange slices and mint springs "It's an American tradition—the blog said so."

"Not right now," I decline, politely abstaining from pointing out that I've never heard of pomegranate punch on Thanksgiving. "I've got to update this cost efficiency model."

"Or the world stops turning, yeah?" Jules teases. "It's nearly 'alf six. Rory'll be here soon, won't 'e? And don't tell me your wearing *that*." She eyes my sweatpants-bottom-professional-blouse combo with overt disapproval.

"It's an American tradition," I say dryly. "Let it rest."

"Go get changed," she commands. "I'll run the control center while you're gone, fear not."

The idea of Jules managing my work computer is nothing short of terrifying, but Nina steps in. "I'll make sure she doesn't touch anything," she promises.

So after making a few more tweaks to the model based on Oliver's feedback (he wants us to overpromise how much Turpi can automate so it makes it look like we're saving them more money), I disappear into my bedroom and try on a few different outfits. Nothing seems quite right, but I settle on a plummy velvet top with high-waisted corduroys. I finish the look with heeled boots and hoop earrings that probably went out of style years ago, but I haven't had the time to notice. My fringe is finally long enough to swoop out of my face, so I wrap it around my curling wand for a wavy curtain bang effect and pull the rest of my hair into a fishtail braid at the back of my neck.

Jules whistles as I reemerge into the kitchen. "You look smashing," she says. "Rory's not going to want to eat my cooking after seeing that, if you know what I mean." She sniggers at her own joke while I scowl.

"He has a *girlfriend*," I remind Jules.

"Thought you said they were broken up?" Jules asks.

"Technically, yes. But effectively, they're still together. It's complicated."

Jules grins, as if "complicated" indicates a green light. It makes me want to launch into all the reasons Rory and I aren't compatible anyway, but the buzzer to Marlow House rings promptly at six thirty.

My armpits start sweating even more excessively than usual. Probably just the nerves of hosting my first holiday dinner. And sure, maybe I'm slightly worried that Rory might think I've tricked him into a double date. I haven't, of course, but the optics aren't exactly in my favor.

"Hey there," Rory greets as I open up the door to my flat. "Happy Turkey Day!"

He's in dark wash jeans and an untucked flannel shirt that makes him look lean but not scrawny. It's more casual than his Mr. Cooper look, and I get the feeling he went home and changed after school. His hair is still damp from the shower, and it looks like he's combed his cowlick in an (unsuccessful) attempt to get it to lie flat. He's wearing a faint cologne—something woodsy and natural that makes me think of summer nights on the lake where I grew up, back before I had anywhere I needed to be.

Rory goes in for a hug that I'm not prepared for. I pat his shoulder instead, bungling the whole thing.

"Deligh'ed to *finally* meet you, Rory," Jules croons as Rory takes off his threadbare Nikes and lines them up neatly next to the door. "Kat 'as told us all about you, of course."

I could swat her and her big mouth, loosened by a couple glasses of punch.

"This is my fiancée, Nina," Jules says, proudly presenting her partner. "She's quite tidy, hey?"

Jules and Nina are both beaming, as if they're just the luckiest humans in the world.

It's impossible to be very jealous of them, but I am *slightly* jealous. It just seems unfair that some people fit together so seamlessly while others of us try so hard to fit square pegs into round holes, sawing the edges off puzzle pieces so they might fit into place, but always coming up short.

Rory doesn't bat an eye at a lesbian couple, which is a relief. I didn't think he would, but you never know with Midwesterners. An alarming percentage are still homophobic.

Jules and Nina wiggle their hands in Rory's face so he can see their engagement rings. "Which one do you like better?" Jules wants to know.

Rory looks entirely out of his element as he studiously examines both rings. Jules's is a prominent halo-cut rock, while Nina's is a tasteful solitaire. "I don't think I can pick," he says. "They're both great, and if I'm being honest, jewelry all kind of looks the same to me."

It makes me smile to myself. Somehow it seems fitting that Rory's future bride forgo a diamond ring. She'll wear a simple band of brass or maybe wood. The thought of an oak ring on my own finger makes me feel snug and serene for a split second, before I remember the utter nonsense of it.

"Typical men. Completely useless," Jules says with a good-humored humph. "Ooh, what've you got in there?" she asks, catching sight of a blue cooler that Rory's brought with him.

"I told you not to bring anything," I chide Rory.

"It's only a few small things," he says. "My mom would disown me if I showed up empty-handed. This here is her corn casserole recipe," he says, pulling a dish out of the cooler. "Though I definitely didn't do it justice. And I brought some Bell's too. Thought it might be a little taste of K-Zoo for ya."

He takes out a case of Bell's, a craft beer brewed in Kalamazoo. Now stocked internationally, it's the town's single claim to fame. That and the fact that Derek Jeter grew up there.

My dad used to love sipping Bell's on the back porch, watching the sun dip down over the water. During my teenage years, he'd let me take a few sips here or there.

Rory's taking something else out of the cooler—a chocolate pie covered in Saran wrap. "This one was a bit of a gamble," he says. "Never made it before."

"Excellent," Jules says. "Now it won't matter so much if my pumpkin ones turn out to be rubbish."

"We're saved," Nina teases, dropping a kiss on Jules's lips. "What flavor is it?" she asks Rory.

It's . . . a Kit Kat pie," Rory says, ears turning pink as he glances at me. "Since you said your family used to call you that."

Something happens inside my body and outside my body too. It's not a stomach flip, nor a heart flutter, but it's a lifting sensation, a levitation of parts of me I thought were tethered to the ground.

"Blimey," Jules says as Nina looks like she's fully melting. "Might have to nick some of that before dinner."

"No rules against a-pie-tizers," Rory says. "Sorry, my puns get pretty terrible from being around kids all day."

"We're all children here," Jules says cheerfully, wasting no time in cutting us all slices of the Kit Kat pie. We eat it as our starter course, standing around the kitchen counter and rotating the side dishes through the microwave as the turkey finishes cooking.

Jules and Nina stick to the pomegranate punch while Rory and I opt for the Bell's. I feel safe drinking with Rory, especially this beer. It's the "Lager of the Lakes," and it tastes better than I remember. The flavor is light and low key and washes down like a guitar-string song.

As Jules carves the turkey and gives Rory a primer in cockney rhyming slang, we set the table with the stuffing, gravy, sweet potatoes, green beans, Brussel sprouts, corn casserole, and crescent rolls. I've cancelled the delivery order, and we still have difficulty fitting all the food on the circular table as we take our seats.

"Now, before we eat," Jules commands, "please can we all go around and say what we're thankful for?"

"Do you really do that in America?" Nina asks Rory and me.

"Yes," we say in unison, with mutually raised eyebrows.

"My family rambles on so long," I say, "that the food's all cold by the end."

"Grace winds up being longer than a Sunday sermon," Rory commiserates.

Jules doesn't like the sound of that. "Let's just do one collective thanks, shall we?" she suggests. "C'mon, hold hands then."

I take Jules's hand on one side and Rory's on the other. Rory's palms are leathery and dry, like he hasn't been introduced to body lotion. The texture is oddly comforting, giving me something to grip.

Jules starts in, talking extremely quickly. "Dear God or Goddess or whatever spiritual forces may potentially be listening, we're thankful for food, footy, bloody good mates, and rub-a-dubs. Who can tell me what rub-a-dubs are?" she asks, quizzing the audience.

"Pubs?" Rory guesses.

"Well done, laddie. You already know more cockney than Kat. And we're thankful for my cheese and kisses—*missus*," she says with a cheeky wink at Nina. "And double-decker buses," Jules finishes, casting a knowing look my way.

I kick her shin under the table, but she doesn't wince, just grins wider. The last thing I want is for Rory to know that I was obsessed with him, or at least the fictional version of him, for weeks before we actually met.

"Alrigh' that'll do," Jules says, dropping my hand and reaching for the nearest dish. "Let's eat and get pissed!"

There's a second or two where Rory and I don't drop each other's hands. We keep holding on. It's not long enough for Jules or Nina to notice anything, but it's long enough to notice it ourselves. It feels like something old and new all at once.

Then it's over, and we both let go.

I wipe my clammy palms on my napkin and start dishing out the food, trying to act like everything is normal. Like Rory and I didn't just share some kind of moment.

It probably wasn't a moment at all. He was probably just too polite to drop my hand, and I was the one lingering. Or if he *was* holding on as well, it's just because he too is suffering from Lack of Physical Touch syndrome. We're both a little lonely, and I was a random hand to hold during grace. That's all.

"Turkey?" I offer Rory, passing the serving plate with feigned nonchalance.

"I'm actually vegetarian," he says, "but I'll definitely have thirds of everything else. It all looks amazing."

"Credit to Chef Jules," I say. "I'd planned to order takeaway, but she wouldn't hear of it."

"I prefer the Cockney Cook, thank you," Jules says as she tops up her punch glass. "Might start a food blog, what d'you reckon? And I've been considering going vegetarian for a while now, but I fancy my Sunday roasts too much. And besides, I wouldn't want people ter think I'm doing it for health reasons." She scrunches up her face at the unpleasant prospect of anyone thinking she'd be conforming to a wellness trend. "I'd be doing it for the animals. Is that why you're doing it, Rory?"

"That and the carbon footprint," Rory says. "Once I started teaching about science and climate change, it only felt right to walk the walk. Sorry, that sounds preachy," he adds hastily.

"Not preachy," I say. "I respect that."

And I do, though I don't respect myself much in that moment, feeling a fresh wave of embarrassment over the fact that I'm consulting for an oil conglomerate. I should've pushed harder on the renewable energy pitch. "Not too many vegetarians in Kalamazoo, are there?" I ask. The way I remember it, it's all hunters, carnivores, camo hats.

"You'd be surprised—it's a growing movement," he says. "I'll have to show you some new spots downtown. If we're ever back there at the same time, I mean."

"Right," I say, trying not to thumb my nose at his use of "downtown," which refers to two and a half streets of half-vacant low-rises. "If we are."

I actually like the idea of walking around Kalamazoo with him, maybe because I know it will never happen.

There's a lapse in conversation as we eat. It's the quietest I've ever heard Jules. "Feel the food coma coming on. The telltale sign of a successful meal," she says happily when all our plates are scraped clean after third helpings. "Need ter get some kip before the pumpkin pie."

She plops down on the sofa for a nap. Nina joins her, sliding in at Jules's side, like they were shaped to fit together just so. They look to be out cold within thirty seconds.

Rory helps clear the table and load the leftovers into Tupperware. He starts washing all the dishes in the sink. "I really don't mind," he says, when I tell him he doesn't have to do that. "I like to feel useful."

We've each only had one beer, and the huge meal has negated any effects. Still, there seems to be a buzz in the room, like the light is filtered by not being filtered at all. By being completely natural and normal.

I'm not fumbling around for something interesting to say. I'm not pouring drinks or turning on music or checking the emails on my computer. We're just there together, washing and drying dishes at the sink, not needing to fill the space because it's not empty in the first place.

Rory's phone rings from its spot on the counter. A blonde woman's face lights up the screen. She's mid-laugh, wearing a floppy sunhat, and looking like she doesn't have a care in the world. *Emily.*

CHAPTER TWENTY-TWO

"You want to take that?" I ask, passing the phone to Rory, who's drying his sudsy hands on the dishtowel.

A shadow flits across his face, but it's gone before I can be sure it was ever there. "I'll call her back later," he says, stashing the phone in his pocket as he resumes scrubbing.

"So you're still talking?" I ask as casually as I can.

"She's been calling a bit more often. Things have been good." He looks cautiously hopeful, and it triggers a certain protectiveness in me.

"But she still doesn't want to put a label on it?" I press.

"Not yet. We'll talk over Christmas, she says. But I think we're headed in the same direction."

I try to hide my distrust, but I don't try that hard, and Rory picks up on it. "What?" he asks. "You don't like her?"

"It's not that," I say, and then elaborate because I can't help myself, but maybe I can help him. "I just . . . I worry she's trying to have her cake and eat it too. She's not willing to commit to you, but she's not willing to let you go either."

At least I broke up with Mateo in one fell swoop. I didn't keep him hanging around in case I changed my mind. Though maybe that was because I knew I wasn't going to.

"It's not like that," Rory says. "She's not trying to play games. She's just making sure she's fully able to commit before making a lifelong decision like marriage. I respect that she's taking it seriously."

It makes me wish someone would defend me that way, even when, like Emily, I might not deserve it. "Okay," I say, not wanting to probe into the areas Rory doesn't want to go.

"Hey, Kat?" he says, voice quiet, cradling my name with care. I wonder if he's going to ask about my dating life and the kind of person I'm looking for. It would be nice to rattle off my nonnegotiables—someone who's princely and romantic and preferably European—so I can remind myself that's what I'm holding out for, and nothing less.

His question isn't about love, though.

"I've been wanting to ask," he goes on. "Any update with the HR investigation?"

"Nope," I say, chapped lips pursed as the weight of it all lands on me again. "Radio silence."

"I'm losing patience with them," Rory says, and I see the wheels turning in his head, trying to find alternative paths to justice. I know there's nothing he can do, but it still feels good to have someone on my side. Like I'm not shouldering it all by myself.

"Let's talk about it another time," I murmur, nodding to the couch at Jules and Nina. I don't want them to hear, not that Jules would probably remember in the morning.

"Top me up, top me up," Jules bleats in her sleep, then flips over on her back and keeps snoring.

Soon after, Nina wakes up and tries to rouse Jules. She doesn't budge, only burrows further into the couch. "Reckon I need to get this one into bed," Nina says. "The punch has finally caught up with her."

Looking more than a little dizzy herself, she attempts to heave Jules off the couch, but physics aren't on her side. Rory jumps in to help, easily lifting Jules and carrying her next door. It seems he's stronger than he looks. As Nina hugs me goodnight, she whispers in my ear. "He's a keeper, that one is."

You can't keep something that's not yours is what I think to myself but don't say aloud.

Alone in my flat, Rory and I return to our dish washing and drying routine. "I should probably get home soon," he says once we've finished. "Said I'd Facetime my family."

"Yeah," I say, thinking of Emily and how vivacious she looked in that photo on his phone. So unlike someone who's consumed by her corporate job. "I should call mine too." I wonder if they even feel my absence around the table. Between work deadlines and trips with Mateo, I've been absent for more than a few Thanksgivings over the years, and it's started to feel like the norm rather than the exception.

I hand the remainder of Rory's corn casserole and the Kit Kat pie back to him.

"Keep the pie," he says. "It's for you."

"But don't you want the pan back?"

"Give it to me next time. No big deal."

I like that thought: *next time.* "I've never had anyone name a pie after me," I say. "Or name anything after me, for that matter."

"Well, there's a first time for everything, right?"

"First time for everything," I agree. And I surprise both of us by leaning up to kiss Rory's cheek.

It's not at all like the passionate make-out session I once fantasized about with Alexander. It's just a G-rated peck, but it stirs something deeper. Because as unromantic as it sounds, the place where I feel the kiss is in my feet. They're light and heavy at the same time. Light because I get the notion that if I kicked off the ground, I could stay suspended in the air for a while. And heavy because they feel firmly planted on the slanted floorboards of my flat. Like nothing can knock me over.

Rory seems as taken aback as I am.

"Sorry, I was just keeping with European tradition," I say quickly, already wondering what came over me. "It's good manners to kiss cheeks to say goodbye." I feel myself reddening to the color of the pomegranate punch.

"Can't mess with tradition," Rory says. He doesn't kiss me back, but he gives a homey kind of hug, which transports me away while also keeping me present in a very pleasant sort of way. "Thanks again for hosting," he says as we break apart. "Cheerio then, as they say around here."

I've never actually heard a real British person say *cheerio*, but I grin and go along with it. "Ta-ta for now."

Rory heads out, down the rickety staircase of Marlow House and out the front door. Heading to the window, I watch as he waits at the bus stop. Once he boards a northbound bus, I close the curtains and take another forkful of Kit Kat pie, feeling more thankful than I have in a very long time.

CHAPTER TWENTY-THREE

The Thanksgiving spirit doesn't last long. It plummets the next week when Oliver pings me to see if I can swing by his office for a quick catch-up.

It's either about the promotion or the Harold investigation, and my stomach is writhing with nerves as I take a seat in his office, facing out onto the monochrome gray and steel of Canary Wharf.

"Kat," Oliver says, looking up from one of his three computer monitors. He swivels his chair toward me, but only halfway, almost like he doesn't want to face me head-on. "You alright? Miserable commute this morning in the rain, wasn't it?"

"It wasn't too bad," I say, resenting the canned small talk. It rains just about every day in London, so it's really nothing to comment on. "What did you want to connect on?"

"Well, see here," he says, and there's a certain apprehension beneath his placid expression. "I've got some good news and some . . . decent news for you."

My chest tightens as my stomach drops. It's not difficult to intuit that *decent* is a euphemism for *bad*. "Let's start with the bad news?" I suggest.

"Well now, I wouldn't call it *bad*. But there's no point talking around it, is there? Reckon the best thing is to just tell it to you straight." Avoiding eye contact, he rushes out the next sentence. "You're not getting promoted this year, Kat."

The words slap my face like an ice storm as my lungs freeze over too.

I told myself I'd been prepared for this. That the odds of getting promoted weren't great. That I'd be fine either way. But now I know just how much I wanted it. I know just how much I really did believe it was going to happen. That I'd done enough to prove I deserved it.

"I tried everything, I really did," Oliver carries on. "But there just wasn't the headcount this year . . ." He trails off, peeking cautiously at me as if worried that I might unleash a spate of anger—or worse, burst into tears.

But it's not difficult to keep my composure. I feel dazed and deadened. "Does this have anything to do with Harold?" I ask.

"Not in the least," he assures me. "Harold put in a good word for you, he did. It was on the Leo & Sons side. With the macro backdrop, purse strings are tight."

It's the lamest of all lame explanations. It's like they hand out a script or something. I wonder if Harold *did* actually put in a good word or if that's just more fallacious fluff. "So what's the good news?" I ask.

"Ah yes, the good news." He looks relieved to move on. "Well, Turpi has extended our scope of work for three more months. The case will run through April now, given it's more of a . . . nuanced situation . . . than we originally thought."

Nuanced situation is a euphemism for *shit show*, as we both know.

"I'll be stepping off for another case after Christmas," Oliver says. "And I—*we*—would like you to lead it from here. It'll be a brilliant opportunity to demonstrate you're already operating at the partner level. You'll be a shoo-in for the promotion next year, not to mention you'll have your pick of cases to work on when you're done. Dubai, Sydney—you name it." He flashes a rare smile, like I should be wringing his hand with gratitude. "You hear what I'm saying?"

I do hear what he's saying. All too clearly. He's saying he wants to give me more work and responsibility without the benefit of a higher title. He's saying I should keep grinding away with no guarantee that it will pay off.

"Would we be able to put it in writing?" I ask. "That I'll get promoted next year if I successfully close out this case?" I should've asked for this last year, and I'm not going to make that mistake again.

"Ah, I'm afraid not," he says, looking flummoxed, like I've been much too presumptuous. "It's against Leo & Sons policy to put anything in writing."

But letting clients feel up their consultants is just fine? I want to retort. But I'm not bold enough to say it.

Last year, my boss on the Boston case said that if I took an international case, I'd prove my versatility and be fast-tracked to the promotion. And now, here I am, back in the same spot, hearing the same evasive excuses.

"I understand your frustration," Oliver says, and I'd bet my bonus that he got the phrase straight from some "Empathetic

Leadership" workshop he was forced to attend. "You've worked hard for this promotion, and you must be gutted it's delayed a bit. But rest assured, Kat, we've identified you as *key talent*. You're one of the women at the firm we're focused on developing. You have loads of potential, there's no doubt."

I have no desire to scream or spit or sob. I simply want to laugh, but I don't have the energy for it. My boss and all of his management peers might not be experts at solving business problems like I once thought. But they sure are experts at moving the goal post. They have the formula down to a science. How to motivate me to keep sprinting at an inhuman pace and maximize my output before rewarding me with the prize.

Still, I've come this far, and after a decade in the business world, what's one more year?

The exit options I'll have with the partner title on my résumé will make it worth it. After a year or two as partner, I can leave consulting and come in at a senior level at a company that actually does good things for the world—health care, or maybe education. I'll be groomed for the C-suite, and all will be well.

And so I tell Oliver that I'd be happy to lead the remainder of the case. That I appreciate his support. That his mentorship means a lot to me. That I'm determined to be a significant contributor to the firm in the year ahead.

I say all the right things, all the buzz words, and he looks pleased at how the conversation has panned out. "Proud of you, lad," he says, clapping me on the back like I'm one of the boys.

Leaving his office, I find refuge in a bathroom stall, feeling small and shaky as I lower myself to the floor and sit there with my head against the plastic wall.

You're still on track to be a CEO, I remind myself. *You're still on track.*

The phrase doesn't comfort me as much as I'd hoped. It just reminds me of how large the gap is between where I am and where I want to be. Of how many hours of mindless, heartless work are ahead before I can reach something I care about. Something that gives me the influence and autonomy to change the system.

Still sitting on the bathroom floor, I take out my phone and do the one thing that I know will make me feel better. Not a superficial sort of better. Not a Band-Aid or a "better for now." An actual, genuine sort of better.

I text Rory.

CHAPTER TWENTY-FOUR

He calls back soon after and offers to meet up after work in Islington or anywhere that's most convenient for me. I've returned from the office early and am in no mood to go out into the cold, cold world, so I text him that he can come to Marlow House so long as he brings gelato.

Already on it, he texts back. Be there in a jiffy.

And sure enough, he buzzes up just as I'm pulling on my coziest sweatpants after an excessively long bubble bath during which I watched *The Holiday* on my phone. I've rarely felt more in need of an escapist rom-com than today. It doesn't make me forget the sharpness of the day, but it dulls the edges just a bit.

I've meant to freshen up after my bath—brush out my hair, which is slung into a messy bun, and apply some foundation and lip liner—but there wasn't time. My au naturel version will have to do. It's probably better that way. The telltale sign of being real friends with someone is not needing to go out of your way to look more put-together than you feel.

"It's the gelato delivery boy." Rory's voice comes through the intercom, making me feel better before I even see him.

Unlocking the door, I let him in. There he is, in his wool coat and maroon scarf, wearing that old raggedy backpack that makes me feel better about my own lack of elegance.

"Thanks for coming," I say.

"Happy to be here. I mean, I'm not happy that you're not happy, obviously. But it's good to see ya again."

Unzipping his backpack, Rory pulls out three pints of Badiani's gelato. "Now onto the big question," he says. "Tiramisu, salted caramel, or pistachio?"

Those were the flavors I ordered when we went for gelato in Camden Passage. The ones I said were my favorite. It's a small thing that he remembered this, but it gets me sniffling a bit, in an ugly, gunky sort of way.

For some reason, it makes me feel sad that someone might be so thoughtful without a hidden agenda. The notion that there are such kind people in a world that can be so cruel. I want to hug him again, but that might come across as a romantic gesture, or a pathetic one, so I just pluck one of the pints from his hands. "Let's start with tiramisu. But I thought you only liked vanilla."

"I like other flavors too," he insists. "Vanilla is just my favorite, but I can get that anytime."

Grabbing peanut butter and spoons for us, I flop down on the couch, connecting my phone to the TV to resume the movie.

Rory sits down on the couch as well, way on the other end so we could fit three more people between us. I wish he was closer, but

I'm glad he's not. It reinforces the friendship boundaries and how neither of us have any notion of blurring them.

My phone buzzes with an incoming call from Blake. Rory sees the name on my screen, and I find myself worrying that he might think a guy is calling me. "It's my best friend, Blake," I tell him. "She lives in New York." I emphasize the "she" a little too vigorously.

"Take it," Rory says, looking as happy as I feel that my best friend is checking in. Shooting him a grateful look, I hop into my room and listen as Blake drops some big news. She's scaling back to work part-time to have more time with her baby. It's a shocking turn of events, as she's been on partner track at an investment bank. I'm frustrated that she feels like she has to make this kind of trade-off, when her husband doesn't. Blake says she's happy about it, and it's hard to tell if she's lying to me or lying to herself. When she turns the conversation onto me and my London adventures, I ask if I can call her back tomorrow, as I'm currently in the middle of watching a movie with a friend.

"A male friend?" she inquires, curiosity piqued.

"Yes," I say, feeling myself blushing, only because the insinuation is so incorrect. "But it's not like that."

"Of course not," Blake says all too knowingly. "Now go get back to him. Call me tomorrow."

With a surge of gratitude that our long-distance friendship is still holding up, I return to the sitting room and reclaim my spot on the opposite end of the couch from Rory.

"I'm almost done watching *The Holiday*," I say, resuming the movie from the spot I left off at in the bathtub. "Is that okay with you?" I pull the tartan blanket over me and wrap my free arm around one of the throw pillows.

"Cool beans," Rory says. I'd venture to guess that rom-coms aren't exactly his cup of tea, but he has that go-with-the-flow vibe that makes me think he'd be up for any kind of movie. "What's it about?" he asks.

I pause the movie so I don't miss the iconic scene where Cameron Diaz's character leaps out of the cab that's taking her to the airport and runs through fields of snow and mud—in high heels, no less—back to the quaint English cottage where she's reunited with her gorgeous British beau, played by Jude Law. Even the first time I watched the movie, the ending wasn't exactly a surprise—their eye contact gives it away throughout the whole movie—but there's something wonderfully comforting in being able to predict an ending. Maybe because it never happens like that in real life.

I gawk at Rory. "You've never seen *The Holiday*?"

"Is that a criminal offense?"

"Essentially, yes. I forget you've been living under the rock called Kalamazoo."

"Kalamazoo isn't a rock," Rory defends. "There's a lot going on."

Holding in a sardonic rebuttal, I just tell him that I'll start the movie back at the beginning so he can get the full experience. Partway through, I ask for his critical review. "So, what do you think?"

"It's not bad," he says, unconvincingly.

"Rory," I implore, "tell the truth."

It doesn't seem like he'd be able to lie even if he wanted to. "It's just," he says, pausing as he searches for a diplomatic answer, "I'm not the biggest chick flick fan, I guess."

"*Chick flick* is a demeaning and stereotypical label," I shoot back. "Why do we need to pigeon-hole love stories as being gender specific?"

"That's a good point," Rory says, but it still feels like he's holding something back.

"What?" I ask expectantly.

"Nothing." Then after a short pause, he keeps going, seeming to decide that he can trust me with what he really thinks. "I just—I think a lot of guys don't like these kinds of movies because of the unrealistic expectations they can give women. It's a pretty impossible standard to live up to, to be honest."

I feel attacked before remembering that he's certainly talking about Emily, not me. "We don't expect guys to be exactly like the movies," I refute. But as I say it, I feel the untruth on my tongue. How obsessed was I with Alexander precisely because I thought he was delivering me a cinematic love story? "Okay, well maybe just a little."

"It's a lot of pressure for guys to have to be *this*," Rory goes on, gesturing to the screen, where a misty-eyed Jude Law is paused in an impossibly handsome frame, looking adoringly at Cameron Diaz as she arrives back on his doorstep. "The grand gestures, the sappy speeches, the animal sex. Women get conditioned to think that's what love is. And then when their real-life relationship doesn't look like that—when it's regular day-to-day life without the intensity of a ninety-minute film—they think there's something wrong. Something missing. So they break up with you over Cracker Barrel hash browns, and then you find yourself in London trying to change into the person they want you to be." He grows suddenly quiet, fidgeting on the sofa, like he's trying to find a comfortable position. "Okay, sorry. End rant."

"Rants are allowed," I say quietly, taking it all in. I'm disliking Emily more than ever. But I also want to defend the movies.

Defend my outlook. "And you're right, rom-coms aren't real life," I say. "But they do represent the best of what real life can be when you find the right person."

"I don't know," Rory says. "I think movies represent the impersonation of love, not the real thing. They make it seem that once the heart palpitations and butterflies and goose bumps are gone, the love is gone too."

"Well, that's not wrong, is it?" I say, thinking about how those symptoms have foretold all of my past breakups.

"I think it *is* wrong, though. Love isn't fireworks or adrenaline, is it? It's the stuff that's still there after the spark fades."

The notion frightens me terribly. "But the spark doesn't have to fade!"

"It does, though," he says. "That's just the natural progression. Or at least the spark *changes*. And that's not a bad thing. I think love can get better with time. That it's supposed to. But movies say the opposite. That the very best moment is some exhilarating first look or first kiss or first night in bed. The box office makes money from selling the love-at-first-sight cliché, even though the screenwriters and actors must know it's complete garbage."

"Love at first sight exists in real life," I fire back. "It's rare, but it's real." And then I go off on my own rant about *Married At First Sight* and the success stories and also the celebrities I've read about who saw their partner across the room and *just knew*.

"Maybe it's like that for some people," Rory says. "I'm just saying that it's not the only way. And it's not always what lasts." Falling silent again, he looks awkward and regretful. I get the feeling he's not exactly prone to outbursts about love and emotions, and he doesn't seem to know what to do with himself. "Sorry, I'm making this all about me," he mutters. "I was supposed to come over and cheer you up, and all I've done is throw myself a pity party."

"Well, good thing I much prefer dissecting other people's problems than my own," I say.

We share a look that feels like an unlocking. The softness of his golden-flecked eyes seems to extend outward, cushioning the austere angles of my flat and adding a splash of sunlight to the baren walls.

"The right person won't compare you to the movies," I add. "They'll just want you to be you." My not-so-hidden message is that Emily is not the right person for him.

"Yeah," he says, looking glum. "I guess so."

"I know so," I say. "Now come on—I need help with this gelato before it melts. Scooch closer—I don't bite."

He straightens up at that and moves over closer toward me. Our shoulders still aren't touching or anything, and I keep my blanket all to myself, but we sit side by side, scooping gelato from the same pint, with separate spoons.

"Forget the beer," Rory says. "This is my kind of pint."

"Same." It feels good to be sober tonight. I'm more in control of myself, less likely to spiral into the depths of despair or do anything I'd regret in the morning.

Like kissing Rory.

It's not that I'm tempted to do that; it's just that I think I might be if I were drunk. But that's not saying much, as I'm apparently tempted to get frisky with anyone when I've been drinking. Even Harold. I shudder as I think about it.

"You okay?" Rory asks.

"Yeah," I say, and I mostly mean it. "All good."

A bit of gelato drips onto Rory's sweater. "Dang it," he says, looking stressed, though it's only a tiny mark.

He's someone who doesn't like things out of place. Like how he sits on the exact same seat on the bus every morning and meticulously washed every dish after Thanksgiving. I feel a rush of compassion for how hard it would be to have to have everything be so neat and orderly.

I offer to let him use the washing machine, but he says he'll just handwash it. Taking off his sweater, he wrings it out under the sink, then hangs it on the clothes rack in the corner of my flat. In just his thin undershirt, his lean arms show through. He's not as big or muscular as I'd imagined Alexander, but his wiry physique is more approachable, the kind of build that holds up over time.

When he sits back down, I toss half the blanket his way so he won't be cold. And then, following the prod of my intuition, I lean my head on his shoulder, repurposing it into a pillow. His shoulder is bony and shouldn't be comfortable, but it is. Incredibly so.

Rory doesn't pull away or nudge me off, so I stay there, liking the view of the TV from this angle. Everything looks a little bit brighter, a little less sharp. The light makes me sleepy. My eyelids droop, and I have to keep them from closing altogether. "Thanks for being here," I mumble into Rory's T-shirt.

"Of course," he says. "What're friends for?"

Right, I think to myself. *Friends.* The word should reassure me, but it irritates me instead—how it circles my brain, swooping down into my body and nipping at my heart, asking for more.

CHAPTER TWENTY-FIVE

By the time I wake up the next morning, rain tapping against the slate roof like a staccato metronome, I'm back to being convinced that Rory and I could only ever be just friends.

Sure, maybe I ever so briefly wondered what it would be like to be with him when we were sitting on the couch. And okay, *fine*, maybe I reread our old texts after he left. And yes, alright, there's a non-zero chance that I went to bed wondering what it would be like to fall asleep curled up in his arms. But people have crazy thoughts all the time, which have little to no correlation with their actual desires. Sometimes the mind just goes rogue and entertains things for the shock factor. Or because you're drained and exhausted and not thinking clearly, which I definitely was after the whole promotion debacle.

Yes, Rory is someone I feel comfortable with. But comfortable is not what I want in my love life. Comfortable is basically a synonym for complacent and an antonym for romance.

I imagine a conversation with my future husband.

What's your favorite thing about our relationship, darling? he asks. (His voice is still British.)

Oh you know, I reply. *That we're comfortable.*

Even imagining that dialogue leaves me in a panic. Like I've failed to find that soul-quaking love.

The whole scenario that I might "like-like" Rory is absurd. And even if, hypothetically speaking, I *did* have feelings for him, it would be a moot point because he's still in love with Emily, and all signs point to their getting back together over Christmas.

Still, our movie night was exactly what I needed, and it's calmed me down enough to keep my composure at work in the days that follow. I go through the motions as swiftly as ever, prepping Oliver with all the detail—and more—that he requested for the cost-savings implementation rollout, and civilly declining Harold's unyielding invites to Annabel's.

At least now there's clarity with where things stand for the promotion. I'm confident in my decision to stay on and take the case over from Oliver, and I'm not going to let my injured emotions derail my path to the top. And the path is still there, just one year delayed.

The fact that I'll be staying in London a few more months makes me less upset than I expect it to, despite being under Harold's reign. I guess I'm just tired of moving around all the time, and now that I'm making friends, it's not so lonely.

I tell myself that Rory and Jules's faces appear in my thoughts at exactly the same time, in exactly the same order. But that's not entirely true. Rory's appears first, though that's probably just because of some biological programming that conditions me to cling to someone from my hometown so that local clans can procreate and save the gene pool.

The word *procreate* careens my thoughts down another rabbit hole, in which I'm trying hard not to picture this verb taking place between me and said *friend* Rory.

Jules comes to the rescue with a welcome distraction, texting me to clear my calendar for Friday night because she's booked us tickets for Winter Wonderland in Hyde Park.

The sun sets around four PM these days (assuming it ever rises, which it doesn't seem to half the time), so by the time I meet up with her at seven, it feels like midnight. Nina has the night shift at the hospital, meaning it's just Jules and me walking into the park together.

The grassy acres have been transformed by transportable carnival rides and ice rinks, market stalls and model trains, inflatable snowmen and circus acts, and an enormous Christmas tree that's bedazzled with colored bulbs. A saxophone band is playing carols from a stage, and kids are running here and there, sloshing hot cocoa and popcorn as they race to the next roller coaster.

"You Americans might 'ave Thanksgiving, but no one does Christmas quite like the Brits," Jules says, happily sponging up the scene. "This spot is proper touristy, but you've got ter do it. And besides. it gives me an excuse to be a dustbin lid again."

"Does 'dustbin lid' mean kid?" I guess.

"There you are!" Jules says with the proud look of a tutor whose student has finally caught on. "Not that I need an excuse to act like a child, mind you. C'mon, let's join the Dumbo queue."

And so she yanks me along with her toward a flying elephant ride. I try to talk my way out of it, but Jules won't hear of it. In the end, it's worth the wait—not so much for the way the plastic elephant jostles me from side to side as it rises and dips, but for Jules's reaction. She squeals with glee, frothing at the mouth with laughter, egging her elephant on as if it can hear her. "That's a good lad," she coos. "Just a bit 'igher now, got ter beat Kat down there."

Next up, she leads us to a pendulum-style roller coaster, described as "sixty-five meters of pure adrenaline—guaranteed to turn your breath to ice." I used to love these kinds of rides when I was little, but now I feel preemptively queasy, so I send Jules without me while I watch from the ground. She meets back up with me after, pure joy plastered on her face. "You don't know what you're missing," she insists, then proceeds to detail the glorious sensation of how she thought her intestines were going to fall out of her mouth on the rocket-speed descent. "If I 'adn't clamped my mouth shut, I surely would've vomited up my bowels," she brags, as if she's half wishing she'd kept her mouth open, just for the thrill of it.

"Sorry to have missed that," I comment dryly.

Jules orders beer and a Cornish pasty from a food truck, and I opt for hot chocolate and chips. We sit down at a picnic table.

"So," Jules says. "'Ow's our Rory?"

"He's fine, I think," I say, bristling at her suggestive tone. "Haven't seen him in a couple weeks."

We've texted a bit after our movie night, but I haven't wanted to suggest hanging out again. It would feel a bit *too much*. Pushing the line of how much you can see a friend of the opposite gender without one or both of you thinking it might mean something more. Rory hasn't suggested getting together either.

"Righ'o," Jules says, eyebrows arching in that cartoon-character way.

"What?" I ask, because it's clear she's bursting to share her opinion. "Just spit it out."

"Well, it's not rocket science, is it?" Jules says. "Nina saw it too. You're both bloody brilliant together, you are."

In the brief moment before I remember to scowl, I want to smile. But I don't. "We're good as friends," I say. "*Just* friends."

"I dunno ' bout that," Jules says in a tone that indicates that she *does* know, and that she disagrees. "He thinks you're the bee's knees, 'e just doesn't want to put 'imself out there when you're not exactly giving much affirmation. Can't say I blame the bloke."

"False," I say, as I catch myself wishing it might be true, just because my ego is greedy. "He's still in love with his ex," I remind Jules—and myself. "They're getting back together over Christmas."

The thought of Rory and Emily curled up together in front of the fireplace is enough to extinguish any feeble flame my own heart might be harboring (and feeble the flames are, if they exist at all, which they probably certainly do not).

"Breaking my heart, you both are," Jules moans, going back to the beer stand to top up her cup.

As she sits back down, my phone chimes with a text. I check it reluctantly, expecting it to be a request from Oliver asking me to pull together a presentation over the weekend. Or a proposition from Harold.

Instead, it's an invite from Rory.

Hi there! Any chance you want to come to the school Christmas party on Friday the 18th? Know it's a work day, so no worries if not—just thought I'd check. Mala's been asking about you!

Jules reads it over my shoulder, cackling triumphantly. "What I'd tell you?" she says, like this proves she should be a professional tarot card reader.

"It doesn't mean anything," I protest, though the text feels like a hug. "He's a good teacher, he's just inviting me for Mala's sake."

"Bloody 'ell 'e is," Jules says. "The lad is keen to have a snog, mark my words."

"There will be no snogging," I assure her, but my mood is a bit bouncier, and I allow myself to be persuaded to come along with Jules to the next ride. It's one of those drop towers that tries to convince you there's nothing more fun that plummeting to your potential death. Strapped into my seat, the ride rises slowly until it comes to a stop at the top.

Jules lets out a whistle from beside me, and the kids on the ride are oohing and aahing at the view. I've got to admit, it's pretty magnificent. London is all dressed up with a million and one places to go. The sprawling web of lights wiggle and wink for attention, and low clouds hover over the city, magnifying the radiance rather than muffling it. Off in the distance, the Thames weaves like a graceful serpent. Everything is sparkling and beautiful and looks like B-roll from a rom-com.

But just for a split second, right before the tower drops, I find myself thinking that this movie-worthy panorama doesn't fill me up quite as much as the mundane view from my couch, when my head was resting on Rory's shoulder.

Then the tower drops, and my nonsensical thoughts are sucked away with my breath, leaving me screaming with the kids— screaming *like* a kid—as we fall.

CHAPTER TWENTY-SIX

It doesn't take much for me to decide to go to the Christmas party at Rory's school. It's an innocuous setting, and I'm not going to decline just because I'm worried about pushing the boundaries of the friends-only line—a line which seems very thick and clear to both of us. And it's the day before I fly back to Michigan for Christmas, so it feels like a nice kickoff to my vacation.

I work from home that morning, then slip over to the school around lunchtime. Rather than taking the afternoon off, I just put a personal appointment in my calendar. I've always been scared to do things like this—scared that one little thing like that would give them (the all-powerful *them*) reason to dock me of points. And so for years I've taken virtually no vacation, put off doctor's appointments, missed lunches with friends, and delayed picking clothes up at the dry cleaner for weeks, all for fear of what would happen if I was caught being away from my desk. If my little green dot on the company's instant message server turned yellow for too long. But it feels different now. I've already had the promotion denied, so there's not much else they could do except fire me, which would leave them in an even bigger mess than it would leave me (or so I like to think).

I'm emboldened enough to sneak out to the school party for a couple hours and deal with whatever consequences come my way. It's a small thing maybe, but it feels big and rebellious.

Wanting to show up in theme, I wear an ugly Christmas sweater that I've bought at a charity shop in Camden Passage. The sweater features a prominent Rudolph, whose 3-D nose lights up when you press it.

I make sure the nose is glowing when I walk into Rory's classroom. DIY snowflakes dangle from the ceiling, and a table full of cupcakes and candy stretches across one side of the room, the students swarming it like a bee hive.

It takes me a moment to locate Rory. Then I see him, standing at the snack table, monitoring to ensure the students don't take more than their fair share. He's wearing his typical trousers and button-down, but his face is masked under a white cotton beard and Santa hat.

"Please put those sweets back in your jumper, Charlie," Rory says, lightly scolding a little boy who was covertly repurposing his sweater into a candy pouch for Smarties and Tony's Chocoloney bars. Reluctantly, the boy unloads his loot and lopes sullenly back to his desk.

Rory and I make eye contact—the friendly, unexciting kind. "Hey there," he says. "You came!" He seems like he wasn't expecting me to.

"I told you I was going to," I say defensively. "Nearly didn't recognize you as Santa though."

"I go by Father Christmas over here," Rory says cheerily. "And if you're thinking of pointing out that that I'm too skinny for the role, don't bother, because the kids have already torn me to shreds." He gives a self-deprecating grimace.

"I wasn't going to," I say, though I probably was.

"At least I can finally grow facial hair," Rory says, stroking his beard appreciatively. "Love the sweater, by the way. I'll be needing you to light the way on Christmas Eve."

For an odd moment, probably just because I'm standing in a classroom full of little kids, I imagine flying through the sky with Rory in Santa's sleigh.

"Bonkers," Rory says, and at first I think he's talking about my daydream. Then I see that he's looking around the room at the students. The ones who aren't raiding the desserts are tugging at Christmas crackers, opening them with loud popping sounds and trading the riddles and trinkets inside.

"It's a combo of the sugar high, plus knowing it's the last day of school before a two-week break," Rory says. "Can't blame 'em though . . . I used to be the same way."

"You used to be a troublemaker?" I ask dubiously. It's hard to picture.

"I mean, not *trouble* trouble," Rory clarifies, flushing in that rule-follower way. "But I definitely talked during movies and stuff like that."

I gasp dramatically. "You rebel, you. Having the audacity to whisper in the middle of *The Polar Express*? The most condemnable of all mortal sins."

Rory grins good-naturedly. "It *was* always *The Polar Express* that we watched right before winter break, wasn't it?"

"Indeed." It feels like sharing a memory with him. One that we never experienced together but experienced collectively at the same time, and sort of in the same place.

As Rory makes his way around the room to collect trash and wrappers, Mala runs up to me. She's wearing knee-high candy cane socks with her uniform and donning a tissue-paper crown—one of those Christmas cracker prizes.

"Miss Kat!" she squeals, rocking back and forth with glee. "I knew you'd be here, Mr. Cooper said so! Say, have you seen our Christmas tree, Miss Kat? Do come have a look!" Tugging my hand, she leads me to the back of the room, where a pile of empty cans and bottles are stacked in a massive, messy pile, reaching the height of my shoulders.

"Isn't it lovely?" Mala says, beaming at the pile of plastic like it's the most magnificent sight in the world. "It's not a real tree, of course, because we don't believe in cutting down trees. It's bad for Mother Earth—Mr. Cooper says so." Without pausing for air, she whizzes right along. "But see here, this plastic tree is still shaped like a tree, isn't it? We made it ourselves, from old bottles. And when we're done with it, it'll all go into recycling. No rubbish at all."

Like a proud parent, she strokes the plastic "branches" of the tree. I squat to see it from Mala's height. Sure enough, it does look slightly more like a tree from this angle. At the base, there's a hand-written sign, spelling out, in wobbly letters, *We're dreaming of a green Christmas*.

"It's beautiful," I tell her.

Mala beams at my approval.

Rory appears beside us. "And who put the star on top, Mala?" he asks, smiling through his beard as he points to a yellow lemonade can atop the pile.

"*I* did," Mala says, as if there were no greater prestige. "Had to stand on the step stool because I was too short. Reckon I'll be able to reach the top next year, though. I'll be *eight* next year, did you know?" She enunciates the number with great awe, as if eight is the indisputable entryway into adulthood.

Rory and I exchange a look that says something like *Please don't go growing up too fast, Little Mala.*

Actually, Rory's look probably says something a bit more casual—something like *Aww, kids. So dang innocent, huh?* but it feels like we're on the same wavelength at least.

"Please, Mr. Cooper, can Miss Kat sit with me?" Mala asks. "I have a surprise for her, *remember*?" She shoots a knowing look at Rory, and upon his approval, yanks me back to her table.

"Here it is!" Mala says, bursting to reveal the secret. "We did a gingerbread craft yesterday. And I made one in the shape of a mitten because Mr. Cooper says that the place you're from in America, it's shaped like a mitten! I traced my hand to do it—look here." She holds up her hand against the ornament. They match perfectly and do justice to Michigan's mitten shape.

The idea that she thought of me of all people during the holiday craft fills me with a sturdy sense of importance. And it also makes me feel very thoughtless not to have brought anything for Mala—or Rory.

"Well, thank you," I say, accepting the gift in my hand. It fits in the small of my palm and though the gingerbread texture is sandpapery and rough, it feels softer than any glove. "It's gorgeous. But I'm so sorry, I didn't bring you anything."

"That's quite alright," Mala says, prodding the Rudolph nose on my sweater so it lights up again. "You can bring me something back from America. You're going there for the hols, aren't you?"

"I am," I say. "Do you like popcorn? I could bring you back some Kalamazoo Kettle Corn. It's drizzled with chocolate and caramel and all sorts of good stuff."

"Loads of caramel popcorn, please," she says, pronouncing "caramel" with three elongated syllables and smacking her lips together like she can taste it already. "And how do you say the name of that place? Mr. Cooper has said it before, I remember. Cow-a-la-moo?"

"Kalamazoo," I say with a chuckle, thinking that Cow-a-la-moo might be a more fitting name, given all the farmland in the area. "That's where Mr. Cooper and I grew up. It's kind of a tongue twister, isn't it?"

Mala nods and proceeds to practice the name over and over until she nearly gets it right. "I'm going to go to *Kalawazoo* someday," she announces. "You must tell me all about it when you're back. I do want to know *everything*."

"Alright," I agree. "And you can ask Mr. Cooper about it too."

"Oh, but he's not going back to America," Mala says. "He's doing Christmas in London—he told us so."

I figure she's just misunderstood, but I bring it up to Rory later, when the students are cleaning up their desks and packing up for the end of the school day, squirming and squealing with the prospect of being set free by the bell any second.

"You're going back to Michigan for Christmas, aren't you?" I ask him.

He shifts a bit as he folds up the snack table and puts it back in its place. "No," he says. "I decided to stay here. I bought a ticket home a while back but ended up getting it refunded to go toward a trip for my parents' thirty-fifth anniversary in the spring. They've never been to Europe, so I'm saving up . . ." He trails off, leaving me self-conscious about all the extra money I have in my investment accounts, just from sitting in front of a computer all day, helping rich companies get even richer.

Rory's pouring himself into educating the next generation, and he can't even afford a plane ticket home. It doesn't seem right. I'd buy him a ticket, but I know there's no way he'd let me.

"But what about Emily?" I ask. "I thought Christmas was when you were going to see each other and talk about getting back together and everything?"

Rory seems to swallow a thought or two before he speaks. "We'll just have to wait a bit longer I guess," he says. "If it's meant to be, it'll be, right?" He doesn't do a good job hiding his disappointment. Manipulating expressions isn't one of his talents.

Selfishly, there's part of me that's glad he won't be seeing Emily. Once they're back together, it'll make our friendship harder—maybe impossible. But I can't be rooting for them to stay broken up either, not when I feel how it's quietly splitting Rory's heart.

And then it lands on me, as softly as a snowflake. Maybe there *is* a way that he'll let me buy his ticket home. If I don't ask for permission.

Once I consider the idea, it's impossible to eject it.

When the bell rings, I hug Mala goodbye and then excuse myself to the bathroom, booking Rory's ticket right there on the airline app on my phone. Five minutes later, it's a done deal. I purposely buy the nonrefundable option, with no travel insurance, because I know that's my only hope of his accepting it—if he knows that the money is down the drain, and his seat will be wasted if he doesn't go.

Hurrying back to the classroom, now empty except for Rory, I'm bursting to tell him the news. But I'm equally hesitant, anticipating how he'll protest.

"You alright there?" Rory asks, and I realize that I'm shifting around, as if I haven't properly relieved my bladder.

"Hunky-dory," I say in an affected English accent because apparently that's my nervous tick. "I have your Christmas gift," I say, suddenly very shy, like I'm still in my awkward braces-with-rubber-bands phase (a phase that unfortunately extended into my junior year of high school).

Trying to tap into my self-assured businesswoman side, I walk up to Rory at his desk and hand him my phone, where the itinerary for *Rory Cooper: London Heathrow to Kalamazoo, Michigan*, is displayed.

Rory takes my phone and stares down at it. "What's this?" he asks, eyes scanning the screen. As he reads the words, his expression bends into a frown. "No," he starts. "Absolutely not."

"It's a plane ticket home for Christmas," I say matter-of-factly, like I'm leading a work presentation. "It's already purchased. Nonrefundable."

"No," he repeats, and it's the closest to being upset I've ever seen him. His voice doesn't rise in volume, but he's firm and decisive. "There's no way I can accept this. Zero chance."

"Yes you can," I say, though I find myself wondering if this was too ridiculous a thing to do for a new friend. I've only known him two months, if you take out the time that I spent thinking he was Alexander, which seems like a logical span of time to exclude, considering I got absolutely everything wrong about him. Everything except the fact that he was someone I would enjoy being around.

I picture him and Emily holding hands as they walk through the sleepy, shabby streets of Kalamazoo, from burgers at Burdick's over to beers at Bell's. The image fills me with a mix of grumpiness and graciousness, knowing it's what Rory wants and that I can help it come true.

"I've racked up an absurd amount of airline miles from consulting travel," I tell him, with the persuasive air of a consultant who's ticking through the numbers in a PowerPoint deck. "A bunch of them are expiring soon, so you're doing me a favor really."

He keeps staring, looking down at my phone, then up at me, then back at the phone. It still takes another fifteen minutes to convince him to consider the idea. Even then, he remains unsure.

"Rory," I say, getting exasperated, "if you don't get on that plane, it's a wasted ticket. And it'll be a waste of a carbon footprint, too, for a plane to fly with an empty seat."

This finally does the trick. "Are you sure?" he says, and I feel his mind racing to come up with a hundred more reasons that he shouldn't accept it.

"Extremely sure," I say in my brusque corporate manner that doesn't take no for an answer. "We leave tomorrow, so you'd better get packing."

Excitement seeps onto his face. Eyes widening, he looks boyishly adorable from under his Santa hat and beard. I want to take a picture but decide just to snap a memory instead.

"I can't believe this," he says, physically bouncing on his toes with giddy jitters. "I'll repay you, I promise."

"You'd better not," I warn. "That violates the definition of a gift."

I can tell he's not going to let the matter drop, but he stops bringing it up—for now, at least. "You're the best, Kat," he says, looking me squarely in the eye, though the shape feels circular somehow, too gentle for boxy edges. "Seriously."

"I know I am," I say, passing it off with sarcasm so I don't have to dwell on how his words make me feel like I can do anything I want—and more than that, like I've already done *everything* I want. Like this one little gesture has filled me more than all my work-related accomplishments.

I stay for a little longer, joining in as Rory cleans up the classroom. Meticulously, he lines up the book bins and chairs just so, sorting all the folders and markers by color and erasing the whiteboard over and over until it looks scrubbed brand-new. As he's checking and rechecking the plugs and wires and windows, he keeps apologizing for taking so long.

"Sorry, it always takes me a while to leave places," he explains. "Especially when I'll be gone a couple weeks." He says it in an informative sort of way that makes it clear that he understands his quirks, and this is just the regimen he needs to follow so he can feel well when he walks out the door.

"Take your time," I say, though I catch myself wishing he'd hurry up so we could walk out together and maybe go look at the Christmas lights on Oxford Street before returning to our flats to pack. I try to hide my impatience, but Rory picks up on it, and it's clear I'm only adding to his stress.

So, pretending to be late dialing in for a work call, I head out so I won't be hovering. I don't want him to feel any pressure to go faster. I don't want him to have to change or apologize for who he is or how he is.

I hope Emily doesn't want him to change either. I hope she loves him the way I would love him if I loved him.

Which I don't, of course. It's hard to explain, but it makes sense in my head.

Or maybe in my heart, but there's no point lingering. He's as good as engaged to Emily at this point.

And so, scowling at the nerve of my imagination, I walk myself home. Or at least I walk myself back to Marlow House and the warped-floorboard apartment that I'm calling home until I settle down in a proper one. If I ever do.

The thought of a nomadic life used to feel so exotic, so *free*, back when I started out in consulting. Traveling all over the country or even the world, with no attachments or anchors. But now it just feels depressing, like I'll always be drifting around the globe, carting my carry-on suitcases from one place to the next. Always getting ready to pack up and leave again, all by myself.

CHAPTER TWENTY-SEVEN

I offer to share an Uber with Rory the next morning, but he says that he'll just meet me at the airport. Something tells me he's one of those people who insists on arriving at airports a full three hours early.

Sure enough, when I reach our gate in Heathrow's international terminal, I find him hovering beside a few other overly eager passengers who are waiting for the boarding process to begin. With both hands, he's clutching his passport and printed-out boarding pass, as if worried they might stage a getaway.

"There you are!" he says, looking hugely relieved to see me. "We're about to start boarding."

"Still have five minutes to spare," I say easily. "I've perfected the art of getting to the airport forty-five minutes before the flight leaves."

Just the idea of it makes Rory wince. "I've been here for ages," he says. "Wanted to build in extra time in case something went wrong."

I have to work not to roll my eyes at how overly cautious he is. But it touches me too—what a big deal this flight is for Rory. "All good so far?" I ask.

"Yeah, but my Christmas crackers got confiscated by TSA," he says. "Apparently they have some sort of powder in them that's on the banned substance list."

"Seriously? TSA can be such Scrooges."

"No big deal. I just thought my family would have fun with them. But at least the Big Ben puzzles made it through. Nearly had to pay for an oversized bag with all the gifts I stuffed in, but the guy helping me was super nice and let me off."

I've hardly brought anything back for my family—just some tea and shortbread in my compact carry-on luggage. I've planned to load up on gift cards when I got back in Kalamazoo, but now I feel like I should've purchased more souvenirs. I'm tempted to run into the nearest airport tourist shop, but I don't think Rory would appreciate my disappearing on him right now.

Glancing at my boarding pass, I see I've been upgraded to first class, courtesy of my platinum status. I want Rory to get the full experience too, especially since it's an eight-hour flight to Chicago. "Come with me," I tell him. "Going to try to get you upgraded to first class with me."

"How're you going to do that?"

"Tell the gate agent it's our honeymoon," I say, like this is a given. "But I need you with me—you're way more charming than I am."

Rory might not have the suave, sophisticated manner that suits my own taste, but he's got an authentic country-boy sort of charm that I suspect will work well with the middle-aged woman gate agent.

"I can't do that," Rory says. "I can't lie. It's a character flaw."

"Not being able to lie is a character flaw?" I clarify with a do-you-realize-how-backward-that-sounds? expression.

"Correct. Even white lies, surprise parties, that kind of thing. You can't trust me with a lie."

I smile at the irony of it. It's actually very refreshing and quite the contrast to Mateo, who was always using the fake honeymoon/birthday lines to get us all kinds of special treatment.

"Fine," I relent. "I won't say it's our honeymoon. I'll just see if they have any ability to upgrade."

"I don't need an upgrade, though," he says. "Really, it doesn't matter to me at all. Give it to someone else." Scanning the bustling gate area, his eyes land on an elderly couple—a white-haired man pushing his frail-looking wife in a wheelchair. "That couple over there!" Rory exclaims.

My heart expands, then contracts with a groan. How can I possibly feel like a decent person sitting in first class, lapping up the luxury, when now I'll be picturing this cute old couple cramped in basic economy?

"Alright," I grumble, trying to get in the charitable holiday spirit but finding it rather difficult at the prospect of giving up my fully reclining private pod and gourmet meal service. "Let's see what we can do."

Rory accompanies me as I tell the gate agent that I'd like to trade in my first-class seat. And that I was wondering if I could redeem some frequent flyer miles to have a second seat upgraded so that the elderly couple over there could sit together in first class?

"You're asking to sit in coach *instead* of first class?" the gate agent asks, and I get the feeling it's the first time someone has ever made such a request.

"That's right," I say, casting Rory a look that says, *"Darn you and your Midwest morals."*

"That's just lovely of you," the gate agent says, beaming at us both. "I'll go ahead and upgrade them both now." She calls a Mr. and Mrs. Garrison up to the desk.

The old man slowly wheels his wife up. "What's this all aboot?" he says in a thick Scottish accent. "We were just up here. Is there an issue with muh wife's chair?"

The gate agent fills them in on the events. "This young couple here has volunteered to give you their first-class seats, free of charge. How does that sound?"

Ever the honest one, Rory interjects. "Oh, we're not a couple," he clarifies.

The old woman in the wheelchair looks like she's sure her hearing aids are acting up. "You didnae say first class?" she says. "Gregor?" She looks up at her husband, who appears highly skeptical of the whole thing until the gate agent prints out their new boarding passes, along with confirmation that there's no additional charge, no hidden fees, no terms and conditions.

Then, waving the first-class tickets in the air like winning lottery tickets, the man's wrinkled face breaks into a youthful grin. "First class for me and my bonnie lass!" he says. "Never thought I'd live to see the day!"

They tell us how they're going to visit their son and the wee grandchildren for Christmas in Chicago. And how their doctors told them the trip probably wasn't the best idea, but they said to hell with it.

"No better medicine than family time, aye?" the wife says, as her husband squeezes her skeletal shoulder affectionately.

I've got to admit, the whole thing does make me feel glowy inside, knowing that we've made their day, maybe even their year.

After finishing with the couple, the gate agent assigns Rory and me new seats. "I've made sure you two are seated together," she says, handing us fresh boarding passes. "But you're a bit toward the back of the plane, I'm afraid."

"No worries," Rory says as I try my best not to pout.

It turns out that "a bit toward the back of the plane" is a British euphemism for the second-to-last row. I can't remember the last time I've sat this far back. Probably never.

Rory lets me take the window. He's wedged in the middle, pressed up close to me, as there's nowhere else to go.

We're both quiet as the plane taxis out to the runway. I'm catching up on BBC news podcasts, and Rory seems half asleep, no doubt drowsy from waking up at three AM or whatever ridiculous hour he left for the airport. But as we start picking up speed on the runway, it strikes me that he's nervous, not tired. He's gripping the armrest with all his might, as if holding on for dear life, and I can viscerally feel him sending *"Dear-Lord-please-keep-this-plane-from-crashing-and-I'll-never-ever-sin-again"* vibes up to Heaven.

I think back to how he said that moving to London was his first time abroad. He probably hasn't flown too much in his life. A lot of people in Michigan haven't. You can drive up to Traverse City in the summer and down to Orlando for a budget-friendly road trip in the winter, so there's no real need to deal with the cost or hassle of airplanes.

I've flown so many times since graduating from college that I've forgotten how nervous I used to be too.

"It'll be okay, Rory," I say as the engines groan louder and louder. The front of plane tilts upward, then the back. "All the stats say flying is way safer than driving."

Beads of sweat trickle from Rory's hairline down onto his pasty forehead, and his veins are all but popping out. "But I'm in control when I'm driving," he grits out. "Or at least, more in control than this."

His body unclenches once we've reached a steady altitude, but at the first patch of turbulence, he's back to gripping the armrest and holding his breath.

"Just pretend we're on a boat," I tell him, knowing he likes the water. "Rocking on the waves." I take his sweaty palm and give it a squeeze. Just like at Thanksgiving dinner, it doesn't feel weird to hold his hand—or perhaps it does feel weird in that it doesn't feel weird. Still, I'm about to let go because he probably thinks it's weird.

But before I can release my grip, he squeezes back, just slightly, like he's telling me thank you. So I keep holding on until he manages to fall asleep, his head bobbing awkwardly in front of him.

There's no actual meal service (the joys of coach), but the flight attendant comes by with bottled water and Biscoff cookies. I forgo the bottled water to reduce my plastic consumption, inspired by the recycled Christmas tree that Rory's class made, but I scoop up the cookies and take a pack for Rory too.

Taking off my shoes to release my swollen feet, I spread the flimsy airline blanket over my lap and turn on *Love Actually* on the seat-back TV while crunching my way through the cookies.

They're not the gourmet chocolate mousse of first class, but I'd forgotten how good Biscoff cookies are, with that satisfying gingery snap. I'm tempted to eat Rory's too while he's sleeping—he'd never know the difference—but I decide to save them for him, which freaks me out a bit because it reveals how much I care about him. Saving someone the last cookie is as good a gauge as any of your level of affection.

I think about what it would be like right now if Alexander were the one sitting next to me, coming to meet my family over Christmas like I'd once imagined. How different it would be.

I'd feel too self-conscious about my smelly socks to take my shoes off, and so my feet would be throbbing. I'd be worried about dribbling crumbs down my chin, so I'd forgo snacking altogether, and I'd be watching some dry political documentary instead of a rom-com, just to try to impress him.

Traveling with Rory is far less romantic than traveling with Alexander would be, but so much more enjoyable. I don't have to worry about being on my best behavior.

Even with Mateo, I was always trying to act just right to fit into his high-flying life and be the version of me that he wanted to see. I pruned and paraded the sides of myself that he liked and let the other ones fall away and atrophy.

Here, it feels like I can just sprawl out beside Rory exactly as I am, with none of the pressure to be shiny and desirable.

Perhaps induced by these thoughts, or the cookies I've just inhaled, a loud belch escapes me like a blow horn.

Waking at the sound, Rory looks over at me. "Was that you?" he asks.

"Oops," I admit.

"Just glad it wasn't the engine malfunctioning," he says with a teasing smile, and goes back to sleep. A little while later, his head bobs sideways and rests on top of mine. He doesn't yank it away, just leaves it there, like he's found a safe place to land.

I stay very still so I won't wake him, wishing, just for one absurd moment, that there wouldn't be an Emily waiting for him. That it would just be the two of us, suspended forever up here in the sky that feels very much like Mala's crayon-drawn picture of happiness.

CHAPTER TWENTY-EIGHT

"That Rory certainly seems like a delightful young man," Mom says on the car ride from the airport to my parents' house, as I stare out the backseat window at the acres and acres of dormant cornfields adorned with red barns and green John Deere tractors, all blanketed by bright white snow. "And so *handsome*."

His parents were picking him up too, and our families did that classic Midwest bonding thing where you stand around and gab for an hour as if there's nowhere else you need to be.

There's absolutely nothing my mom would love more than for me to fall for a local guy and settle down on a house across the lake. She's always dropping not so subtle hints about how great it would be if the *whole family* lived nearby. I'm the only holdout, so no pressure.

"We're not dating, Mom," I dismiss gruffly, tired from the two flights (the second one was a propellor plane to the teensy tiny Kalamazoo Airport and made me perspire nearly as much as Rory). "We're just friends."

I had to explain the same thing to Blake when I caught up with her during a layover phone call. She, of all people, should know that Rory isn't my type, but she was infuriatingly skeptical when I insisted there was nothing going on between us.

"I wasn't implying anything," Mom defends. "Just don't rule out having a friendship *evolve*."

And then she launches into the age-old story about how she and my dad had started out as friends in their high school science lab, and though there hadn't been chemistry initially (she always pauses for a chuckle here, then fills it with her own hearty laugh), the Bunsen burner of their flame had heated up over time.

"Friendship is a good foundation to build on, that's all I'm saying," my mom finally concludes when we're finally pulling in the snow-covered driveway of the small, split-level house where I grew up.

"Very enlightening," I mutter dryly, kindly not pointing out how I don't want a hohum relationship like hers and my dad's. I want passion and romance and everything theirs lacks.

*   *   *

Christmas plays out in its typical fashion. Mom shoves trays of home-cooked food at me, rattling off every single ingredient she used, as if adding red onions to the chili instead of green onions is a life-changing development indeed. Dad cracks the beer and fills me in on how U of M's football team would've and should've made the playoffs if the idiot coach hadn't decided to go for it on fourth down instead of kicking a field goal.

My brothers, Sam and Dylan, join in the football rants too, while their wives, Krista and Lauren, fuss over their kids and compare proud notes on when they last slept through the night.

Unfortunately, they're not too exhausted to interrogate me on my love life. They're are part of the Marriage Evangelist Cult (not an official organization to my knowledge, but it might as well be) and are convinced that life only starts when you have a ring on your finger. I can pretty much hear the pitying thoughts: *Poor, poor Kat. Single and over thirty—practically an old maid!*

Krista and Lauren ask me if there's anyone special in my life this Christmas.

There are lots of special people in my life, I'm tempted to retort. But I don't want them to think I'm bitter when I'm clearly not, so I just tell them no, I've gone on a few dates but no one has caught my eye.

Except the guy I was obsessed with on the double-decker bus, who's actually also from Kalamazoo, I could add. *But I fell out of love with him the moment he opened his mouth, so it's irrelevant.*

"City guys never want to settle down," Lauren says, though I doubt she's ever spent more than a long weekend in a big city.

"There's still time for you," Krista chimes in, as if she genuinely thinks she's being helpful and not triggering my stress about how my biological clock is tick-tick-ticking.

Sam and Dylan tease that they'll launch a podcast where bachelors can submit applications to be my trophy husband, and they'll screen and interview the candidates for me. Mom snaps at them to stop making a joke out of my love life, but it actually makes me feel better that they can find some humor in all of it.

After a five-course feast, we waddle out of our chairs to go for a family walk to see the neighborhood lights, per tradition.

Night is falling but taking its time. The inland lake my parents live on is half frozen over, and late afternoon light reflects off the thin sheets of ice, like sunshine on solar panels. Small houses made of synthetic siding are all cramped together, none hogging too much waterfront. Colored bulbs are strung joyfully from the roofs, and huge snow banks border the street. Most mailboxes are crooked, presumably from collisions with the pickup truck plow.

Walking this old route makes me remember little snippets of my childhood. Racing my brothers to the bus stop at the top of the hill. Building igloos and snow forts, pounding each other with ice balls. Tubing behind the McAllisters' boat on the last day of school, four of us kids piled on one tube, bouncing and hollering as we veered out of the wake. And then devouring Mom's famous grilled cheese sandwiches back at our house.

I don't usually linger on the good parts about growing up here. The stories I tell myself are the bad ones. How awkward and shy and friendless I was. How I didn't fit in and I didn't *want* to fit in because fitting in here would mean having to make myself small to squeeze into a small box where the best you can hope for is mediocrity.

During my obligatory trips as an adult, these are the stories I've repeated. Cementing them in my memory helps prove to myself, and to other people, that I'm on the right path now.

But the daylight has slipped away, taking my smugness and sense of superiority along with it. I should feel more successful than my family, given how I'm raking in a large salary at a prestigious consulting firm in an international city and am on track to make partner.

But I don't actually feel more successful. Not right now. I feel just as stuck as they are. More stuck, maybe, because they don't seem to think they're stuck. They think they're free, whereas I feel trapped by the weight of everything I haven't accomplished yet.

The thoughts cut me like an icy wind, and I'm newly aware of just how freezing it is out here. I ball up my fists in my gloves, trying to warm up, but it doesn't help much.

Ever since I moved away at eighteen, I've been pushing myself so hard to reach my potential. To not stop or pause or hardly even breathe until I reach my dreams.

And yet what do I really have to show for all of the work? I've sacrificed relationships, morals, and sleep, and I'm barely more than a stranger to my own family. My salary is big, but I have little time to spend it—and no one to spend it with. Blake's decision to scale back at work starts to make a little more sense, even though I'm not sure I want it to, because it threatens the narratives that hold my own life together.

There's a certain empowerment in knowing that I don't *need* a partner—that I'm capable of providing for myself. But that doesn't keep me from wanting to find that person who completes me and makes me feel like I was never actually living before meeting him.

What I haven't wanted is to end up like my parents, two people who've managed to stick it out together, it seems, because they haven't expected too much out of each other or out of life. Or at least that's how it's always looked to me.

But as the stars start poking out of the sky like rustic diamonds, I take a closer look at Mom and Dad, walking one in front of the other through the snowy street. I'd assumed they were spaced so far apart because they were too sick of each other to walk side by side, let alone hold hands. But now, suddenly yet slowly, I notice little details I haven't before. Like how Mom, walking ahead of Dad, tests each footstep with her boots and reports back to Dad if there's an icy patch (Dad had a hip replacement last year, so falling could be bad). He grumbles that he knows how to walk, but I can newly discern the gratitude beneath the gruffness.

Dad starts complaining about how stuffed he is, how he must've packed on ten pounds from dinner. But he does it in a way that compliments every single dish Mom made, and her whole posture perks up.

What I see in my parents is not a movie-worthy love story. But it's a love story, nonetheless. Here are two people who are still choosing each other after thirty-some years together. Still trying to affirm each other in their respective love languages.

It's more than a bit disorienting, thinking of my parents being this way. Being in love. But rather than making me feel lost, it makes me feel found.

Through my fresh lens, I observe my brothers and sisters-in-law too. Their gender-role dynamic might not be what I'd choose, but it's what they've chosen, and it's clear they're glad for this. They don't have fireworks leaping between them, but there *is* a spark there—a slow-burning bonfire that lights things up instead of burning them down.

My family isn't perfect, but they're happy. Or maybe they're happy *because* they're not perfect. Because they're free from the pressures of needing everything to be flawless. Because they give their spouses and their kids and themselves the grace to be human. The grace to understand that relationships aren't ninety-minute Hollywood movies.

I'm reminded of Rory and how peaceful I felt sitting next to him on the Marlow House couch. How I always thought that comfort implied complacency, but maybe it's just the feeling of being fulfilled exactly where you are and as you are.

It makes me wonder, not just in the abstract anymore, if I might be in love with him. I don't linger on the thoughts because they don't really matter, not when he wants to marry someone else and might even be proposing at this very moment.

When we return to my parents' house, I shake off my snowy boots in the mudroom. There's an old family portrait hanging on the wall. We're all sitting out on the dock with sunburns, ice-cream cones, and bad tan lines. I'm probably six or seven, about the age when I first declared I wanted to be a CEO. It was a dream then— something whimsical that made me squeal with glee to think about. But as I've grown up and gotten closer to the reality of it, it's devolved into an obligation—something I feel like I *should* go after because it would be good for me and good for women. Not because it lights me up inside.

I miss you, Kit Kat, I hear myself telling my younger self in the portrait, only realizing how much I mean it once I let myself think it. How much I wish I still had her spunk and innocence.

The little girl in the portrait doesn't latch onto any of my own worries or regret. She just smiles back, gap-toothed and beautiful with her wide eyes and bushy, untamed hair—long before the years of keratin treatment made it sleek and flat.

"I'm still inside you, silly goose," she seems to say, and it punches me in the stomach with the force of a tiny but mighty fist.

For so long now, I've been trying to grow up, trying to get away from my past self, leave her in the dust. But she's stayed with me the whole time. Like she knew I'd want her back someday. Like she knew I'd finally start loving her. Loving me. Loving *us.*

Dabbing a finger kiss on my face in the picture frame, I go into the family room and hang Mala's mitten ornament on the

Christmas tree. Then I sit down on the couch with a mug of Mom's hot cider and hold my baby niece, carefully cradling her head. This is first time I've met her, but she doesn't shriek or even whine. She seems to trust me, even though I'm not sure I even trust myself.

Like a sponge, her huge blue eyes absorb every little thing. Her raw awe becomes my own, and we watch together in wonder as the family room shines under the lights from the tree and the fire and the love packed into this house—love that, only an hour ago, I could hardly feel or even see, and now seems so completely obvious. Like only a fool could miss it.

A fool, or someone who's turned rom-coms into her bible on love.

Which, on second thought, might in fact be the very definition of a fool.

CHAPTER TWENTY-NINE

My big revelation doesn't make me want to quit my job and move back to Kalamazoo and settle down in a cottage across the lake from my parents.

It doesn't make me want to drive over to Rory's house and knock on his door and say, "Oh hey, so funny story, I think I might actually have romantic feelings for you. How about we head over to Culver's to talk it out over frozen custard and curly fries?"

Sure, I've contemplated those scenarios, but the more I think about them, the less sense they make.

If I moved back here, I'd get bored and restless in two seconds flat. I'd regret giving up on my goals. One day in eight years or so, I'd be at the grocery checkout line in Meijer and see a display of Forbes magazines featuring a glossy woman on the cover with a power suit and formidable blowout. *That could've been me,* I'd think bitterly. And then I'd run some red lights on the way home just to let out some steam, and next thing you'd know, my mug shot would be plastered on the front page of the Kalamazoo Gazette—*Local Soccer Mom Wreaks Havoc on Westnedge Ave.* On the plus side, perhaps the story might go viral and kick Little Miss Forbes right off her high horse, but that's beside the point.

As far as Rory goes, it's not like I'm actually in love with him. He's a good guy, and I'm tempted to give good guys more of a chance after spending more time with my family. But Rory and I are still too different. If this were a Hallmark movie, there'd be a chance for us with the big-city-girl-falls-for-wholesome-home-town-guy plotline, but as we've established, life is *not* a movie, and my newfound realism tells me I wouldn't be able to give him what he needs—someone who wants to live in the same zip code for the rest of her life and raise a bunch of kids (without ending up in an orange jumpsuit). And I don't think he could give me what I need either—the adventure and spontaneity and kissing-in-the-rain date nights.

Yes, I can make more time for my family, and yes, I can open myself up to people who don't fit the typical Prince Charming type. But that doesn't mean I have to run back to my hometown and profess my love to Rory. I'm not going to let fear hold me back. And that's all this is—fear. Existential spirals are normal at the holidays, especially when you're the last single one standing.

The rest of the visit at my parents' house isn't exactly ideal. Cranky and on edge, I throw myself into work, leading Q1 planning Zoom calls from my childhood bedroom while my mom clanks pots and pans from the kitchen below. With each hour, I get more antsy to leave. Jump back on the corporate treadmill and sweat out all the angst. Seek refuge in the rat race because at least I belong there. Or even if I don't, there's no time to pause and dwell on it when I'm jamming to meet a deadline.

Maybe it's not the most mature solution, but the most expedient one is just to move up my flight back to London. Before I do, though, I check with Rory to see how things are going with Emily. If they're back together, that's an extra reason for me to leave ASAP and avoid having to be on the same return flight and see his glee juxtaposed to my gloom.

How's it going with Emily? I text him, hoping the strictly platonic, supportive-friend tone comes through.

It takes him a while to text back. Not at all like his typical time lines. Finally, my phone chimes, and my mood lifts at his name, then sinks at the message: She wants to get back together.

It feels like losing a friend, only worse because of the part of me that was wondering if just maybe we might be more than friends, in another universe or potentially this one. The thought of Rory being there and available was highly comforting. And now it's gone, just like that.

Knew she'd come around, I reply because I did. No one with an ounce of common sense would let Rory go. Congrats!!!

I'm hoping the three exclamation points do the trick to make him believe that I'm being genuine. He probably will think that— he always likes to believe the best in me and other people. The thought paints me even bluer.

I tell him something has come up for work, so I have to fly back to London a few days early. Then I pack up my carry-on bag, and both my parents drive me to the airport, even though I tell them I don't need them to.

As they hug me goodbye, they ask when I'll be transferred back to the States, and I say hopefully soon. But on the flight back to Heathrow (back to first class this time), I send some emails to request that my next case be in Dubai or Singapore or any English-speaking place east of the prime meridian. I might not know exactly where I'm heading in life, but I refuse to go backward.

Then I recline my seat one hundred and eighty degrees, spreading out in my private pod, somehow less comfortable than I was when I was crammed in next to Rory at the very back of the plane.

*   *   *

Back in London, the city feels too crowded, too loud, too frenzied. Though it's less densely populated than New York, there's still a suffocating atmosphere with cars and lorries and cyclists piled up on top of each other, always impatient to get somewhere. Sirens and construction equipment relentlessly split the air, and the parks feel small and claustrophobic after the wide-open spaces in Michigan. Time skips and sprints here, and I find myself missing the slower, shuffling pace. City life offers no refuge for real peace and quiet or undomesticated nature, and it gives me a persistent, low-grade headache. It doesn't snow, but just rains, and the damp coldness cuts to the bone without the benefit of Michigan's winter-wonderland splendor. And after a week back in a small town where the neighbors all knew my name, it feels brutally anonymous among the throngs of strangers who don't even offer eye contact.

I'm more homesick than when I first moved over, and a vibrant vision of a house of my own in Michigan with dogs and kids and a husband who makes Kit Kat pies on my birthday keeps flitting through my mind like a fly I can't swat and don't want to.

I start going into the office every day. The last thing I want is to be sitting alone in my flat, looking out the window to catch a glimpse of Rory on the bus. And now that I'm leading the case, I feel an increased level of investment in my work. Though I still don't agree with Turpi's fossil-fuel business model, I want the project to be successful so it clinches my promotion at the end of the year.

Going into the office is worth it, even if I do have to endure Harold and his obnoxious airs. What HR is doing—or not doing—about him is still very much on my mind, but I'm not in the headspace to check in about it just now, especially with all the increased pressure I'm under as the proxy partner.

During my first week back after the break, Harold calls me into his office. I expect him to want an update on the projected cost savings, or to make another snide remark about how I never join him for drinks. But it goes differently than I expect.

"Kat," he says, looking up from his swiveling desk chair. His spray-tanned face is splotched with more orange than ever, and his sagging cheeks look reinflated with fresh fillers. "No more Kitten this year—how's that?" He smiles his seedy smile, looking like I should be thanking him for this.

When I don't say anything, he carries on, clanking his pinky rings together for something to do with his hands. "I did just want to . . . apologize," he says, like the word is difficult to grit out, "if you didn't quite enjoy that night at Annabel's."

There's a flicker of something in Harold's eyes—maybe embarrassment for his actions or more likely just trepidation about what might happen if I escalate this up the chain and involve the board of directors. "Thought it was just a bit of fun, but I sense you might view it differently," he goes on. "And I'm sorry about that—I am."

Abruptly, he comes to a halt, as if he's reached the end of his earnings call script.

Now is my chance to say something. To speak up and stick up for myself. To protect any women he might prey on in the future. But I find myself oddly disarmed by his apology—or half apology at least.

"It's okay," are the words that come out even as my brain is screaming, *It is not okay! Make him pay for being the pig he is!* "Let's just move forward?"

Harold's face splits with relief. "Brilliant," he says, stroking his head with his hands as if he thinks he still has hair. "Just brilliant. Well, glad that's sorted."

And just like that, he switches the conversation over to the latest metrics from the automation rollout plan and the bottlenecks we're facing on the operations side.

Back in my own office afterward, I gaze out the window, at the cluster of clouds hanging over the Thames, dulling the water. Everything feels as monochrome as it looks.

Replaying the conversation that just took place, I launch into a string of self-attacks. I shouldn't have rolled over so easily. Maybe it's because of how conditioned I've been to be a people pleaser. To be the good girl and not cause conflict. Or maybe I let it go because I'm just desperate to move on and forget what happened.

That afternoon, I get an email from Helena in HR. Heard you connected with Harold—glad all is well. Wishing you a Happy New Year.

It lathers my skin with a grimy, guilty feeling.

When I get back to Marlow House that night, I collect my mail, which gets dropped through the slit in the door every day. Amid the water and electric bills (which I have no intent on opening, thanks to online payments), there's a coupon for Nando's on Upper Street and then a plain envelope that just says *Kat*.

Opening it, I find a thank-you note from Rory for the flights, signed by his whole family. Rory's handwriting is just about the opposite of calligraphy—stick letters that aren't straight, but it looks like he's tried very hard to make them even at least.

I wish he'd written Kit Kat, not Kat. The one syllable feels very stiff and formal. Like it's proof he doesn't want to be friends with me now that he's back with Emily.

There's no stamp, so he must've come by to drop it off in person. I wonder if he buzzed up to see if I was home.

I text him a thank-you for the thank-you. I nearly tell him that I spoke to Harold today. I nearly see if he wants to come over for gelato and a movie (no rom-coms). But I don't. He's with Emily now. Our friendship is as good as dead. As is the potential for more than friendship.

It's all gone now, before it ever really existed.

* * *

Things are manageable in the weeks that follow.

Harold tones down the level of his comments from crude to cringeworthy, and he mostly leaves me alone in my office. As I lead the case into its final stretch, we're on track to meet the deliverables and time lines.

As part of those time lines, Turpi announces another round of layoffs. I feel more than a little responsible since it's part of the cost-savings plan I've helped come up with after Harold and his team shot down the clean energy idea. Because they've refused to invest in new revenue streams, their only option is to slash costs, which means that thousands of people in Turpi's factories, and the headquarters where I work, are suddenly made redundant.

I soothe my conscience by telling myself that this is just how the corporate world works. Everyone knows that going in. Businesses aren't married to their employees. They don't have to commit to them for their whole lives. Firing people is just a natural part of the economic cycle.

But it's harder to stay unattached when there's a forlorn-looking man in the elevator with me at the end of the day. He's carrying about ten different plastic bags, all stuffed with different office supplies, as if he cleared out his desk in a hurry, without forewarning.

He drops something on the elevator floor. I bend over to pick it up for him. It's a framed photo of the man with a little girl hoisted on his shoulders. Above the photo, there's one of those fill-in-the-blank prompts: "My hero is . . ."

The little girl had filled it in with shaky handwriting: *My Daddy.*

"Thanks," the man mutters, stowing the photo back in one of the bags. It's only then I notice that his eyes are red and puffy. He seems determined to keep his head ducked so no one will notice.

A pang spreads through me at the thought of this man going home for dinner tonight and telling his family that he no longer has a job. I want to reassure him that his daughter will still think of him as her hero. That the job market is strong and he'll land on his feet. That Turpi is going to be in a tenuous financial position in the coming years, so it's actually better he's getting out now with some severance.

But there's no time for that. The elevator doors open, and the man skirts out, rushing out of the building as if determined to be rid of this place as quickly as possible.

On my commute home, wedged shoulder to shoulder on the crowded tube, I try not to picture where that man is right now, or if he's stopping by his local pub for a pint before facing his wife and kids. If he's stashing the bags away so his wife won't see them. So he'll have more time to come up with a plan before telling her what's happened.

None of this would be happening if Turpi had agreed to invest in clean energy. They'd be needing more people for that, not fewer. I tried to prevent this.

But beneath my defensive posture, I know I didn't try that hard. I gave one little clean energy pitch in a meeting, and then, when it wasn't popular, I gave the higher-ups what they'd asked for, instead. I let my values be steamrolled for self-gain.

I wonder what Rory would say about it. He wouldn't approve of so many employees being let go. But he'd still have a way of making me feel better about myself, making me believe I'd find a way to make up the damage.

Back at Marlow House, it's the creaky, quiet type of night when I'd like to have Jules around. But she and Nina are off in the Cotswolds, visiting wedding venues, so I soothe myself with *Married at First Sight*. The newlyweds are off on tropical honeymoons with cerulean ocean views that make me miss Michigan and the raw beauty of the water.

As I watch the couples Jet-ski on TV, I picture zipping across the tame lake behind my parents' house, racing Rory to the dock on a bet that loser buys ice cream. The unpolluted breeze makes it easier to breathe, and the fresh water sprays playfully in our faces, redeeming the youthful parts of me I'd left for dead.

Stop that, I chide myself. *That's not a productive thought. That's the opposite of productive.*

But the vision sticks anyway, latching on like a memory. I'm homesick for what I used to have—and also for what I'll never have.

CHAPTER THIRTY

Jules bursts onto the scene again when she's back from the Cotswolds.

Me and Nina are having a spontaneous hen do tomorrow! she texts me that Friday night. Pub crawl starting at King's Head at midday. Leotards required.

Upon Googling *"What is a hen do?"* I find out it's the British term for a bachelorette party. Even if I not so secretly wish I were the one having a hen do, I'm not going to be the bitter single woman who refuses to celebrate her friends just because she's moping about how she's going to wind up alone while everyone else is basking in marital bliss.

Noon seems aggressively early to start drinking, but when I walk into the King's Head the next day at quarter past, the party is already in full swing, streamers dangling from the antique light fixtures and helium balloons tied to pint-glass anchors at the bar.

Jules and Nina are surrounded by a gaggle of women. Jules is in a bright magenta leotard, with a plunging neckline and spaghetti straps. No matter that it's the middle of winter, she's boasting bare legs with over-the-knee boots. Glitter eyeshadow covers most of her face, and massive hoop earrings reach nearly to hear shoulders. She's wearing her most voluminous false eyelashes, and her flaming hair is teased at the roots so it adds an extra few inches to her already tall frame.

Nina is wearing a svelte, long-sleeved bodysuit that makes her look like a professional ballerina. They're both wearing matching tiaras that say "Future Mrs."

Their friends are all in various-colored, various-shaped leotards, and everyone is wearing "Team Brides" sashes (the "s" looks to have been added on in permanent marker).

"Babes!" Jules exclaims, spotting me. Her expression swiftly drops from delight to disapproval as she looks at my casual jeans and T-shirt outfit. "Where's the leotard?" she demands.

"I've never owned a leotard in my life," I say. "I thought you were joking."

"You should know I'd never *joke* about leotards," Jules says reprovingly. "You're lucky I've got a few spares back at my flat. Do come along now."

And so she drags me out of the pub and up to her flat. "Take your pick," she says, laying out the options flat on the crisply made bed (something tells me that Nina is the bed maker in their relationship).

I'm tempted to refuse altogether, but it is her day after all, so I oblige and choose the most conservative of the choices, not that that's saying much. It's basically a scoop-necked black swimsuit, ruched in the stomach to make it slightly more forgiving. I change back in my flat, pairing it with the thickest tights I have, plus a cardigan.

"Oh c'mon, it's poor form to wear a bloody jumper with a leotard," Jules vetoes when I emerge from my bedroom. She looks as horrified as if I've dared to pair beer with green juice.

As I reluctantly shed the cardigan, Jules waves lipstick and mascara wands over my face before I can stop her. Rummaging through my closet, she pulls out my highest heeled boots and jams them onto my feet, paying no mind to the fact that they're way too fancy for a grimy pub.

"'At'll do," she says proudly, like she's my fairy godmother. "Now c'mon, time to get Scotch mist. *Pissed,*" she clarifies in cockney. "Comes from how the mist in the 'ighlands fogs your vision like drinks do. Though to be fair, I never see more clearly than when I'm sloshed, do I?" She grins happily, as if this is a very fortunate character trait.

Back at the King's Head, I keep my knee-length parka zipped up for as long as I can, adorning it with a sash that one of the women hands me. But by the time we're at the Bull's Head for our second stop on the pub crawl, I'm too warm to keep it on any longer. The bar is filling up with soccer fans who are crowding in front of the large-screen TVs, and I'm sweating through the layers of down. Slinging the jacket over a barstool, I let the leotard free.

"Bloody 'ell," Jules says, looking over at me. "Who invited the supermodel, hey?"

"As if," I say, but there's a certain thrill from the costume, like I can swap out my story for someone else's.

The bartender starts passing out Craig Davids. I know tequila is a bad idea, but I don't have too many good ideas at the moment, so

I go along with it. Jules raises her shot glass in the air. "To my last days of freedom before being cut and carried!" she hoots.

One of the bridesmaids, a school friends of Jules's from East London, tells me that *cut and carried* means *married*, dating back to how brides were cut off from their parents and carried by their husbands. "Good bit of irony in the context of a lesbian love story, innit?" the woman says. "No men needed."

We all clink tequila shots, then toss back our heads. My face pinches as it goes down. I chug the pineapple-juice chaser, then wash it down with a few thick-cut chips.

It doesn't take long to feel the effects. The rest of the hen doers start to feel like long-lost sisters as they pull me into their circle, gushing over my American accent and insisting that I rank their own attempts at one. The Maid of Honor wins the contest with her Valley Girl California accent, but Jules gets runner-up with her sorority-girl Southern drawl, only because it's too rib-splittingly atrocious not to award points to.

I try to pace myself as we move over to the Old Queen's Head on Essex Road. (When I ask Jules if there's an unwritten rule that every pub in London must include the word *head*, she just sniggers and says she knows where my own head is at.)

By the time we reach the Camden Head, a haunted-looking castle-type building at the spout of Camden Passage, dusk is falling, and the night is spinning. Not enough to make me dizzy—just enough to make me curious about where I'll land on the roulette wheel tonight.

The outdoor terrace is closed for the season, so everyone is packed inside around the circular bar, with overflow at the rowdy comedy club upstairs. The pub's classic Victorian furnishings are similar to those at the King's Head, but more torch-style lights dangle from the wood-beamed ceiling, so everything feels a bit brighter. Or maybe that's just the work of the pints and shots.

"I haven't had a girls' night out in so long," I confide to one of the bridesmaids, and then all the others, as we stash our coats in a musty corner, à la the college frat party days. "Didn't realize how much I needed it." There's a pang of longing for Blake and our other friends from the New York days. All those nights out together that we took for granted.

Jules overhears and blows me a tipsy kiss. "This is a cracking start to the wedding fun, this is," she says. "You'll be a bridesmaid, Kat, won't you?"

"You don't mean that," I say, though I hope she does. I've never actually been a bridesmaid before. I've always seemed to rank just beneath the cutoff in my friends' lists, ousted by sisters and cousins and childhood best friends I'd never heard them mention before. "Ask me again when you're sober."

"I'm dead serious. Don't we, Nines," she asks, pulling Nina into the conversation. "want Kat to be a bridesmaid?"

"'Course we do," Nina says with a cherubic smile. She seems significantly more sober than Jules, and I get the feeling she's been tossing the shots over her shoulder. "Eleventh of May—put it in your diary."

"You'd best take Rory as your plus one," Jules says, a scheming look breaking over her sweaty, glittery face.

A dull ache rises from somewhere far down. It doesn't quite reach my outer layers, and I take a hearty sip from my pint to keep it that way, but it still pokes and prods from within. "I can't," I say glumly. "He's back with his ex."

Jules looks appalled, as if there could be no worse news. "Not that Kal-a-wa-choo bird?" she laments. "Gimme all the goss."

As briefly as possible, I fill her in about how we haven't seen each other or even talked since Christmas.

"What a faff this is," she says, looking as despondent as if her own happy ending has been thwarted. "Reckon 'e figures 'e doesn't 'ave a chance with you, so 'e's going for the backup choice so 'e doesn't get hurt."

"No," I say, though I'll admit that I like how that scenario sounds. "He loves her. That's all there is to it."

"'E's being a bloody idjit, 'e is," Jules says, false lashes blinking indignantly. "Never liked that bloke anyway."

I roll my eyes at how obvious the lie is, but it still makes me feel a little better. "He didn't do anything wrong," I say. "We were only ever friends."

Jules gives me a dubious look but thankfully lets it go. "Righ'o then," she says, briskly changing tempers as quickly as London changes weather. "So who're you shagging tonight? Let's have a gander." She scans the pub, which has filled up to the brim. "Those rugby blokes over there are quite fit, ya reckon?"

"Stop it," I grumble. "I'm not in the mood." But I can't help but glance over to see who she's pointing to.

A group of burly, athletic-looking guys is gathered across the pub, still in muddy, grass-stained jerseys. They have a self-important air about them, as if they've just won a big match.

Though they're all decently attractive, one of them stands out. He's a bit taller than the rest, with the swagger of someone who nominated himself to be captain. His sandy blond hair falls wet and tousled onto his scruffy face. He's exactly the type of guy I would've gone for ten years ago. But I've grown up since then, and people like him haven't. I'm way beyond needing to flirt with a gorgeous man-child just to feel better about myself.

Oh come on, the drunk voice chastises. *Just loosen up and have some fun, won't you?*

Fit Rugby Lad must feel me staring because he looks up. We make eye contact, and I watch as he takes in my leotard-and-lipstick ensemble. Drinking it in slowly, like he wants to linger over the flavor, he looks thirsty for something more than beer.

That old excitement courses through me. I'd forgotten how fun it was to play the eye contact game. To seduce and be seduced with the delicate exchange of facial expressions. My confidence in my ability to read and speak eye contact was ruined by the whole Alexander/Rory debacle. It's gotten me wondering if maybe I've lost all my talents. Left them back in my twenties with my toned glutes and hangover-proof drinking abilities.

But there's zero doubt that Fit Rugby Lad is looking at me. That he's interested. He's already defied British cultural norms by holding eye contact for more than two seconds, so that's basically the equivalent of a five-page love letter in this day and age.

I need to prove myself right. After a large swig of beer, I hand my pint to Jules to hold. "Be right back," I tell her, then shimmy my way through the crowd until I emerge right in front of Fit Rugby Lad.

He's every bit as attractive up close. There are a few stray blades of grass on his forehead, as if he slid headfirst in the rain for a match-winning score.

"Hey there," I say over the din of the crowd, feeling wholly unstoppable.

"Hiya," he says, like he's enjoying this as much as I am.

"Were you looking at me?" I ask.

"Um," he says, flustered. "Sorry about that." His accent rises and falls in that effortlessly magnetic English way.

"I wasn't asking you to apologize," I clarify. "I was asking if you wanted to kiss me."

He looks taken aback, like he's not sure he heard correctly. "You serious?"

"Very serious." I take a half step closer. We're so close together that his eyes aren't quite in focus anymore. I prefer it that way so I don't have to concentrate on him. I can focus on the game and how I'm winning.

"I bloody love American girls," Fit Rugby Lad declares, leaning in. It's a rough and unapologetic kiss, like we both have something to prove.

Jules and the rest of the hen-do crowd are watching on, cheering manically. The rugby squad are whistling too, as if they've just brought home the trophy.

I tell Fit Rugby Lad that I've got to get back to my friends' hen do but that he should find me before he leaves. He takes my number and promises to do that.

"What a snog, babes," Jules says when I return to her side. "Never knew you were so shameless." She looks enormously impressed.

"I'm not shameless," I say. "I can just tell when someone's into me."

"Except with Alexander," Jules notes without filter. The moment it's out of her mouth, she seems to realize that was the wrong thing to say, so she proceeds to laugh loudly to cover up her tracks.

I'm not bothered, though. I'm too busy riding the drunken high that comes from being desired by someone desirable.

A little while later, Fit Rugby Lad comes over to say good-bye. "We're heading back to my mate's flat," he says. "Give a shout later?" He gives a cheeky wink, and I feel it between my legs where my leotard meets my tights.

I think about the last time someone touched my tights. It makes me want to have someone else's hand there so the new memory can fully usurp the old one. And more than that, to satiate the ravenous hunger I haven't realized I've been repressing until now.

"Yeah," I hear myself telling him, as if I'm back in college again. "Text me."

He taps my bum, almost like a high five, and then is out the door with his teammates.

I'm left buzzing. Here it is, the proof that I've still got it. That I can still speak eye contact and land the hottest guy in the room.

But one pint later, the whole thing is filling me with that hollow feeling. Here I am, over thirty years old, waiting for some guy I've just met to text me to see if I'll come sleep with him. The fact that his name (which I can't even remember) hasn't lit up on my phone screen is making me feel old and unattractive.

I don't want this to be who I am—someone whose self-worth is tied up in a stranger's decision of whether I'm worth hooking up with. I just want to have that one person who I know loves me, flaws and quirks and cellulite and all.

I don't want the hot passion of hormones that quickly dissolve and fizzle and fade. I want the kind of love that makes me feel sane and secure and snug. Not with a bad boy or some arrogant adrena-line seeker who lies his way to the top. With the good guy, someone who's responsible and respectful and texts me on Sunday mornings, not Saturday nights. Someone who's patient and kind and rejoices with the truth. Someone who makes me feel like I'm always enough for him, even on the days I don't feel like I'm enough for myself.

The thought drops into me, or drops out of me, like it's been there all along, waiting to be released.

I don't want someone. I want Rory.

*   *   *

It's not in the hesitant or hypothetical ways I've contemplated that I might love Rory in the past. It's firm and full of unflinching conviction. And maybe this isn't the perfect time to fully accept this, when Rory is with someone else. When I'm drunk in a pub, trying to flirt with other guys so I won't have to think about how the one I want doesn't want me.

But maybe it *is* the perfect time because it cuts through all the clutter and deception I've been telling myself about how fine I am. How I don't want a life like my family has. How I'm destined for bigger and better things than the places and people of Michigan can offer.

But here it is, the cold, hard truth. Except the truth doesn't feel cold and hard at all. It feels warm and soft and relaxing, like putting my feet up after a long day at the office.

I love Rory and I want to be with him. I want to settle down in a little yellow house on a lake near Kalamazoo. Close to our families but not *too* close that we can't enjoy a bit of privacy. I want to slow down and slow-dance in the kitchen and host game nights on the back porch in the glow of firefly light. I want to have a few kids and take them tubing and roast peanut butter s'mores together on long summer days, serenaded by crickets and bullfrogs. I want to watch college football in the fall with Rory and my dad and brothers on Saturdays. Sundays will be for church and homemade pizza, without the incessant stress of work emails and deadlines.

I want to make pancakes in the morning before Rory and the kids leave for school and let Rory scoop me ice cream at the end of the day. I want to fall asleep curled up next to him every night and wake up beside him each morning and do it all over again. I want to grow old together and take our sweet time doing it so we notice every single gray hair that appears and tease each other for it.

It feels so sunlit and safe. Not the safety net kind of safe—not a fallback or a backup choice. The first-choice kind of safe. The security that comes from knowing there's no place you'd rather be and no one you'd rather be there with.

On one level, there's the relief that I'm finally being honest with myself. But on another level, there's the regret that it doesn't matter. Because although Rory might want that life too, he wants it with Emily, not me. I'm not going to come between them. You never try to sabotage the person you love. You just try to support their happiness, however best you can. Even if it means staying away and moving on.

Jules is doling out another round of Craig Davids. My phone buzzes with a text from an unknown number.

U still up?

Perhaps it's the idea of more tequila or letting a stranger use my body for his pleasure, but I feel like I'm about to vomit. I tell Jules I'm not feeling well, that I need to go home. Fumbling around, I search for my parka but can't find it. Giving up, I bolt out of the pub in just the leotard.

Ankles wobbling on the cobblestone, I hurry back to Marlow House, trying to seek refuge in the possibility that my thoughts about Rory and our life together are nothing but inebriated ruminations and that by the time the alcohol wears off, all those thoughts will be dead and gone and buried.

But the idea doesn't comfort me. It just adds to the sense of loss that's mounting. Because as scary as it is to think that I'm in love with Rory, it's even more frightening to think that I'm not.

CHAPTER THIRTY-ONE

The thoughts and emotions hang over me in the days that follow, like I'm perpetually walking through the London fog. The only solution to gaining some clarity seems to be getting together with Rory again in person.

I haven't seen him since Christmas, and even if there's some validity to my feelings, my imagination is likely exaggerating the whole thing by inventing all the ways we might be compatible. In reality, if there were some grand connection between us, we'd be together by now.

So, early in February, I finally text him. Or at least I type out the text, keeping it in my iPhone notes until I'm ready.

Achieving the "ready" status involves talking myself in circles about how Rory hasn't reached out, so he clearly doesn't want to be friends, so I should just take a hint and leave him alone. But also I do need to see him for my own closure, so I shouldn't worry about reaching out—I should just woman up and do it. Or maybe I should just let the whole friendship fizzle out completely and delete his number from my phone.

One day at the office, Harold assembles the management team, plus me, to vent about how some of Turpi's largest shareholders are asking Harold to diversify into clean energy. "They're such puppets," he vents. "Just worried about the optics, no spine to think for themselves. It's all the media's fault, of course," he carries on, pounding his hands on the conference room table like a tantrummy toddler who's been denied a third serving of pudding. "Those clean energy charlatans are hogging the spotlight. It's a bloody joke."

Turpi has been on the negative end of some recent PR stories that have been praising their competitors for going green. It's not hard to see through the veneer of his business motivations and into the deeper reason for his concern. If Turpi loses its stature, his stock options will plummet in value, not to mention that the models at Annabel's won't be as impressed by him.

I feel an unexpected pity for him, that his net worth and identity are so wrapped up in his business and the opinions of strangers. Then the pity turns inward as I wonder if that might be me someday—hopefully leading a less dreadful company but still defining my success by what I do rather than who I am.

It's in that moment of frustration that I decide I'm ready to text Rory. I do it quickly, before I can talk myself out of it. I copy the draft from my phone notes and press "Send."

Hey, hope you're doing well! Any chance I could come by the school on Friday and have lunch with Mala?

I do want to see Mala, very much so, but it's also a defensive strategy for deflecting the message from Rory himself. For making it seem like I'm entirely indifferent about him specifically, since he certainly doesn't seem inclined to see me—thus the total silence of the past six weeks.

It's late enough in the afternoon that the school day will be done, but I still try to prepare myself that I won't hear back for a while, perhaps not at all.

But the texting bubbles appear right away, along with bright bubbles of hope that—I'm bracing myself—could pop any second.

They don't pop, though. They just inflate further as I read the message.

Of course! Sorry I haven't reached out, been a bit of a crazy time. Will be great to see you ☺

I'm relieved and a bit exultant. There was a part of me that was worried I'd never see or hear from Rory again. I thought he might be gone for good, the way Mateo blocked me after our breakup. In fact, the way every ex has blocked me after a breakup. I guess that's the type of person I've gone for in the past—the passionate, tempestuous type who drops out of my life as quickly as he popped into it.

But it's not going to be like that with Rory. Yes, he's with someone now but that doesn't mean we have to cut each other out completely. It doesn't mean that he can't still be there when I need him.

And I do need him now. I need him to help me see all the ways we're not right for each other.

*　*　*

When I arrive at Hendrick Primary School on Friday, the children are scampering about the playground, spinning on the tire swings in their puffy winter coats, racing down the twisty plastic slides, cackling with ebullient amusement at nothing and everything all at once.

When I reach the classroom inside, it's empty except for Rory. He's sitting at his desk, filing papers, wearing a pair of round glasses that give him an even more earnest expression than usual. His hair is cropped tightly around his ears and forehead, like he asked for the barber to cut it shorter than he wanted so he'd be able to go longer in between cuts and save a bit of money. He has a sunlight-deprived look about him, his skin paler and his hair darker. His cowlick remains as stubborn as ever, an upturned tuft that's the only rebellious part of him.

Lingering in the doorway, I arrange my face in my most believable oh-hey-friend-for-whom-I'm-harboring-zero-repressed-romantic-feelings expression.

"Hi there," I say, talking a bit too loudly to mask the nerves.

Rory looks up from his desk, and his face breaks open into that stretchy smile that used to look too large and now seems just right, like anything less would be a rip-off. "Hey!"

Something expands inside me, something I didn't even realize was contracted.

"I didn't know you wore glasses," I say, because that seems like a slightly better line than, "Shoot, I might actually be in love with you for real."

"Ah, forgot I had these on," Rory says, taking them off and wiping them carefully with the cleaning cloth before putting them in their case. "They're not prescription. Just got 'em real cheap because one of the boys in my class recently had to start wearing glasses, and he's feeling kinda self-conscious. Wanted to show him there's nothing weird about it."

My heart folds in some origami pattern, far more beautiful a shape than I could ever create on my own. And it's confirmed in one horrifying, glorious sweep.

It wasn't just that I was making everything up in my head. I wasn't idealizing him because he was out of sight and out of reach.

I love this man in front of me.

I love him, in fact, for all the things I was disappointed about when we first spoke. For how he's from my hometown and has that earthy Midwest twang. For the simple life he leads and how he doesn't care about the flashy, fancy things. For his grounding energy and stability, so much rarer and more valuable than constant spontaneity. For how he views love as a choice as much as a feeling and believes that it can get better even after the corporal chemistry fades. For the way I don't have to worry about being shiny and "on" around him.

I love Rory precisely because he isn't Alexander. If it *were* actually Alexander standing before me (presumably in a penthouse suite, not a school classroom), I know that whatever I'd feel—the rapture, the awe, the infatuation—would be so superficial, so ephemeral compared to this.

Unsettled by how settled this all makes me feel, I look away from Rory, down at my phone. Mindlessly, I check a few work emails to achieve a determinedly disinterested demeanor. No need for him to catch onto the untimely and inappropriate feelings churning within me.

I play out the scenario of what would happen if I just laid it all out there and told him how I felt. He'd be way too compassionate as he tells me he's engaged to Emily, or about to get engaged. And his reaction would only make me love him more, which would not help the whole getting-over-him-ASAP endeavor.

The silence stretching between Rory and me isn't awkward, but it has me wishing that it were because that would provide some welcome evidence that we're not really compatible after all.

"How've you been?" he asks.

I look back up at him. He's taken the glasses back out of the case and has resumed wiping them down. That's when I notice he looks a bit nervous, jaw pulsing in uneven increments, and the thin veins at his temples more prominent than usual. He looks tired too, with crescent-shaped bags under his eyes, which look more wideset than ever and have taken on a forlorn puppy-dog quality. "Sorry I haven't reached out," he says, repeating what he said via text. "Just been a lot going on . . ." He trails off, like he knows that was a very lame excuse.

"No worries," I say, eager to keep things normal. "I've been busy at work anyway," I tack on. It's nice to have the excuse to hide behind. Something that the world accepts as important and worthy of my full devotion.

Though I know that Rory doesn't see it that way and never has. Still, he tries to show interest. "How's it going leading the case?" he asks.

"Not too bad," I say with a shrug, because that's as good as work gets these days—not too bad. I could linger on the sad implications, but I'd rather not. So I tell Rory just the very shortest summary about how Harold apologized and we're moving on.

Rory asks a slew of follow-up questions about whether Harold is being held accountable, and seems less than pleased when I tell him that the apology is the extent of it.

"It's bullshit," Rory says. "Excuse my language, but he can't get away with it."

It's the first time I've ever heard him curse. He has a big-brotherly posture, which makes me feel protected but also confused because I want to kiss him.

"So you had a good time with your family over Christmas?" I ask, to divert from the topic of Harold. And also to unearth the latest with him and Emily. Rip the Band-Aid off.

"Yeah," he says, in a reluctant tone. "It was very . . . enlightening, I guess you'd say."

"How's Emily? Did you get engaged?" I blurt it out, trying to prepare my most believable happy-for-you-and-not-at-all-dying-on-the-inside expression.

But it turns out I don't need to wear that expression after all.

"No," Rory says, shuffling the folders on his desk. "We broke up. For good." He doesn't look at me when he says it, just focuses intently on organizing and reorganizing.

"What?" I expect to feel happy about this turn of events, and there's a small, ugly part of me that does, but the rest of me—the better part of me—is devastated for Rory and with Rory. It's the extra proof I didn't need to confirm that my love for him is the real thing.

CHAPTER THIRTY-TWO

"Why didn't you call me?" I ask Rory, feeling like the worst friend of all time. "I would've brought gelato over—every flavor of vanilla that exists—and we could've thrown darts at pictures of Emily's face."

I'm rambling on because I don't know what to say, and I'm scared to stop talking because I'll have to hear him explain the heartbreak, and I don't want him to have to explain it or have to feel it. I just want to heal it.

"No dart throwing," Rory says somberly. "I was the one who broke up with her."

Now my head is really spinning. I thought this was the woman he wanted to marry. And she'd told him she wanted to get back together. It's not adding up.

"Sorry I didn't tell you," he goes on. "I've just needed to process things alone." He has an anxious look about him, like he's been trying very hard to stick to a routine to provide some order since things have fallen out of place, but it hasn't exactly worked.

The ache in him becomes an ache in me, and I feel the true essence of empathy. Physically taking on someone else's emotion and holding it in your heart exactly as it is, without changing or reshaping it.

It's not as heavy a sensation I expected. There's a certain sweetness in the sadness. Even in pain, his heart is still so pure.

My first impulse is to go over and wrap him in a hug. To bury my head in his chest, and breathe in his wholesome, homey scent and tell him everything will be okay.

I refrain because I don't think he'd appreciate that, not in a school setting. So I just stow my hands in my coat pockets as he keeps tidying up his desk. He's onto the pens now, making sure all the caps are on as tightly as can be and that they're all stashed the same way in the wicker cup.

"How about you?" Rory asks, as if there's nothing more to talk about. As if I'm not bursting with a million follow-up questions. "Any rom-com princes swept you off your feet?"

I let out a gritty chortle at the irony of it. "Hardly," I say. "I don't think princes are my type."

"I thought they were every girl's type."

"Apparently not."

We don't say anything for a moment, just stare at each other. His golden eyes finally hold mine again, like they used to, with that cozy texture that makes me want to snuggle up on the couch and take a nap together.

A bell rings. It's a short, high-pitched thing that cuts the moment short and takes me back to my own school days—the feeling of coming in from playing soccer at recess, sweaty and grass stained and brimming with life. Little did I know Rory was doing the same thing the next school over (though probably without the grass stains).

"The kids will be going into lunch now," Rory says, standing up from his desk and smoothing the nonexistent wrinkles out of his button-down shirt. "Want to see Mala?"

So I follow him out of the classroom and down the hall. His loafers drag on the rubber tile floor rather than bouncing to their usual beat. Again, I feel like a terrible friend for not being there for him in his lows.

The circular cafeteria is stacked with long tables with bench seating. I always used to like lunch tables with benches versus the ones with individual seats, because it was easier to just slide onto the end of a bench and pretend like I belonged. Benches made it less obvious if there wasn't a seat for me.

Rory tracks down Mala, who's unpacking a pink lunchbox at the middle of a window table. I'm glad to see she has a few friends to sit with.

She leaps out of her seat when she sees me, and it makes me feel all filled up inside. "Miss Kat!" she exclaims. "Mummy packs the best sandwiches—look here," she says, when I sit down to join her at the table, and Rory heads to the teachers' lounge. "Even though she never gives me chocolate biscuits like I ask for. Chocolate biscuits are my very favorite thing in the world."

Opening up her Tupperware, she takes out a stack of chutney and cheese sandwiches, all cut out in different shapes—a star, a rainbow, a smiley face. My maternal instinct is triggered in an uplifting sort of way, and I feel it in my veins, that I do want to be a mom someday. The kind who packs my kids' lunches and cuts their sandwiches into festive shapes.

I think back to the time that Rory said he wanted Emily to be able to stay home and not have to work. It had felt insultingly anti-feminist of them both. But maybe the only way you can be anti-feminist is if you force a certain path upon a woman or judge her for not living how you think she should. And right now, the prospect of being a fully present mom makes me feel I'd be more successful than by being a famous CEO. It's just a fleeting thought that passes quickly, but the aftertaste lingers and is alarmingly palatable.

"You can have the heart-shaped one, Miss Kat," Mala says, doling out a sandwich. "Say, do you have a Valentine, Miss Kat?" she wants to know.

"No," I say, trying not to sound too glum about it, though I've seen all the red-and-pink-heart decor filling up the shops. I'd been hoping that Valentine's Day was just an American holiday, but no such luck. "Not this year."

"Me neither," Mala says. "Mummy and Daddy reckon I'm too young, but I quite disagree." She makes a sad little sigh that's far beyond her years, and it makes me wonder what she'll be like as a teenager. "Why don't you have one, Miss Kat? Aren't you in love? You're rather old not to be in love, wouldn't you say?"

"Um," I say, and it's impossible to get offended by the innocent way she's asking and the soft intonation of her accent. "It's complicated."

Mala's shoulders slump. "Grown-ups always say it's complicated," she laments. "It's like they think I won't understand. I'm seven and a *half* now, did you know?" She squirms importantly in her seat.

"It's not that I don't think you'll understand. It's just—" I pause, trying to find the right words. "I'm in love with someone who doesn't love me back. Does that make sense?"

"Indeed, it does," she says very solemnly. "I'm in the same situation, see." And then she proceeds to spill her heart out to me, says that she's in love with a boy in her class. His full name is Jeremiah Bartholomew, but that takes too long to say so everyone calls him JB. But he doesn't like Mala at all, he's always stealing her Percy Pig candies at snack time and tripping her on the playground.

"Sometimes boys tease the girls they like," I say.

"No, that doesn't make sense," Mala decides. "He just doesn't fancy me, that's all." She sighs heavily, then starts peppering me with questions. "Say, who are you in love with, Miss Kat? Is it someone from America?"

I nod.

"Reckon Mr. Cooper knows them?" She looks excited by the prospect.

"I think he might."

Then an idea lands on me in that stubborn sort of way that makes it clear it won't be rid of me until I see it through. I know it's completely ridiculous to let a seven-year-old be leading my love life. But I also know that I have to tell Rory how I feel now that he's not with Emily. And I want Mala to get the answers her young heart needs too.

"How about we make a deal?" I suggest to Mala. "I'll tell my person that I like him if you tell JB."

Mala scrunches up her face to consider the deal. "What happens if I don't do it?"

"Nothing at all," I assure her. "But if you *do* tell him, then no matter what he says, I'll bring you three sleeves of chocolate biscuits. How's that?"

Mala's eyes light up. "Really truly? You're not joshing?"

"Not joshing."

So we agree to it, and after lunch, I procrastinate heading back into the office, with a long walk around Clerkenwell, talking myself in circles about why it's probably better if I renege on my end of the deal. Why Rory and I still might not work out just because Emily's not in the picture. Our lives are still going in different directions, and although we have a foundation of friendship, that wouldn't necessarily translate to romance. And even if I do decide to say something, I should wait longer so I give him more time to move on from Emily.

But I know that if he were to get back together with Emily or start dating someone new, I wouldn't be able to forgive myself for not speaking up sooner.

So I find myself walking into the Boots down the street from the school, perusing the cards aisle just to take a look. I leave the store and return three times before I end up buying one—not a Valentine's Day theme or anything romantic, just a blank card with a floppy-eared hound dog on it.

And then, after more internal waffling, I sit on a bench in one of the grassy squares and start to write in the card. I don't pen sappy poetry or sentimental verses, just a few plain-sounding sentences saying I've realized I like Rory as more than a friend. The words that would be too difficult to say aloud are alarmingly easy to put down on paper, like they've been waiting for their chance to flow out.

Once it's done, I nearly drop it in each rubbish bin that I pass on the walk back to the school. But some force more powerful than my doubt keeps me holding onto it.

Too nervous to deliver the sealed-up envelope to Rory in person, I give it to the woman who works at the front office of his school and ask her if she could pass it onto Mr. Cooper. The woman assures me that she will, so I leave it in her hands and dart out the door, to be as far away as possible when Rory opens the card and learns the inconvenient truth.

CHAPTER THIRTY-THREE

I work from my flat for the rest of the afternoon, turning off my phone off and stashing it under my bed to keep from checking to see if there's any reply from Rory.

It's a childish game, I know, but the antics can't be helped. I'm in love and I've finally admitted that to myself and the other person, and I won't be held responsible for the way it's making me crazy.

Although the thing with loving Rory is that it actually makes me *less* crazy. Even as my mind and heart are agitated, my soul breathes with peace when I think about him. He centers me and cuts through all the noise and clutter to make way only for what's real and good and true.

But I can't let myself dwell on how wonderful he is. How all the other times I've been "in love" were just vacuous emotional highs, disparate sequences of Instagrammable moments that never had the strength or substance to hold up. No, I can't linger on any of that because at any moment I'll be getting a voicemail or text from Rory saying how much he values me as a friend.

Unless . . .

There's a little voice wondering if, just maybe, he might say something different. That he actually does have feelings for me, and that's why it didn't work out with Emily. The odds are slim, but knowing there's some kind of chance makes it impossible to focus on anything else. At six PM, I retrieve my phone and turn it back on.

When I finally get myself to look, a flurry of email notifications fill the screen, but no new texts or missed calls.

The implications of the silence sink in.

He's definitely read the card by now. The woman in the school office assured me that she'd deliver it right away. If Rory had good news to share, if the feelings were reciprocated, he'd have gotten back to me immediately. He would have called me and said, with endearing awkwardness, that he liked my card. He would've asked if we could get dinner or gelato. But as that hasn't materialized, he's clearly just trying to plan out how to let me down easily.

The weight of it all presses in on me, and I feel dreadfully delicate. Reckless too. I never should've made that childish deal with Mala, never should've written those words in ink that I can't take back.

I should've given him more time before springing the "L" word on him so abruptly. I should've considered that he's not someone who likes to be surprised and dropped some hints along the way to help him get accustomed to the idea of being with me.

Still, if he were really the right guy for me, telling him too soon or in the wrong way wouldn't be able to mess it up. He must just not be my person after all.

Pacing my flat, I go into a cleaning frenzy, putting the vacuum on full force to block out the inner dialogue that keeps reprimanding my boldness, then applauding it in the next moment, then cursing it once more.

Once the flat is sparkling clean (a very disorienting state), I draw a hot bath and stay in there for a long time, overloading the tub with salts and bubbles. In the background, I have on a relationship podcast called *Perks of Being Single*. The women cohosts are in their thirties, and I'm hoping they'll instill some gratitude or inspiration, but they just annoy me instead. All their self-proclaimed benefits of being single are man-bashing reasons like "The only way not to get cheated on is to not be in a relationship," and "Men don't remember anything we say anyway, so now we save ourselves the trouble of having to talk to a brick wall."

Turning off the podcast, I recline in the tub in silence with just the routine creaking of Marlow House to keep me company. I don't want to become jaded. There *are* good guys out there. Rory's one of them, even if he doesn't love me back.

When I finally get out of the tub, I pat myself dry and pull on my sweatpants pajamas. Instead of lying down on the couch and watching *Married at First Sight*, I attempt a more mature form of coping in the form of lighting soy candles and dabbing my wrists with lavender-scented essential oils. Spreading the tartan blanket on the clean floorboards, I sit in a cross-legged posture in the dark. Palms turned open on my kneecaps, I breathe in and out, attempting a meditative chant because this seems like the sort of thing that a well-balanced woman who has her life together would do.

Jaw clenched in a masculine posture that I've learned to associate with toughness, I repeat a mantra to myself about how I don't need anyone else.

Though I can't help but entertain the idea that maybe there's nothing inherently wrong in needing other people. Maybe codependence is actually an essential part of being human. And we just have to make sure that the people we depend on are the ones who are good for us.

There's a fiddling of a door handle, and Jules bursts through the connector between our flats. "Can I borrow your Hoover, babes?" she says. "My earrings got sucked up in ours and broke it, and Nina's been on about tidying up." Flicking the lights on, Jules finds me in my (previously) peaceful trance. "Bloody 'ell," she says. "You're alright? 'Aving a seizer or summit?"

"I'm cultivating inner calmness and tranquility," I tell her solemnly, reciting the verbiage from the essential oils label.

"What's all this faff about?" she asks, looking around at the candles and oils, as if she's walked in on some kind of blood-drinking cult.

I don't want to tell Jules about the letter I wrote to Rory, but I do. The story leaks from me, and once it's out, I'm glad I've unburdened myself. There are few surer ways of lightening your own load than by sharing it with another woman. Especially a woman like Jules, who's guaranteed to side with me no matter what. Blake would too, but I haven't filled her in yet. It would require too much backstory, and I'm not in the mood to have to explain.

"It was deffo the right thing to do, babes," Jules declares confidently. She's plopped down on the floor to sit next to me, back slouched against the sofa. "And it's only been a few hours. Rory's probably at the florist, loading up on roses so he can come stand outside Marlow House and toss stones at your window until you come out."

"Zero chance," I protest. "This is *Rory* we're talking about."

"Wouldn't put it past 'im. The bloke knows you like that rubbish."

But I don't need or even want flowers or serenades or any grand gestures. Just the chime of a text or a buzz of the doorbell would do. But there's nothing, only the static of my imagination as it formulates potential explanations, each one more dire than the prior, plus the rise and fall of Jules's cockney accent as she tries to comfort me.

"Stop checking your dog and bone," Jules says, plucking my phone out of my hand. "At least now you'll get your clarity. Even if it does turn out that Rory's a proper arse."

"He's not an arse," I defend. "He's just sensible enough not to get involved with a maniac like me."

"You're not a maniac," Jules says. "An overachiever, maybe, but it's all from the right place, innit?"

"Is it?" I question, turning inward to examine the root of my motives for my insatiable need to be the best.

"Dunno," Jules admits candidly. "Just said that ter make you feel better." She hands me a whiskey flask that she seems to have conjured from thin air. "This'll help you forget all your barney rubble—*trouble*."

"I'm not drinking tonight," I decline. "I'm keeping my vessel clear." I saw that phrase on a wellness Instagram account, and it seems to fit the occasion.

"Sounds like a load of shite to me," Jules says, crinkling her pierced nose in disapproval. "But 'ave it your way."

So she takes a second gulp of whiskey on my behalf and stays there a little while longer, listening to me hash and rehash how I shouldn't have written that note, how it was a completely imprudent and irrational thing to do.

Jules takes the vacuum back to her flat, determined to clean before Nina gets home. I check my phone again. Still no word from Rory.

For the first time, I consider the possibility that he might never reply. He might ignore the message in the card to avoid the confrontation of an uncomfortable conversation. He might just ghost me, like the players I was sure he was so different from.

My judgment might be off with him, like it's been off with so many people from my past, as I blindly saw their best and blocked out their worst.

Blowing out the candle, I smear more essential oils on my neck and turn on some mindless show to try to drown out the refrain that's coursing through my brain. The refrain is something about how it couldn't actually have been true love with Rory because true love is reciprocated, and this clearly wasn't. I was just latching onto another counterfeit connection, fanning the flames of my fantasy until the fire burned my face and reminded me that I'm still farther than ever from my happily-ever-after-ride-off-together-into-the-sunset-as-the-credits-start-rolling moment.

* * *

By midday Saturday, I've accepted that I'm never going to hear from Rory again.

Or at least I've told myself that I need to accept it, which is the first step . . . well, perhaps the second; the first was eating an entire pint of gelato for the therapeutic value and also because I'm determined to reclaim gelato as something that's just *mine*, not mine and Rory's.

Anger starts to push out the humiliation and hurt, and I'm glad for this. It's much more enjoyable to be angry than sad. Anger gives you permission to sling blame this way and that, all while vindicating yourself and assuming the role of the irreproachable, underappreciated heroine.

I'm whizzing through the stages of grief. Within no time, I'll be back to normal. Though the thought doesn't exactly cheer me up. *Normal* is a state before Rory. *Normal* is that vacant way of life where I elevate everything unimportant and de-prioritize the highest-value parts. *Normal* is backward.

Thoughts like these are entirely unhelpful, so I preoccupy myself with a long walk along Upper Street, all the way up to Highbury Fields, the largest park within walking distance. The dewy green acres are far off the tourist track, more serene than the always bustling Hyde Park, though it's still too cluttered for my liking. Children hustle in youth soccer scrimmages, hovering parents coaching from the sidelines as off-leash dogs yap at seagulls and sparrows. The damp dirt paths that zigzag through the park are filled with an inordinate amount of hand-holding couples, and it feels highly insensitive for them to be parading their partnership so conspicuously.

I try to curl up into a hostile shell and repeat some feminist quote about how I don't need a man. How I'm alone but not lonely, thank you very much. I try to scorn all the suckers who latch onto each other just because they're too lazy to do the work and stand up on their own two feet.

But I can't do that. The next couple I pass—arms looped together as they balance coffee thermoses and croissants, quietly giggling at some private joke I doubt anyone else would find funny—is too adorable for me to slash with my serrated cynicism. It's not the in-your-face PDA sort of happiness. It's the subtle kind of bliss that's exceptional precisely because of how ordinary it is.

And in that moment, as the squally English wind scuffs against my face, I stop regretting how I put myself out there with Rory and start respecting it, even if it led me here, to a pain that's tender even in its sharpness.

And though my mind keeps spiraling and my chest keeps clenching, there's a certain stillness at my core. Not a lifeless stillness but a serene one. The type of stillness that comes when you know that you've done what you're supposed to do, and regardless of the outcome, you wouldn't take it back.

Because it was born from loving someone good, and when you lose someone good, your heart can be bruised and bent and dented, but it can never quite shatter because that person brought out the best in you, and the best is still there even when they're not.

Love doesn't change you or make you better. It just reveals the goodness that's already there.

In my pocket, my phone vibrates. I know it's him before I even see the four-letter name on my screen.

There's an initial lurch of hope, quickly superseded by fear. I'm terrified of picking up, but I don't want it to go to voicemail either, in case he leaves a message and the rejection is recorded.

You can do this, I tell myself, akin to the pep talk I gave myself before I boarded that double-decker bus for the first time. *You can pick up a bloody phone.*

"Hello?" I eke out. My voice is thin and pinched, highly unattractive to my own ears.

"Kat?" Rory says, pronouncing my name with that earthy arc that makes me feel protected before I can remind my body that it's not supposed to respond like that, that this person isn't my safe place anymore. Never really was.

"Yep," I say blandly, hoping that a blasé voice will correlate with a blasé heart. "It's me."

"How's it going?" Rory asks.

The question feels cruel and callous with its nonchalance. Maybe the small talk is just a nervous tic, and I should give him some grace, but it's tough to come by at the moment.

"I'm okay," I say, keeping my answers short and generic so I don't give him any more of myself than I already have. "How about you?" Immediately, I regret asking because I don't really want to know.

There's a pause, so long that I have to check to make sure the call didn't drop. "I got your note," Rory finally says.

"Oh," I manage. "Right." Unable to bear the silence and all of its suggestions, I prattle on. "You don't need to say anything. We don't have to talk about it. It's fine, really. No hard feelings."

I chide myself as the words fall out. Why do women always lie like that? Are we so accustomed to trying to please other people that we'll say whatever they want to hear? Or do we actually lie for ourselves, so we don't have to confront the consequences of the truth?

Rory's voice preempts me from mulling over the question any more. "Would you have time to meet up for coffee tomorrow?" he asks.

My stomach scrunches like it's been stepped on. Nothing says "friend zone" more than a coffee catch-up. It's the same thing Rory suggested the very first time we hung out. Here we are, coming full circle, without much of a story in the middle. His feelings toward me haven't changed this whole time. Only mine have, and I'll just have to figure out how to change them back. Or release them altogether.

"Sure," I hear myself say, because I aspire to be the type of emotionally mature woman who can have difficult conversations in person, not the kind who childishly hangs up the phone on her friend/could've-been-lover and promptly blocks his number forevermore, like I desperately want to do. "I could do coffee."

"Sounds good," Rory says. His tone sounds stiff and formal, and I'm already missing the way he used to say "cool beans," though I used to find it goofy and uncouth.

"I'll come by Gail's?" he suggests. "Does eleven work?"

"Sure," I say. "See you tomorrow." The phrase feels sacred, like I may never be able to say it to him again. Because there's no way I want to do the dreaded "just friends" thing, if that's what he suggests.

I want all or nothing. And if he wanted to give me his all, he would've told me by now. He would've at least hinted that he was glad to read the card. But there's been no kind of positive affirmation at all, which makes his answer obvious.

The only thing I can do is show up with dignity and poise tomorrow and hear him out as he lists out all the reasons he thinks I'm so great but just doesn't see me like *that*.

CHAPTER THIRTY-FOUR

"Dignity and poise" is more than a little bit difficult to find the next morning.

I can't help but compare the day to the first morning that I met up for coffee with Rory. How I woke up so hungover, feeling slimy and soiled and irredeemable after what had happened with Harold the night before. How I threw on the first clothes I could find and schlepped across the street to Gail's out of a sense of duty.

Today I rise sober and alert, my body feeling clean even as my stomach writhes and ties itself in knots. I take a long time getting ready, putting in far more effort than I ever have with Rory (except when I thought he was Alexander). The trick is making it seem like I haven't gone to special lengths at all, like I've just rolled out of bed like this, with beachy waves and dewy skin and a cobalt blue jumper dress that hits me in all the right spots and cleverly hides the wrong ones.

Rory is no longer someone I can let see my unfiltered self. And I'm not above a little spite either. I want to look extra good so he'll have to see what he'll be missing out on. So he'll have fresh images to haunt him, rather than the last memories he has of me, sitting beside him in those cramped airplane seats, shoveling Biscoff cookies into my mouth as new zits popped out of my chin while my face simultaneously flaked with dryness because apparently it's somehow possible to have parched skin and oily skin at the exact same time, even in your thirties.

Ten minutes before we've planned to meet, Rory texts me that he's just gotten to Gail's and is holding our spot in line. Peeking out my curtains, I see him there, at the back of the queue, which is winding all the way back to the St. Mary's bus stop.

He's wearing a different coat than usual—a forest-green down puffer that only reaches his waist and adds some bulk to his body. He's not wearing his scarf either, and it makes me feel like something's missing, like a stranger is standing there, rather than my friend.

Leaving Marlow House, I cross Upper Street, avoiding looking at Rory until I'm standing right in front of him.

"Hey," he says quietly. His face is somber, with none of its typical levity. He's looking at me intently, like he's trying to apologize for not loving me, which is potentially the worst expression in the world to be on the receiving end of.

"New coat?" I ask, peeling my gaze away.

"Yeah," Rory says. "My grandma got it for me for Christmas. Even she said that it was time for me to replace my old one, which is saying something, what with how frugal she is."

"I liked the old one," I mumble, more to myself than to Rory.

The music from Gail's blares out into the street, far too loud, and it's clear that the place is packed to the brim. My stress levels rise before we even step inside, and the prospect of a private conversation feels impossible.

Rory seems to be thinking along the same lines. "Want to check out another spot?" he suggests. "Kinda loud in there."

So we keep walking down Upper Street, not talking much. "I like Islington," Rory comments, swiveling his head this way and that, perhaps to avoid having to look at me. "It's kind of like Traverse City, except way bigger."

"Mmm," is all I say back. I don't want to think about how this neighborhood reminds him of a Northern Michigan beach town. I just want to get this over with. But Rory doesn't seem like he's ever going to broach the real reason we're here.

When we've walked all the way to the southern juncture of Angel, at the four-way cross leading down to Clerkenwell, an open-topped double-decker bus hums past us. It's one of those hop-on, hop-off buses for tourists.

"I've still never been on one of those," Rory says, looking up at the bus as he continues to fumble around for small talk to avoid the big talk. "Should we get on?"

I wouldn't have picked a double-decker bus to be the spot where this all ended. Though perhaps it's a fitting lesson for me, given how a bus was how this all began.

"Sure," I say, in no mood to keep walking or trying to fight for space in overcapacity cafés. "Let's do it."

So we chase the bus to the next stop and get on, heading up the stairs to the open-air top deck, which is mostly empty. For maximum privacy, I take a seat toward the back. Rory sits down right next to me.

The bus lurches into motion, wind snagging my hair and undoing all the effort I put in to look put-together. On a different day, this bus ride might be a London bucket list adventure that makes me squeal with childish glee. But today, it's defiled by the distress of the occasion. Even the clouds seem to be darkening all of a sudden, like they're preparing for the worst.

"It's nice up here," Rory says, and he's still looking all around—forward, backward, out the sides at the balconies and fire escapes and Victorian townhomes we pass by. Anywhere but at me.

My patience is peeling off, exposing the coarse temper underneath. Rory doesn't even have the spine to start the conversation. This is the behavior of a boy, not a man, and I'm too old for these games.

I'll just have to be the more mature person and start it off. "So," I say, not bothering to pad my voice. "You wanted to talk?"

Rory looks down at his lap, fiddling with his hands, head drooping a bit. He glances over at me, then back down at his lap, and I wait for him to launch into the slick speech he's no doubt prepared about why we're not meant to be.

"Did you mean it?" he asks, voice scraping out like it's stuck on something. "What you said in the note? It wasn't a prank or a dare or something?"

He seems genuinely uncertain, and it punches my gut, the notion that he'd think I'd try to dupe him like that.

But here it is, an opportunity to preserve my pride. To tell him that I didn't actually mean it. That it was a dare or a lonely whim getting the worst of me. I could get out of this mess right here, right now.

I can't do it, though. I can't lie to Rory, especially a lie I know would hurt him. "I meant it," I say, voice thick with unwanted truth. "Every word."

Rory lifts his head and looks at me—really looks at me—for the first time all day, and I accidentally taste the sweetness of his honey-colored eyes. "Really?" he asks, and he starts blinking quickly, almost like he's fighting back tears at the fact that he can't reciprocate my feelings.

I'm in no mood to comfort Rory, not when I'd planned to be cold to him, but I can't help myself. "I don't want you to feel bad that you don't love me," I mumble, as the bus rattles along, south-bound toward the Thames. "It's not your fault."

In the midst of the intersecting emotions, my heart bends even more because I can't imagine ever having this level of selfless compassion for anyone else. I can't picture ever looking at another man and knowing that I'll always, always, always go out of my way to put him first. Not in a toxic sort of way that makes me lose or abandon myself, but in a redemptive way that helps me find myself and elevate my wants and needs to something higher than they were before.

CHAPTER THIRTY-FIVE

"That's what you think?" Rory asks, forehead pinching into a frown. "That I don't love you?"

"I mean, yeah," I say, feeling a dangerous lurch of hope at how surprised he seems by this. "If you felt the same, you wouldn't be acting all weird and avoidant."

Rory lets out a helpless sort of laugh. "Of course I would be," he says. "You know I'm not good with emotions." He gives a self-deprecating smile, the dimple in his cleft chin deepening. It makes me want to smile too because I think this might be a positive sign, but I'm still unsure and need to hear him say it.

"Okay, here's my side of things," he says, sneakers tapping the floor as his knees jitter. "You know that day we met on the bus?"

I nod. How could I forget it? Not to be dramatic, but it was one of the most disappointing days of my life.

"Well, I had a crush on you right then," Rory says, eyes shifting my way again. "It wasn't just that you were really attractive, though obviously that's true." It's the gushiest thing I've ever heard him say, but he drops it like it's no big deal, like it's something I must've assumed. "I just—I felt like we knew each other already," he goes on. "I actually thought our first coffee at Gail's was a date."

"What?" I ask, thoroughly confused now. There was nothing romantic about that day in the least.

But replaying the scene in my head, I note how he showed up early, a bit overdressed. How he took an interest in getting to know me and tried way too hard to hold the umbrella over us. How he comforted me when I told him about what happened with Harold.

Maybe that *was* romance and *is* romance. The real, stripped-down thing that I was too dense to recognize at the time. Repentance gnaws at me. I wish I could go back and do that day differently. Appreciate him right from the start.

"I actually told Emily about it before I asked you out," Rory says, talking to his twisting hands again. "I know I didn't need to ask for her permission, but it felt right since we were still talking. So yeah, that was a big deal for me. But I could tell pretty quick you were friend-zoning me. And that was fine. You'd just been through that whole thing with Harold, and I just wanted to get to know you."

The space between where I'd expected this to go and where it's actually going continues to widen, in the best way possible.

"So I was telling myself that I was okay being friends," Rory goes on. "That I was still hoping it would work out with Emily because that made more sense. I could picture a life with her fifty years into the future. With you . . . I didn't know where you'd be moving next. Everything felt up in the air.

"And over Christmas, Emily said that she wanted to get back together," Rory continues. "Said she did see herself marrying me after all. And I don't know . . . I kept thinking about you during the whole thing. Thinking about how you'd probably never love me or want to do life together."

My stomach dips down at that, then swoops back up at his next words.

"But I realized that I *wanted* you to love me, and I *wanted* it to work with you and me, and there was no way I could commit to someone else. So I ended things with Emily and just sat on it for a while. I needed to make sure I was thinking clearly, not just feeling clearly. That's why I haven't reached out."

A chilling sensation is spreading over me, but instead of making me cold, it's making me warm.

"And then when I got your letter on Friday," he says, "it seemed too good to be true. I genuinely thought it might've been a joke or something."

"It wasn't a joke," I tell him again. "I'd never joke about that."

"I know that now. And I know we'd have a lot of life stuff to figure out. I don't want to hold you back in your career or make you move back to Michigan if you don't want to. And you know I'm the kind of person who likes clear plans. But what I know is that I'd rather be with you and have some uncertainty than have the certainty of a life without you."

The words run through me like a stream through a dessert. I'm praying they're not a mirage.

"I'm not a words person, as you know," Rory carries on in a diligent tone, like he's determined to express himself the best he can. "It's hard for me to say what I'm feeling, but it's not hard for me to feel what I'm feeling. And what I feel is that I love you, and I want to be with you. If the stuff you wrote is still true."

I wait for a moment before saying anything, just to make sure that I'm not about to wake up from a dream. When the reality wriggles its way into my skeptical soul, I let myself reply. "Of course it's true. I bloody love you, Rory," I say with an English lilt.

He looks joyful, which means he *is* joyful because he doesn't have the ability to disguise his emotions. "Smashing news, I reckon!" he says in a completely butchered accent of his own, and we double over with laughter, like we're just the funniest, luckiest people on the planet.

It's not polished and perfect like the movies, and there's so much more depth and texture to it this way, two people awkwardly jumping from friends to lovers, each trusting the other to help ease the transition.

"Lookit," Rory says, gesturing to our surroundings, which we both seem to have forgotten. "We're on Tower Bridge. Didn't you say once that this was your favorite place in London?"

I look out in front of us. Sure enough, the bus is starting across the iconic bridge. It's ridiculously picturesque, the robin's-egg-blue suspension rods swooping regally from the turreted towers, the Thames glistening beneath it as the rain lands lightly and radiates out in a million concentric circles. Rory's right—this has always been my favorite landmark in the city. But I don't have any impulse to stare at the landscape or snap a picture. The view is only beautiful because I'm sharing it with someone beautiful.

"I changed my mind," I tell Rory. "My favorite place isn't a landmark anymore. It's a person."

"You stole that line from one of your movies, didn't you?" Rory asks with good-natured skepticism.

"It's a Kat original," I assure him.

"Alright, I've got a line for you," Rory says. "You know I love dogs, but guess it turns out I'm a Kat person after all."

The corners of my mouth twitch. "Good one."

"A solid supply of dad jokes is one of the duties I take very seriously as your boyfriend," Rory says happily.

Boyfriend. The word lands happily on my ears, with the promise of all to come.

It starts raining, some mixture of mist and droplets.

"The sky is too chuffed to keep in its tears," I declare, catching the rain on my outstretched palms. "Do you want to go down below?" I ask Rory, since I know he doesn't like getting his clothes out of sorts.

"Nah, it's okay," he says, checking his new jacket to make sure it's holding up. "It's just water—it won't ruin anything."

And how true that is. Water doesn't ruin anything. It rejuvenates everything.

All along, I've equated fire with desire. I've built love up to be the flames, the burning, the ashes. I've idolized destruction in the name of passion. Gravitated toward the color red because I thought it was romance. But the truth is that love is the clear, blue water, washing over me after a long, long drought.

I don't need to tell this to Rory. Words alone wouldn't mean much to him. I just need my actions to show him that I understand. That I can finally see him and me and us without my blinders on.

We look at each other, and it's the most magical eye contact of my entire life. Not because of the whimsy fantasy of what it might be, but because of the sturdy fact of what it *is*. Of how he's seeing straight through all my walls and veneers, into all the parts of me I thought I'd never want to share with anyone. The flaws and fears, the mistakes and regrets, the splotches of sin and selfishness and greed. And the good stuff too. The caring core, the resilient hope within me that good will triumph over evil, the resurrected belief in happy endings and the sureness in my soul that I want to be with him in this moment and all the ones to come.

Rory sees everything exactly as it is. Exactly as *I* am. And instead of it making him retreat or rethink, it just makes him come closer. "Can I . . . kiss you?" he asks with the innocence of a teenager and the intentionality of an adult.

"You can do, kind sir," I say, faux accent returning with youthful merriment.

Smiling at ourselves and the situation and how we're both a bit unsure what to do, we lean into each other, hesitating to make sure we're lined up right.

Our lips touch. We try it out tenderly, giving each other the grace to acknowledge that it's not the world's sexiest kiss, and that's absolutely okay.

It lifts the pressure from the first moment, the first kiss, needing to be some flawless thing. There's such liberation in that, such a joy that comes from knowing that all the best times are still ahead. That a first kiss can really just be a first kiss. The starting point for all to come.

The kiss doesn't make my breath skip a beat. It steadies my heartbeat instead, making me feel stronger than ever before.

The kiss doesn't steal my breath away either, like I used to dream of how it would be when I met my true love. And thank God it doesn't. Because this first kiss with Rory, it feels like giving my breath back. Like after everything I've been through so far, and before everything we'll go through together, I can truly breathe in peace.

CHAPTER THIRTY-SIX

Curled up on the Marlow House couch the next week, the traffic from Upper Street has mellowed to its late-night purr, and the bass from Jules and Nina's sound system seeps through the walls as they're watching some show that makes Jules shriek dramatically every few minutes.

Sitting up straight on the couch, Rory is going over his lesson plans, and I'm sprawled across the cushions, my head resting on his lap as I'm curled up under the blanket. I'm reading a bestselling business book titled *The Affliction of Emotion: Why Women Shouldn't Use Exclamation Points in Work Emails*.

Each page is making me increasingly agitated. I don't use exclamation points at work—I had the habit squashed out of me by my very first boss—but I'm increasingly wanting to revive them and break the bounds of the little corporate box I've been conditioned to stay in because that's how you rise up.

From the coffee table in front of us, Rory's phone screen lights up with a reminder. *Tell Kat she's beautiful.*

Raising my eyebrows, I pass the phone to Rory. "You have a reminder to tell me I'm beautiful?" I ask. Accuse, more like it, because what my tone says is, *You can't just remember that yourself?*

It strikes me as a highly robotic expression of affection, lacking spontaneity and sincerity. I start pouting, giving Rory the cold shoulder as I sit up and slink to the other side of the couch.

Setting his school folders aside, Rory adjusts the blanket to make sure that my toes are covered. "I'm always thinking it," he says. "I want to remind myself to express it. That's all."

I steal a glance at him, only it doesn't feel like stealing. It feels like returning. And something about his good-to-the-core aura makes it impossible to begrudge him.

Feeling sheepish, I close the anti–exclamation point book and curl up next to Rory. "There should be a movie about this kind of love," I say with the lisp that comes from my retainers. "The little things. The real things."

"Would people watch that kind of movie?" he poses.

"I would." Though if I'm being honest, the old me wouldn't have watched it. Or she would've started watching it, then turned it off after twenty minutes because it wasn't sensational enough. *"Too boring,"* she would've thought.

But I'm starting to realize that this kind of stable love is far more interesting than anything I've experienced before. The space that's available in a drama-free relationship leaves so much room for exploration. For really getting to know the intricacies of each other's hearts and hopes and habits. It goes so much deeper than all the surface-level sparks.

And it's not like the spark *isn't* there. It's like the depth of my attraction overflows from all sides, making me want Rory more than I've ever wanted anyone. It's just that the spark is the frosting on top. The deeper connection will be there either way.

"I like your little phone reminder," I assure him, letting my grudge loose. "It's kind of sexy, actually."

"It's not sexy," he says, wrapping me up into his arms. "It's just me."

"They're one and the same," I insist, dropping a kiss on his smooth cheek, then his lips. He has no idea how good-looking he is—or how incredible he is in general—which makes me want to treasure him that much more.

When I'm snuggled up beside Rory, it doesn't feel like there's any gap between us. With other people I've dated, no matter how close we physically were, I'd still feel far away. All of that empty space—it's gone now.

"How's your back?" Rory asks me now.

My lower back has been aching from some combination of period cramps, sitting at a computer for too many hours, and approaching my thirty-second birthday. "It's alright," I say, though it's not feeling great at the moment.

"Turn over," Rory says, seeing through the lie. "I'll give you a back rub."

"No, you have to get to sleep. You have a big day tomorrow."

Rory makes a face. "I wouldn't call the primary school science fair a monumental occasion."

"Of course it is," I counter. "It's a big deal." He's shown me the demos and dioramas that he's helped the students make, including a balloon-powered toy car for Mala.

"I'm not going to bed until you accept my back rub," Rory says resolutely, so I gratefully accept the massage.

Rory isn't the best at giving back rubs, to be honest. Scared to hurt me, he doesn't knead forcefully enough to get the knots out. But his gentle touch heals something deeper in me than my muscles.

"Alright," I say with a yawn, pretending to be tired so he can get some sleep. "Time for you to get home."

I want him to stay, of course, but I know he'll feel better if he keeps with his routine of being at his own place tonight, and I like the trust that comes from taking things slowly. After he checks my flat a few times to make sure he hasn't left anything, he heads out, kissing me goodbye on my lipstick-free mouth, and then my shoulder, through my old T-shirt.

It's a light little peck, but I feel it with force. Because the real power of love comes from its gentleness. The small, quiet moments when it doesn't think anyone is watching.

Warmth radiates from the spot where his lips touched, and my body relaxes in that way it only does around Rory. Locking the door behind him and watching at the window until he gets on the bus, I can start to feel just how clenched and cold I've been for so many years.

I didn't even know I was frozen until I started to thaw.

* * *

In the midst of the bliss, there's something weighing on me, attempting to sabotage the happiness. It has to do with the future and logistics of how Rory and I will maintain our relationship after my case and his school year wraps up and we might not be living in the same place.

I try to stash the fears away, but I end up voicing them to Rory the next day, when we're seated next to each other on the morning bus. Though it's not my most efficient commute, I've boarded at St. Mary's so I can spend some time with him before work.

"What's wrong?" he asks, looking intently at me as the stormy thoughts brew. "Don't like this seat?"

He said I could pick somewhere new for us to sit, since he knows I like variety, and we're seated up in the front. It's the best view from the bus, with the windowpanes facing out on the foggy London morning as the bus jostles along. Everything has a silhouette quality about it, and I can almost feel the cloudy vapor seeping inside the bus, clinging to my fears.

"It's not that," I say, slouching in my seat. "It's just . . . I'm trying to figure things out."

"Figure what out?"

"Everything." I sulk. "You're moving back to Michigan in June, right?"

With our relationship so new, we've been too swept up, or maybe just too scared, to tip the balance by broaching the subject of the future. But as Jules and Nina prepare to tie the knot, I want to be reassured that Rory and I have a viable future too.

"That's been the plan," Rory says. "To keep teaching in Kalamazoo next year. But if you're staffed on another London case, I could see if I could stay over here a bit longer."

"But you want to go back." It's a statement, not a question, and he doesn't dispute it.

"Ideally, yeah," he admits, "but we could do long distance." He rests one of his hands on top of mine, which are clenched together in my lap.

"I don't want to do long distance," I say, more curtly than I mean to. Maybe I'm tainted from how things ended with Mateo, but I feel like relationships are either moving forward or backward, and long distance sends them in reverse.

"How about this?" I ask, feeling desperate to figure this out right now. Like if we don't resolve it immediately, we never will. "I could get staffed on remote cases and work from Michigan."

"But you don't like Michigan," Rory points out.

"I didn't *used* to like it," I clarify. "But I do now. Things change."

It's true that the idea of living in Michigan has been starting to appeal rather than appall, especially when I picture being there with Rory. I'm increasingly ready to go home. Ready for that quieter life near my family, on the country roads that are never congested with traffic. The vision that's been popping up since Christmas takes a more defined shape now, and I feel myself grasping for it.

Rory looks like he wants to believe me but doesn't quite. "Didn't you say that remote cases aren't as good for your career trajectory, though, because you don't get the same kind of visibility?"

"I mean, sure," I say, feeling the burden of the words. "But my job isn't the most important thing in the world."

It's strange hearing that sentence aloud. But it also feels true and good, like it's something that I've been wanting to say for a while now.

I've always thought it would be crazy to prioritize a relationship over a job. But the truth is that my relationship with Rory fills me up so much more than work does.

I've been holding on to the idea that once I'm in a leadership role, once I'm partner, and then once I'm CEO, the dynamic will change, and work will be something wonderful that completes me rather than depletes me. But I'm less sure than ever that that day will ever arrive. I might keep straining and sacrificing myself for something that will never love me back.

Maybe my chat with Blake earlier today has rubbed off on me. Loving her improved work–life balance, she's even contemplating quitting her job altogether. It didn't seem as crazy a prospect as it once had. The usual edge of stress in her voice was gone, and she sounded happier than I'd ever heard her. Though perhaps some of that was from her smugness about Rory and I being together, as she insisted she called it all along, since I first told her I was having a guy over for Thanksgiving.

"Would you resent me," Rory poses, "if you moved back and didn't make partner this year?"

"No, I wouldn't resent you," I say, and I know it's true, though I might resent myself for not sticking it out, especially since I'm so close to the promotion. "I could also just look for a new job," I suggest. "There are a couple Fortune 500 companies in West Michigan. It's not like it's *entirely* cornfields. I could be a big fish in a little pond."

I expected to be scrounging up excitement for Rory's sake, but I'm surprised and satisfied to find that the positivity is my own. But part of me remains conflicted, wondering if it would feel too much like I was quitting on my career ambitions to actually be able to enjoy living there.

"Let's keep thinking about it," Rory says, never one for rushing decisions. "It'll all work out."

The suave British-accented intercom on the bus announces that Percival Street will be next. It's Rory's stop, and he hoists up his backpack, checking all around to make sure he hasn't left anything behind.

"Yeah," I agree, though I'm agitated that we haven't solved it. "It'll all work out."

CHAPTER THIRTY-SEVEN

We have our first big outing as a couple that weekend. Jules and Nina have spontaneously moved up their wedding to capitalize on a cancellation at the venue, which apparently resulted in a massive discount if they took it. Jules isn't worried if people can't make the new date, she's confessed, as long as they still send gifts. "But that doesn't count you, Kat," she'd clarified. "You'd better be there for bridesmaid duties, which just means standing up there to catch Nina if she faints at the sight of me, and giving a bloody good laugh during my vows. I've gone for comedy over quality."

The wedding is in a quaint Cotswolds village a couple hours outside London. Rory and I aren't fond of the idea of renting a car and driving on the other side of the road through precariously narrow country lanes, so we take a train, then transfer to a bus. It's a scenic ride, winding through one postcard-perfect town after another, each high street packed with idyllic teahouses, Tudor-style taverns, and chippies selling fish and chips with mushy peas to eager tourists. Beyond the villages, public footpaths traverse the grassy farmland, dappled with sheep and cows. It reminds me of Michigan in a soothing sort of way.

But as the bus crawls along at a snail's pace, I start getting stressed that we're going to be late to the ceremony. It wouldn't be a good look, especially for my first time being a bridesmaid.

"It'll be okay," Rory says, much more at ease on buses than planes. "Worst thing that happens is we break down and call an Uber."

"They don't have Uber out here," I say, scowling. "I've already checked."

"Then we'll walk," Rory says. "It'll be an adventure."

"Jules and Nina's wedding is supposed to be the adventure," I retort. "Not showing up late and muddy like Lizzie Bennet after hiking to Netherfield through the moor in the rainstorm."

"Lizzie who?" Rory asks.

"Bennet," I reply pointedly. "From *Pride and Prejudice*."

I never thought I'd be with someone who didn't understand my *Pride and Prejudice* references. It sends me pouting for a few minutes, until Rory nearly breaks his back opening the jammed-shut window of the bus to get me some fresh air.

"You okay?" he asks, fanning me with the paper menu from the teahouse, which he asked the waiter if we could keep because he knows I like to hold onto sentimental souvenirs. "I can ask the driver for a trash bag if you're going to be sick."

It breaks through my bad mood. Rory is no Mr. Darcy, but he's my perfect guy.

When the bus finally huffs up to a stop at Bourton on the Water, a sleepy, thatched-roof town split by a narrow river and flanked by lush parks, we head straight to our hotel. Named the Mousetrap Inn, it's a cobbled stone house at the far end of the high street, with a classic English country pub downstairs. It's only midafternoon, but the barrel-keg bar—which doubles as the front desk—is already rowdy.

The ruddy-faced bartender shows us up to our room on the first floor. "Nice and cozy, innit?" he says with a droll chuckle. "'Fraid the hot water isn't working at the mo', but do give a shout if there's anything we can do." With that, he ambles back down to the bar.

"Sorry it's so small," I say to Rory, looking around at the tiny space with a sunken double bed, linen-sized closet, and scrunched bathroom. "It didn't look like this online."

"What do you mean?" Rory counters. "This is great." His optimism has no edge of irony, and it makes me smile as I unpack my toiletries on the bathroom windowsill since there's no counter space.

Hurriedly, I do my hair and makeup and slide into my bridesmaid dress, a yellow chiffon gown that Nina picked out. It's meant to be tea length but reaches the floor on me. I pair it with a navy shawl and close-toed shoes to adapt the summer colors to the late February weather.

When I emerge, Rory doesn't whistle when he sees me, and his jaw doesn't drop to the floor. But he stops matting down his cowlick with his comb and stares. "You look great," he says. "Beautiful, I mean."

I feel him trying hard to use the words I want him to use. To be the person I want him to be. It hurts, him thinking I might judge him—and the strength of our relationship—based on which adjective he chooses.

"I mean, you always look beautiful," Rory clarifies. "No matter what you're wearing."

"You're allowed to think I look better dressed up with makeup on than in my retainer and zit cream," I tease, though I'm drinking in the compliment like a glass of lemonade.

"But I don't think that," he protests. "I think you're equally beautiful all the time." We both seem a bit taken aback at how many times he's used the word *beautiful* in the past minute.

"You look rather smart yourself," I say, taking in his sleek suit ensemble. It's an old suit but impeccably ironed, and it makes me glad I'm not with someone who has money to splurge on whatever he wants. Rory takes care of his things, and I like the metaphor as it applies to love—investing in what you already have and making it last a while, versus casting it aside to buy some new, flashier version.

He did buy a new tie for the occasion, though, and spent an hour at a formal wear shop, comparing all the different shades of yellow to ensure he chose the one that most precisely matched my dress.

I want to kiss him, but I resist because I know he doesn't like getting lipstick on him, so I just give his hand a squeeze. It makes me smile to myself that the best way I can express my love for him right now is not to kiss him.

Heading out of the inn, we make our way over toward the village hall where the ceremony is taking place, just on the other side of the river. It's a dry but overcast day, with a lukewarm breeze. Pausing on the arched stone bridge, I look out over the water. Families of ducks and paired-up swans swim idly along the gray, glassy surface. Willow trees swoop playfully, lightly brushing the water in the breeze. The locals we pass smile and say hello, a welcome change from the London brusqueness.

"I like it here," Rory decides. "Reminds me of home. Everyone's super nice, and no one's in a rush."

"Except me," I note, furiously speed-walking to our destination, my ankles wobbling in my heels. Rory keeps up easily, bouncing along with his reliably springy step.

The ceremony is taking place in the back garden of the village hall, a historic sandstone manor house nestled right against the river. White folding chairs are sinking into the spongy grass, and a wooden arbor stands at the front, adorned with colored Christmas bulbs that ooze Jules-related joy. The gardens are teeming with pink heather and purple irises. It strikes me as one of my favorite things about England, how the mild climate allows for flowers to bloom year-round.

It's not a large wedding—under a hundred people—and it makes me preemptively nostalgic. Like it's one of those days I'll look back on in a decade or two as a souvenir from a prior era when I was close friends with someone I haven't seen in years.

Jules's grandmother, a feisty old Irish woman with a fabulous Shirley Temple wig and a pint of Guinness in hand, serves as the usher. "The *Americans* have arrived!" she proclaims, overly enthralled by our accents as she proceeds to ask all about life across the pond. ("Have you ever been to *New York City*? Is it true you eat *plastic* cheese? I had a friend named Annie marry an *American*. Have you ever met an Annie Morgan? No, that was her *maiden* name—what was her new second name? Drat, it's slipped my mind. It'll come back to me, it will do.")

With a swift flick of her cane, she shoos me along to join the wedding party inside the hall and points Rory to his seat. Before I even have time to apologize for my tardiness, a modern remix of a classic wedding song starts playing over the speakers, and I follow the queue of bridesmaids down the aisle, taking my place beside the arbor and waiting for the brides.

Jules struts out first, wearing a white tuxedo and a massive smile, her curly red hair wild and free. Her freckles and nose ring—a crystal hoop today—are as prominent as ever, and I'm glad she hasn't toned herself down. Nina follows, in an ivory lace dress with a braided chignon and the aura of a Greek goddess.

Far from being a comedy sketch, Jules's vows end up leaving half the guests in tears, with their tenderness. I choke up during the part when she says she was never good at maths, but she finally understands how, when you meet the right person, one plus one is more than two. I look over at Rory. He's not tearing up, but he's leaning forward in his chair, like he wants to be careful to catch every word.

After the ten-minute ceremony, we gather for drinks and a Sunday roast-style dinner, which Jules admits she cooked half of to ease the pre-wedding jitters. Once we're filled up on meats, potatoes, and Yorkshire pudding (Jules had vegetarian options for Rory as well), we return to the garden for dancing. The chairs have been moved aside, and a portable dance floor rolled out. In an extemporaneous first dance, Nina swirls lithely around the checkered tile while Jules claps and shimmies in place, both of them dripping with delight.

Rory and I join in on the next song. We're not drunk from booze, just buzzed from love. Loosening his tie and collar, Rory shows a carefree side I haven't seen before, spinning me around as we make up dance moves on the spot. It's that uninhibited type of dancing I haven't given into for so long. The silly sort of thing I could never get away with if I were with an aristocrat.

It feels like we're skipping on bright, fluffy clouds, the kind that the sun can't keep from seeping out from. Everything is beautiful. True love is alive and well. Its light has landed on Jules and Nina, and it's found Rory and me, too, despite my best efforts to push it away.

CHAPTER THIRTY-EIGHT

Some songs later, Jules comes bounding over, face aglow with sweat and smeared glittery eyeshadow, breath reeking of whiskey. "You look smashing together," she slurs loudly. "Glad you put an end to that *just friends* kerfuffle. And just think about it, if I 'adn't told you to invite 'im to Thanksgiving, where would you be now?" She looks imploringly at us, supremely satisfied with herself.

"We owe it all to you," I deadpan as Rory grins along.

"I've got ter tell you, Kat," she carries on. "When you said you were going to marry that sod on the bus, I thought you'd lost the plot and were a proper lump of school—*fool*. But it actually was love at first sight after all, hey?"

I try to change the subject because this is the last thing I want to talk about in front of Rory. He's better off not knowing about my obsession with Alexander. It's irrelevant now, and it would just confuse him.

But Jules is babbling on and on, her mouth a leaky faucet. "'Ow many weeks were you watching 'im go by before you actually got on that bus?" she asks me, resting an arm on my shoulder for a crutch or camaraderie, I'm not sure which. "Going on and on about Alexander this and Alexander that. Swore you were mad, I did. But you trusted your intuition, and after a few twists and turns, it's all worked out. I'm bloody glad you're just Rory, though, not Prince Alexander," she says to Rory. "The lad would've been a posh prat, no doubt of that." With that, Jules mutters something about needing to leg it to the bog, then makes a beeline for the toilets.

"What was she talking about?" Rory asks. "Who's Alexander?"

I want to tell him that I have no idea. That Jules is just drunk and talking nonsense. I want to deny the whole thing and say that the first time I'd ever seen Rory was the day I got on the bus and sat next to him.

But like always, my fatal flaw with Rory is also my greatest gift. I can't lie to him. So I rush out the next words, hoping to get them out and over with as quickly as possible.

"I might've seen you pass by my flat a few times," I confess. "Before we met. And you . . . caught my eye, and I had a crush. So I told Jules about you and started to refer to you as Alexander because I didn't know your name."

The crease between Rory's eyebrows deepens. He waves me off the dance floor, so I follow him away from the crowd, over to a cast-iron bench overlooking the river. Night has fallen, and the river gleams under the glow of the wedding lights, plus the half-moon hanging up in the sky.

"You made up a story about me?" Rory asks, as the music carries on in the background and the willow trees continue to sway, insensitively jubilant to the change in our own tune.

"I had a crush on you, that's all," I say, forcing my voice to stay light and airy, so things won't plummet to the ground. "That's why I got on the bus, to introduce myself that day."

Rory doesn't say anything. I'm terrified by the idea that he might not understand. That he might jump to the wrong conclusion.

"What did you think I was going to be like?" he asks. "What did you think this Alexander was going to be like? A rich English royal, like Jules said?"

"Sort of," I admit. "It was silly, I got carried away by the rom-coms and everything. I was stuck thinking that was what love was. Now I *know* what it is, and I've never been happier." I reach to hold his hand, but he pulls away.

"So you were disappointed when you found out who I really was?" Rory says, and I can feel his thoughts racing as he tries to tie things together. "When you found out I was just some poor schoolteacher from America?"

"Not disappointed," I insist. "It was just different from what I expected. Took me some time to realize you were actually my prince after all." I smile at him but get nothing back, just a stoic face stripped of all softness.

"I'm not a prince," Rory says, his voice coated with coldness too. "And I don't want to be. I'm just me. Rory from Kalamazoo."

"I know that," I tell him, trying to keep from sounding impatient. "Believe me, I know that. And that's what I need. That's what I *want*."

Behind us, the DJ spins one sugar bop into the next. It's too happy a backdrop for a fight. In the movies, this is where promises and proposals happen.

My breath rises and falls, unable to find a steady rhythm.

One of Rory's legs is bouncing with anxiety, rattling the whole bench. I want to put a hand on his knee to soothe him, but I'm scared he'll push me away again.

"How do I know you're not just trying to force this story to fit a love-at-first-sight movie plot?" Rory asks. "I'm not a character in a rom-com or some reality TV show."

"Of course you're not," I say. "I had to unlock myself from the fictional story I'd created. That's the whole point. You're not understanding." It comes out almost accusatory because I'm so desperate for him to see my side so everything can be alright again.

"What am I not understanding?" Rory asks with an edge. "That before you even met me, you invented some story that I was English royalty? And that when I didn't turn out to be that, you've still forced yourself to like me so you could have your fairy tale?"

I can't keep my composure any longer. "No!" I blurt out angrily as the insensitively loud music keeps playing, and the insensitively happy people at the wedding keep dancing. "I love you for you. I wouldn't want you to be Alexander."

Rory looks at me, just for a moment, then shifts his gaze back down at his bouncing knees. "I don't know if I believe that." He says it softly, but it cuts through like a knife.

"You don't believe me?"

"I'm not sure."

I can't keep from spiraling, not when he's questioning the entire basis of our relationship. "So you don't trust me?" I push.

There's a pause, which says it all. Then the words follow as confirmation. "I don't know."

I wrap my arms around myself, trying and failing to stay warm. "Relationships don't work without trust," I say.

"I know that." His voice and posture are robotic, and though I'm sitting right next to him, he feels so far away.

Everything is unraveling, and rather than trying to stop it, I'm compelled to speed it up and get it over with. If this isn't going to work, I'd rather know now than postpone the pain to some point in the future, when I'm even more invested, when I've altered career decisions and uprooted my life to be with this man, only to find out that he actually doesn't believe I love him at all.

"So are we breaking up?" I ask. My own voice is equally detached now. Like I'm talking about a work initiative that's on the chopping block.

"I need some space to think," he says. The delivery leaves me feeling like a stranger.

I sit there and nod because there's nothing else to do except fling myself in his arms and beg him to stay, and I have too much pride, or maybe fear, for that.

He tells me he's going to get his stuff from the hotel and head back to London tonight. That he'll leave the room key with the bartender. I just nod along, unable to say anything. We've gone from peace to pieces in a matter of minutes. This was the kind of volatility I didn't think I'd have with Rory. With him, I thought I was protected from the plummets of emotion.

It's the sort of drama I always used to crave. And now I'm cursing it, missing the calm.

"I'll call you when I'm ready," Rory says, standing up from the bench.

"Okay." I watch him walk away, down the path, over the bridge, back toward the high street.

I'm not sure if we broke up or just had a bad fight. All I know is that he isn't here next to me. That it'll take a lot to come back from that.

I want to blame Rory for overreacting. I want to blame Jules for spilling the story. But even as my temper tries to flare with self-righteous smoke, I know the only person I can actually blame is myself. I should've come clean right away and told Rory the whole backstory last week, before we kissed for the first time. Then he would've understood.

Clouds have cloaked the sky, and it starts to rain as I stay there on the bench, unable to join the party. Rather than bringing any rejuvenation, the droplets land on my skin with a rubbery eraser texture, wiping away everything I wanted to keep in place.

CHAPTER THIRTY-NINE

The pain that follows isn't an acute spasm or a sharp slicing open of the heart. It's a mellow ache with no escape, stretching from my limbs into my lungs and back out again.

If Rory had left because he didn't want to be with me or didn't love me, I think I could eventually come to terms with that. But there's no resolution in knowing he doesn't trust me.

That's what keeps me from falling asleep in that rickety old inn the night of Jules and Nina's wedding. And that's what nearly makes me call Rory the next day, when I'm back at Marlow House, eating takeout from Pizza Express on the couch as I sift through the mound of work emails that came through over the weekend and text Blake about what happened because it's too painful to talk about on the phone.

I don't call Rory either. He was clear that he needs space, and I need to respect that. His personality isn't prone to handle surprises well, and once he gets over the initial shock, I'm hoping he'll come around and understand that my feelings are genuine. But I can't force that realization. He has to get there on his own.

Distracting myself from the damage, I throw myself into work. It's a bit disconcerting, how convincingly I can project the image that everything is fine. Dressed in my fiercest power suits, I run meetings with laser-sharp efficiency, and no one seems to notice that anything is amiss.

Rory would notice. He'd be able to tell that something was wrong. The thought makes me miss him before I remember that I'm not supposed to do that.

At the office, the mood is brash and buoyant as we head into the final few weeks of the case. The oil market has been on an upward tear, with barrel prices rising from an attractive supply–demand dynamic (attractive to oil companies and investors, that is; unattractive to environmentalists). Consumer demand has been surging for cars and airplanes, and supply has hit roadblocks because of OPEC constraints and capacity limitations from companies who've diversified away from fossil fuels.

Turpi, given its unwavering commitment to oil, has been well positioned to benefit from this dynamic. The stock has been rallying to new highs, and both the investors and the press are back on Harold's side, praising his judgment.

To say that Harold is smug would be an understatement. He won't shut up about listing off all the reasons that he was right to keep Turpi from entering the clean energy market. "Those chavs aren't critiquing me now, are they?" he says one afternoon the week after the wedding debacle. "I'm the only CEO in the world who has the balls to do what's right economically and say to hell with all the social impact nonsense."

Part of me is tempted to record one of these conversations and post it on YouTube, but if my name were attached to it, I'd be blacklisted in the business world. No company wants an undercover journalist lurking in their midst. It's not worth the risk, though I do wish people could hear him.

And I wish I could tell Rory about it. But another weekend comes and goes without hearing anything from him. The silence is almost less bearable than receiving a formal breakup text, the way it keeps me hanging on to that hopeless sort of hope. But the idea of actually receiving that breakup message makes me welcome the silence, which at least leaves room to imagine a reunion.

It's only been a few days, and I'm not ready to admit defeat. I'm not surrendering to Rory.

And I'm not giving into Harold either. Though Rory isn't at my side anymore, his repeated comments about needing to hold Harold accountable have stuck with me like glue tugging at my skin. And being in the midst of a heartbreak makes me feel more resilient to everything else. Like I can withstand anything right now.

So the week after the wedding, during one of the long days of silence from Rory, I reach back out to HR and say I'd like to discuss the Annabel's situation again. And I post Oliver this time, with an email that provides context about what happened, including Harold's apology and HR's "resolution." I'm less afraid to have the story recorded in writing anymore. In a way, I actually like the idea that there's an email trail. It helps me feel like there's a record of it.

Almost immediately, Oliver emails back saying that he's escalating the situation to Leo & Sons leadership. He thanks me for letting him know, says he believes me and is only sorry he didn't know earlier.

It's as good a reaction as I could've hoped for, but I'm not expecting anything meaningful to happen. Harold is too entrenched to be ousted by the firm he's paying to consult for him. The most that would happen is for Leo & Sons to drop Turpi as a client, though it's highly unlikely given the money at stake.

Still, I feel better having resurrected the investigation, and there's a certain pride that comes from acting on my own accord rather than relying on Rory to shepherd me through it. Although I still heard his voice in my head the whole time.

It was the warm, chummy voice that I'd gotten to know and love so much. Not the cold, clinical tone he'd used when he clammed up into a shell of himself at the wedding. The one that gave me the eerie, searing sensation that I was nothing more than a stranger to the person I'd hoped to spend my forever with.

CHAPTER FORTY

The next Monday, I'm sitting at my desk at the office, watching Harold do a BBC interview about the bull market for oil and commodities. His stringy hair, freshly dyed, has been gelled and fluffed to new heights, and he reeks of ego more than ever. As he evades the reporter's questions about the long-term industry outlook and instead uses the microphone to shout about his own genius, I'm filled with an urge to punch the TV screen perched on the office wall. Instead, I just put it on mute as I receive an incoming call on my work line.

It's Oliver. "Kat," he says. "Thought I'd give a bell and check in. Heard the case is tying up nicely. Nice one—know it hasn't been the easiest."

I fill him in on the key performance indicators and synergies and latest financial projections, assuring him that we're on track to meet the deliverables. The numbers roll easily off my tongue and give me a certain comfort, almost as if I have some kind of control over the future by confidently stating these projections.

"So, I've got some good news," he says after I've given him the rundown. "I pushed again with management, and I've just gotten the green light to promote you to partner. Effective immediately, even though it's off cycle."

A surreal sort of thrill courses through me. I'm sure I must have misheard him. "What?" I say, my corporate tone dropping as I try to process his words. "Are you serious?"

From their desks scrunched up next to mine, I can feel the juniors looking on curiously, straining their ears for a juicy piece of office gossip. The open floor plan leaves little room for privacy, but this is news I don't mind sharing.

"Very much so," Oliver says, as even-keeled as ever. "You'll be getting an email from HR soon, but I wanted to call and give you the good news. You're the youngest woman partner in the firm's history, if I'm not mistaken. Well deserved, and only sorry it was such a faff to get here."

I wonder if he's pranking me, but then I remember he's not the sort of person who believes in pranks or practical jokes.

My heart skips a beat or two, and shivers course through my body. An incredulous grin catapults across my face, and I feel my mouth physically hanging open. Here it is, the shiny accolade I've been waiting for and working for.

It turns out I've gotten it after all.

Oliver says they want to send me to Dubai for my first case as partner. I'd be relocated right after the Turpi case wraps up. Rory's face—and the vision of our hypothetical life together in Michigan—flashes through my mind before I accept.

But I accept anyway. In the rush of this success, the idea of giving up an incredible career opportunity for someone who's effectively broken up with me seems ludicrous. And there's no point moving back to Michigan by myself. I'd be reminded of Rory, and it would just depress me that much more.

My ingrained instinct to run far away is taking over, and I'm in no mood to fight it.

Sure, I'm still hoping Rory will come back, but I can't put my life on hold while he figures out what he wants. He had his chance, he asked for space, and if he wants to try again then he'll have to understand that while we were broken up (or "on a break," as I still prefer to think of it), I made decisions that were best for me, not us, because currently there is no *us*.

The reasoning doesn't go down easily, but it goes down, nonetheless.

"And Kat?" Oliver carries on through the phone. "I know Harold has been . . . difficult to work with, to say the least. I'm glad you told me what happened at Annabel's, and it's not right—absolutely not. But at this point, I reckon let's just try to go out on a high note, shall we?"

There's a stanza of silence as I search for something assertive to say. "Sure," is the meek little word I hear myself say, because it seems like the only thing I *can* say. I'm supposed to agree with the man who just made my career dreams come true. Let everything pass over peacefully because, in the end, it turned out alright. I got what I wanted, even if it wasn't the way I wanted it.

It's not until I hang up that I wonder if the promotion and allegations were not in fact mutually exclusive events. Could the higher-ups at Leo & Sons have wanted to avoid upsetting a client by escalating the matter, so they decided to promote me as placation? Was the partner title nothing but an expedient solution to save a client's reputation, and their own?

I want to think that I got it because I deserve this. That being good is good enough. But I'm not sure. The truth suddenly feels tangled and tainted, like it's a dirty mix of factors.

I tell myself that it doesn't matter. That I deserve it regardless. That I've reached my goal and am one step closer to my CEO dream, so all's well that ends well.

I do my best to push out the uneasy feeling in my conscience and bask in the glow of this milestone. It's not too hard to do, especially when the HR email arrives, confirming the promotion, and I get those giddy shivers all over again.

Since I can't share the news with Rory, and I don't want to rub the partner news in Blake's face, I go to the loo and call my parents. Mom picks up on the first ring. She always answers right away, and I wonder sometimes if she walks around with that bulky landline phone in her hand, just so she doesn't miss me on the rare times I call. The picture, whether true or not, makes me feel like a bad daughter. It makes me yearn for that lake life in Michigan more than ever, not just so I can be with Rory, but so I can be near my whole family.

She seems excited as I tell her about the promotion, letting out some squeals and claps, but I can tell she's doing it more for my sake then her own. She doesn't care what my business card says, so long as I'm still the same Kat on the inside.

Which I'm not sure of. I felt like I was getting that Kat back again with Rory, but I don't know if I can find her again on my own. Or if I even want to.

Mom wants to know if this means that I'll be transferred back to the United States. I tell her that I'm actually being sent to Dubai, and try not to notice the way her whole demeanor deflates. "How's Rory doing?" she asks as brightly as she can.

The question scrapes all over. I never told her that Rory and I were dating, since it only ended up being a week, and I'm mostly glad for this so she won't be disappointed now. But part of me wishes I had filled her in, so more people would know about our relationship and it wouldn't be something that could fade away so easily after one fight.

"Haven't seen him recently," I tell my mom curtly. To avoid follow-up questions, I say I have to go jump on another call but that I'll talk with her again soon.

A bit later, Harold swings by my desk, fresh off the TV set, his face still caked in peachy goo. "Heard the news, Kitten," he says jovially. "Brilliant job. Reckon we round up the team for some celebratory drinks at Annabel's?"

It's a testament to the audaciousness of the male species, or perhaps just to this single male specimen, that he so nonchalantly suggests celebrating my promotion in the very place where he made a pass at me.

I'm inclined to say no and just go back to my flat and order takeaway from Deliveroo. I'm inclined to see as little of Harold as I possibly can before the case wraps up, when I can be free of his seedy stare forever.

But I don't want to live in fear of him or that place any longer. So I put on a smile and say, "Sure. Annabel's sounds great."

* * *

By the next day, the high from the promotion has steeply waned. I feel jittery and hungry, almost like I'm having a sugar crash.

I didn't stay long at Annabel's and only sipped seltzer before slipping out. I was glad I'd gone, if only to prove something to myself, but I'd wound up wishing I were curled up on the couch, eating gelato with Rory instead. I didn't spiral or text him, probably because I wasn't drinking, but I still dropped into a low sort of place like a rapid comedown after what should've been one of the best days of my life.

The juniors cooed over my promotion, asking wide-eyed questions about how they could best set themselves up for success and make partner one day. They diligently scribbled down everything I said in their notebooks, like it was the word of God. Last night, I'd welcomed their idolization as proof that I'd followed the right life track and arrived somewhere wonderful and enviable. That everything I gave up to get here was well worth it.

But this morning, as I lather peanut butter onto my crumpets, it strikes me as tragically sad, the way these young twenty-somethings look at me for answers when my whole life seems to be one giant question.

As I open the sitting room curtains and glance out onto Upper Street, I catch myself wondering if I took a wrong turn somewhere. If there was a fork in the road that I never noticed because I was hell-bent on getting straight up to the rocky, wind-blown summit when a sunny meadow lower down might've actually been a happier landing place that more closely resembled Mala's crayon-drawn picture.

The triumph from the promotion only seems to be touching my skin, which has lost its initial goose bumps. My palpitating heart has returned to its normal pace, and it's eerily comparable to that sinking feeling when a crush starts to wear off. When you're compelled to see the other person for who they really are rather than who you wanted them to be.

Though I'm already dressed for the office, I trade out my pant-suit for joggers and decide to work from home in hopes that the existential dread will pass like a twenty-four-hour flu. As I sit down at my desk, my eyes automatically search for the 4 bus out the window, and I don't stop them. I'm mature enough to be able to see Rory on a bus and not fracture into a thousand fragments.

He passes by right around seven forty-five AM, like always. He's in his usual seat but doesn't seem to be reading anything. My body tenses as I remember how relaxing his presence used to feel.

I want him to look up so he'll see me and be reminded of the love he shoved away, but he keeps his eyes down. Too hastily, the bus leaves the St. Mary's stop, and I'm left gripping Rory's ghost, trying to let go of what I'm unable to hold onto as I repeat all the reasons that we're not right together. How being with him would hinder my ambition and how I don't want someone who doesn't want me.

I'd like him to feel the pain of losing me, but I also don't want him to hurt, and my generosity irks me. I'm at the stage in my heal-ing where I'm seeing how this whole thing is his fault more than mine. I didn't do anything wrong except make up a rom-com story about a guy I had a crush on, and what female on the planet hasn't done something like that at some point in her life?

My head is packed but my heart is void as my emotions rattle around in the empty space where Rory used to fit like a mitten.

I feel an unwelcome urge to jump off my life path and onto his, or at least find a way for ours to intersect again. The C-suite track doesn't feel as reliable as it used to. Part of me is starting to wonder if it was designed by a con artist or perhaps just a clueless buffoon.

Maybe this is what Blake realized too, but she's been reluctant to share her full epiphany in fear of dissuading my own ambition.

But even if I wanted to, I'm too far down the road to change directions or retrace my steps. And I certainly wouldn't know how to do it without Rory. He was the only one who could encourage me to shift my priorities and excavate myself from the shrine of impressive résumés and C-suite status. And now that one person who could help has abandoned me.

Though I wonder, deep down in the places I don't want to go but can't stay away from, if maybe I can't pin the blame on Rory for leaving me, not when I left myself long ago. Maybe I've been looking for the easy way out by having someone else come and save me when the truth is that it's not up to him to show me the way back home. That's on me.

No matter if it's back in my hometown or on the other side of the world, I need to reclaim my life so I'm proud of the person I am right now, not the one I might be down the road. So that I'm living with purpose for today, not just promise for tomorrow. So that I'm making space for grace and joy and play instead of just grinding and gritting my teeth so I can get some shiny prize on the other side.

And I know it's deeper than the job. The job is the symptom of the problem, not the problem itself. For so many years now, I've been looking for things to pour into so I don't have to peer into myself.

Because that's what I do. I throw myself into jobs the same way I throw myself into relationships. I build up the promotion and the proposal to be my savior, latching onto the promise that the perfect position or the perfect person will fulfill me.

When fullness can only overflow from what's already within.

Shutting my laptop, I pour the hot water into a thermos, then add a teabag and a dollop of gelato on top just to feel a little closer to my kid self. Pulling on my squeaky wellies, I take the sweet tea with me as I head outside for a walk. My morning Zooms can wait. Right now, I have to meet myself.

CHAPTER FORTY-ONE

I'm not sure what to do about my job-related doubts, so I don't do anything about them. I keep schlepping to the office each morning and schlepping back at night, lulled by the routine and lifted by the fleeting highs that come from moving into my glass-walled office and depositing my first partner payslip.

I receive a partner plaque too, inscribed with my name. Though I judged how prominently Oliver displayed his trophies, I find myself polishing mine and putting it next to the window, so the sunlight catches it in the rare hours that the clouds peel away.

While swiveling in my fancy new office chair, I update my LinkedIn with my new title, and comments and congratulations come rolling in from old high school teachers and people I haven't spoken to in years. Things like: Always knew you were going places! Keep making us proud.

It's only when I start to question whether people back home *should* be proud of me that I realize how much I want them to be.

Though my title has changed, my day-to-day work hasn't, nor has the amount of power that I feel like I wield walking around the office. The seat at the partner table feels so anticlimactic that it makes me wonder again if it's success at all or just something else that society has manufactured to replicate success so no one will probe into the real thing.

One night a couple weeks after the wedding, I pop by the King's Head. Jules has texted me that they're back from their honeymoon, and she's keen to catch up.

Taking a seat on a barstool, I listen as she jabbers on about the exact shade of turquoise of the water in Mallorca and the wide-open days for sex and all-inclusive buffets and bars, followed by more sex.

"Reckon I was made for the retirement life," Jules declares. She's one of those people who doesn't seem to tan, only burns, and her freckled face is bright pink and peeling, with cat-eye sunglasses lines giving a striking racoon effect. She seems proud to show off her fried complexion, as if it's a souvenir from her honeymoon heaven. "But enough about me," she goes on. "What I'd miss 'round 'ere?"

"Not much," I say dryly. "I got promoted."

Jules whistles through her teeth. "Bloody 'ell. Well done, babes," she says, summoning two glasses of bubbly. "Why aren't you more chuffed 'bout this?"

"It's just . . . not really what I pictured so far," I say as we clink glasses. "And Rory and I broke up," I tack on, hoping to train my brain to make him an afterthought.

"*What?*" Jules says, eyes bugging out in horror. "You're joshing me."

I tell her everything, or mostly everything, except her role in the conversation at the wedding (it's clear she doesn't remember, and I don't want to make her feel bad).

"I ruined it," I lament, sipping very slowly on the champagne because I know by now how alcohol is inversely related to my healing. "I finally found real love, the kind you can build a life on, and I ruined it within a week."

"You didn't ruin it, babes," Jules says. "If Rory can't come around and see sense, then 'e doesn't deserve you. That's all there is to it." She presents me with a basket of chips and a side of fried pickles, and it means a lot to me, how she's taking my side even when I know how much she adores Rory.

"He's talked himself out of it," I say. "I'm sure of it. He's so logical that he's no doubt stacked up all the facts about why I'm not a suitable partner—that I'm too emotionally driven and have unrealistic expectations. Then add on the instability of where I'll be living, and he can't remember anymore why he ever thought he loved me at all."

"I'm not saying 'e's in the right," Jules says. "But you don't need to wait for 'im to reach out. Just pick up the dog and bone and give 'im a bell."

"I'm not going to call him," I say. "I'm moving to Dubai next month for my new case anyway."

Even though I'm going to a place I've never been, the process of leaving is soothing and familiar. I know what to do. I pack up and delete his number. Moving on is something I'm good at.

"It's better this way," I go on, speaking very firmly to try and prop up the flimsy words. "We were just never meant to be."

Jules snorts loudly, not bothering to hide her skepticism. "I don't know if I believe anyone's really *made to be*," she says, helping herself to the chips she's just given me. "I reckon you just *make it be*. Love is a choice every damn day, innit?"

The old me would've been grievously offended by this idea of love being a choice—*"How dare you insinuate that soul mates don't exist?"* I would've ranted.

But maybe this more pragmatic view is just as dreamy after all. Maybe the most romantic thing of all is to continually choose somebody, even—and especially—on the days it's hard and laced with hurt. And rather than leaving our love stories up to the flimsy whims of fate, perhaps we each have the ability to shape our own destiny through the enduring power of commitment.

"Beef bagel's up, be back in a jiffy," Jules says, hopping back into the King's Head kitchen to collect the food, leaving me chewing on the true meaning of love that I've resisted and rejected and rewritten for my whole life.

*   *   *

Early the next week, I use my elevated partner status to pop out for a lunchtime spin class across from the office, without feeling (as) guilty about being away from the desk. At the end of the class, I check my phone and have three missed calls and seven texts from Harold. The top text reads: PR crisis. Get back to office now.

The following messages are just different iterations of his escalating impatience. A quick Google search reveals the headlines. There's been a massive oil spill in the North Sea off Great Britain, caused by the explosion of one of Turpi's oil rigs. It's an environmental catastrophe. The worst in decades, the reports say.

My stomach turns as I read estimates on the number of marine species impacted and how many years it will take for the ocean to heal. The outward disgust at Turpi turns inward as I feel my complicity as their consultant.

When I get to the office in Canary Wharf, I find Harold and his compadres huddled together in his office, barking orders and excuses.

"We don't owe the public anything," Harold is ranting to anyone who will listen. "And the investors will hold steady so long as we can prove the financial impact will be negligible. The stock hasn't sold off yet—we've got to reassure them"

Reassure them that you're not losing money, you're just destroying the ocean? I want to bite back.

"Kat," Harold says, as I put my bag down at the desk. "Go down to the eighteenth floor and build out the PR messaging with the team. They're sure to bungle it."

I'm used to acquiescing to these kinds of requests, but I'm not the junior consultant anymore. I'm the partner. This is my opportunity to speak up. To be the change in the system, like I always said I would be once I had the power.

So I clench my jaw and stand firm. "We need to issue an apology," I say. "We can't pretend like Turpi didn't do anything wrong."

"Are you mad?" Harold sneers. "Of course we didn't do anything wrong. Oil spills are the normal cost of doing business in this industry. Reasonable people will understand that."

"Let's put that in the PR statement," I mutter dryly, under my breath.

"It's not a bad quote," Harold says, unironically. "Now let's get cracking." He shoos me away, like he's a lord and I'm the help.

And so I find myself heading down to the eighteenth floor, per Harold's request. When I tell the internal communications team that Harold wants me to weigh in on the messaging, someone shoves a printout in my hand. It's the latest version of the draft, and it starts off: *While we at Turpi regret the current circumstances, we want to wholeheartedly assure our investors and customers that we take great pride in our unwavering commitment to supporting a healthy planet for all.*

If it weren't such a catastrophic moment, it would be comical. Sitting down at a spare desk, I start typing a new version—a simple apology that takes ownership.

Harold appears at my side as I'm editing it. "What's taking so long?" he fumes. "We needed to put out a statement five hours ago." Reading the document over my shoulder, his face boils over. "Who wrote this piece of shite?"

Folding my arms, I meet his inflamed gaze. "I did," I say coolly.

"This is the problem with girls in business," Harold mutters, half to himself, half to me. "They're too damn soft."

Something inside me switches, or already has. I'm no longer scared of Harold or what he might do if I resist him. "Can you repeat that, please?" I ask him in an artificially subservient voice. "Want to make sure that I caught it verbatim for the statement."

"Fuck off, Kat," he says. "Show some respect."

I'm about to unleash a sarcastic comeback about how he's shown *me* nothing but respect when my attention is snagged by the office TVs. BBC is on, and Turpi has made the headline: *Climate Activists Gather in London Amid Turpi's Catastrophic Oil Spill.*

Video footage turns to a climate rally forming outside at Trafalgar Square in Westminster, a great paved space in front of the majestic National Gallery, dominated by a sky-high memorial column and multiple stately fountains. Packing the square, protesters are holding handmade signs and chanting pro-Earth slogans. The camera flashes to a group of students.

A little girl with long black braids appears on screen. She's in a purple jumper with a pleated skirt and mismatched knee-high socks. It's Mala, being interviewed by a reporter.

"Among the protestors are grade-two students at Hendrick Primary School in Clerkenwell," the reporter says. "Here we have seven-year-old Mala, who's come with her mum and classmates. Mala, what do you think about the oil spill?"

"It's horrid," Mala says, speaking clearly and solemnly into the microphone. "Some people don't care about our lovely Earth. It makes me sad. But also glad because we're here and the big people in the government will have to notice us and change the laws. They will do!"

I feel myself getting choked up as I watch it. Kids intuitively understand right and wrong and are so hopeful that justice will prevail. That their voice will be heard.

After Mala, the reporter moves over to Rory, who's wearing his rain coat over his button-down shirt, like he's prepared for a downpour. My chest clenches and releases at the sight of him. The painful frustration I've felt toward him is replaced by a poignant sort of pride at how he's out there on the street, standing up for what he believes in. Advocating for the Earth that has no voice.

While I'm here in an ivory tower helping the culprit cover his tracks.

"Mr. Cooper," the reporter says, "what was the motivation for coming out here with your students today?"

Rory looks flustered to be on camera, but he answers the reporter's question like he knows it's for something bigger than himself. "Well, when we got into school today, some of the kids had heard about an oil spill and were asking what it meant," he says, looking at the reporter rather than the camera. "We turned on the news, and when we learned this rally was happening, the students asked if we could go. I called their parents to check, and a few came to chaperone. I'm just so proud of the kids for wanting to get involved. This is more impactful than any kind of school lesson, in my opinion. I just hope—"

Harold snaps up the remote and turns the TV off mid-sentence. It zaps to blackness. "What a bunch of wankers," he jeers. "Those people don't understand how the world works. That's why they're bloody skint while I've got five properties around the globe."

If I'd thought my patience had broken earlier, now it's fully snapped. Even though I'm not with Rory, I still have an unshakable need to defend him. I don't fight the instinct, not when it's more important to fight this evil.

"*Those people* are my friends," I say, loudly enough for everyone on the floor to hear. "And they're right."

Harold looks at me like I've just sprouted three heads. "What's gotten into you?"

"Some decent ethics," I say, energized by the thrill of finally speaking my mind.

"That's enough," Harold grumbles. "Turn in the new draft of the press release. You're partner now—this is what you've been trained to do."

It's probably true. Maybe I have been trained to go along and do what the client says. To value profits over the planet. To sacrifice the common good for the bottom line.

But this is the beginning of un-training myself so I can start over and live a better life. Even if I can't live that life with Rory, I still want to live it. For the students in his class. For my nephews and niece. For the kids I hope to have someday, and for their kids.

And for me too, so I can look back when I'm eighty and be proud of my choices.

"No," I say, in a strange, strong voice that I recognize immediately as my own. Like it's returned to me after a long sabbatical. "I quit."

Now it's Harold's turn to laugh—a coarse, phlegmy sound that makes me think of lung disease. "You can't quit," he says, as if this were obvious.

The old CEO dream comes to mind, but it's lost its luster. The closer I've gotten to the top, the more the disillusionment has swelled. What I once worshipped as gold now leaves me cold.

As I stare at the TV that's gone black, it's newly clear to me that success isn't about scale. It's about soul. Not how many people you impact, but how deeply you do it.

I don't need to be CEO to make a difference. I just need to be a decent human being with a backbone. Transformative change happens at the micro level, not the macro.

And though I've been determined to shatter the glass ceiling and advance gender equality in the business world, I'm now wondering if maybe the only thing I owe the trailblazing women who came before me is a thank-you for the doors they've helped open. The doors I can walk into. Or out of.

"Yes, I can," I tell Harold. "And I do."

Without waiting for permission of any kind, I go back up to the thirty-second floor and make a phone call to Leo & Sons HR, officially turning in my notice, effective immediately. Hastily packing up my office, I don't take much, leaving behind the partner plaque, half-filled notebooks, and designer heels stashed under my desk.

The juniors watch me go, looking almost like they want to clap or follow me out. But they stay tethered to their desks without saying a word.

The elevators are taking too long, and I'm overcome by the need to evacuate the building and everything it represents as quickly as possible. Slipping on my trainers, I dash to the stairs. I'm panting a few floors in, but I don't stop until I'm out of the marble lobby and onto the sidewalk.

Flagging down the first cab I see, I hop in the back. "To Trafalgar Square, please," I wheeze. "As fast as you can."

"You late to something, ma'am?" the driver asks, eyeing my disheveled state in the rearview mirror.

"Yes," I say as the cab lurches into motion. "I am."

I'm late to prioritizing the important things and valuing sincere goodness over simulated greatness. I'm late to running toward love, not just sprinting away from it. I'm late to unshackling myself from the hectic, hollow life I've proudly chained myself to for so many years.

I'm late to it all. I just hope I'm not too late.

CHAPTER FORTY-TWO

I quit my job!! I text Blake, from the back of the cab.

WHAT!?!!! she replies, all caps with an excess of exclamation points, like we're back in our early twenties, enchanted by everything and jaded by nothing. YOU SAW THE LIGHT!!!

Finally did!! I assure her, then send her incoming call to voicemail. Will call you later—on a mission now!

The cab gets backed up in traffic a few blocks from Trafalgar Square. Unwilling to wait, I get out and run the remaining distance along the north bank of the Thames. Passing the docked riverboats bobbing on the water, I outpace morning joggers, propelled by my newfound freedom. I'm tempted to toss my work phone into the river, but I don't want to pollute, so I keep it stashed in my pocket, to be deposited at a recycling center later.

As I turn a bend, Big Ben and the Houses of Parliament come into view before me, all their grandiose glory rising up against the textured fabric of pastel, purple-gray clouds. The golden sandstone spires and meticulously etched turrets are backlit by the sun, which, though it isn't out, seems nearer than usual for a London morning.

Exiting the river path and crossing the street (my eyes finally know which way to look for oncoming traffic), I make my way inland a few blocks until I reach the square. Protestors are squeezed together, from the monument all the way up to the steps of the National Gallery. They're not loud, but the hum of their chanting is a distinct change from the clamor of traffic, construction, and car horns.

Trying to locate Rory based on the angle of the earlier TV report, I hear the students before I see them—the youthful voices raising the pitch of the whole crowd: "Clean up and green up!"

And there he is, next to the nearest fountain. Rory, standing there with a little boy on his shoulders so the student can see over the crowd. The boy is holding up a posterboard sign with a water cycle drawing on it.

Squirming my way through the crowd, I hurry toward them. But the closer I get, the slower I move. My nerves start to fail me.

I had the courage to quit my job today. But I'm not sure I'm brave enough to face the man I used to love.

The man you still love.

He asked for space, and here I am turning up without warning. Not only that, but in a setting with his students. I consider turning around and heading back to Marlow House.

But my body rejects the idea with the same confidence that it rejected Harold's requests earlier. I can't waste another moment.

So I walk toward him. But before Rory sees me, Mala comes running over, tugging on her mom's hand. "Miss Kat!" Mala shrieks, reaching out for a hug that I gratefully return. "Guess what, Miss Kat? I was on the telly—you won't believe it!"

"I saw you," I assure her. "Can I have your autograph?"

She's positively giddy, hopping up and down, long braids flapping freely. "I do hope I go viral," she declares.

Smiling to myself, I think of how the world has changed since I was Mala's age, but how it's not all for the worse.

"And also, guess what else happened, Miss Kat?" She gestures for me to lean down so she can whisper in my ear. "It worked!" she hisses. "When I told JB that I fancied him, he didn't *say* it back, but now he gives me all his Percy Pig sweets instead of stealing mine." Mala beams, like this is the most romantic of all gestures. Which, to be fair, it pretty much is for primary school.

"I guess I owe you those chocolate biscuits," I tell her.

"Indeed you do," she says happily. "Say, did it work for you, Miss Kat? Did you tell your *American* person you loved them?"

"I did," I say, lowering my voice. "I'm not sure if it worked."

"It didn't?" Mala's face drops, and she looks distraught. "But who wouldn't love you, Miss Kat?" she asks, eyes stretched and solemn. "That's what I want to know."

The comment breaks my heart a bit, but in the sort of way that's needed to let the light in.

Rory has noticed me. He's lowered the boy off his shoulders and is now standing in front of me. "What're you doing here?" he asks, avoiding direct eye contact by fiddling with the zipper on his raincoat.

It probably deserves to be a loaded question since I'm disregarding his request for space and because my client is responsible for the oil spill. But there's no venom in his voice, just vigilance.

"I quit," I tell him. His impassive expression doesn't change, so I say it again. "I quit my job."

Rory seems to turn the words over a few times, as if checking for fraud. "You did what?"

In a well-timed way, Mala's mom diverts Mala's attention to the news cameras, giving Rory and me a moment to talk, just the two of us.

"I ended up getting promoted to partner," I tell him, and there's a flicker of something in his face, as if he let the mask slip for a second. "I'm not sure if it had to do with the fact that I brought up the sexual assault case again," I continue. "I hope it wasn't related. But anyway, today Harold asked me to help with the press release for the oil spill. And I quit. I know I should've stopped selling out ages ago, but I'm doing it now, so that's something, right?"

I flash a grin at him, trying to force that old friendliness. He doesn't return the smile, and it reminds me how far we are from where we once were and where I thought we were going to get.

"You made partner and then you quit?" Rory asks with the puzzled inflection of someone trying to solve a math problem that doesn't add up.

"Correct." The adrenaline from walking out of the office is still coursing through me, but I know that when it runs out, I'll still be glad of my decision. It's the kind of conviction that's been percolating so long that, now that I've acted on it, there's no part of me that wants to go back.

"Wow." He's still distant, hiding under an invisible veneer.

I want to show him it's safe to come out. That it will always be safe. That I'll protect him and take care of him, just like he'll do for me.

Because standing before him now, all my arguments about why we're better off apart have fallen and flattened. My life will be okay without Rory, but it'll be so much better with him.

"Can we talk?" I ask, too sure of the truth to be shy.

"I can't right now. Gotta keep track of the kids and chaperones." He glances around nervously, then relaxes once he counts everyone.

"Afterward, then?" I pose.

"Alright."

So we stand near each other for the next hour or so, keeping track of the students and doing our best to answer their questions about the oil spill and why anybody would let the ocean get hurt like that. From the outside, people might think Rory and I were coparents. The thought fills me with equal parts of hurt and hope.

"Byeee, Miss Kat!" Mala sings, as her mom takes her home for the end of the school day. "I must go check how many views my video has gotten. Do bring me the chocolate biscuits, won't you?" With that, she trots off.

Once Rory's triple-checked that all the kids have been collected, he turns back to me, visibly uncomfortable without any buffer. His posture is more slouched than usual, and the pep has been zapped from his step.

We wiggle our way out of the crowd, emerging to the outskirts of the square, beside a battered telephone box that's in need of a new coat of red paint.

"I love you, Rory," I say, and it reverberates with relief.

Rory blinks in surprise a few times in a row, looking even more taken aback than when I told him I'd quit. I don't try to discern what he's thinking and feeling; I just whiz along, spellbound by the surrender that comes from speaking my truth.

"And I know we started off in a weird way," I tell him. "I had this fairy-tale idea in my head, and you're different from that. But I don't love you in spite of all that. I love you *because* of that."

I feel the pain again of watching him walk away at Jules's wedding. But I know that wasn't really him. It was a stress reaction, and I'm praying I can break through to the real Rory. That he's still in there.

"If you'd been the prince I'd pictured, I'd be trying to be that rom-com character too, always filtering and polishing myself and feeling like I could never mess up," I go on. "With you, there's no performing. And I know I can't force you to trust me, and I know these are just words that I'll have to back up with actions, but what I'm saying is that I want to have that chance. I want to live near our families and hopefully have a family of our own someday and have a little house on a lake. And I have no clue what I want to do in my career, but I want to figure it out with you at my side, scooping from the same ice-cream pint."

As quickly as I started, I stop. I'm tempted to take back everything I just said, but I'm glad I can't. I stand there, waiting, infused with the atypical patience that I get around Rory, not wanting him to feel like he has to hurry up for me.

I brace myself for a goodbye. But the goodbye doesn't come.

"Separate pints," is what Rory says instead.

"What?"

"We'll eat from separate pints," he says. "So I can have my vanilla ice cream in peace while you go for the fancy stuff." The protective layer is retreating from his face. A smile slips out, and there's my Rory again, his eyes honey and sunshine and everything good.

I'm scared to ask it, but I do anyway. "Is that your way of saying you still love me?"

"I still love you," he agrees, wrapping me up in one of those hugs that feels like home. "And I trust you."

He apologizes for his reaction at the wedding and for his silence since. He tells me he got worried that he wouldn't be what I wanted. That our life together wouldn't be enough. "You've been on this high-power track straight to the moon," he says. "And I'm not on the track. I don't want to hold you back."

The words cut me to the core. "You could never hold me back."

The reality is that I'm the one who's been holding myself back by staying stuck within the small, rigid box of my double-decker expectations. By thinking that the only way to be successful in love was to marry a prince, and that the only way to be successful at work was to reign from the C-suite. And that any other life path would be settling.

"And besides, who needs to go to the moon?" I say, splashing in a bit of our old playfulness. "As long as we take care of Earth, I like it right here."

Rory's shoulders perk up, and he's standing straighter again. "You sure?"

I sense that he's just going to ask me it this once, and then he'll take me at my word. So if I'm having doubts, I need to tell him now. But I'm not.

Because in this pocket of calm amid all the noise from the chanting crowd and honking lorries and squawking gulls circling the parliament spires, I have complete clarity that a low-key life with Rory is exactly the sort of success that best serves me.

I used to think that clarity would come in a lightning-bolt moment. A sudden jolt of "when you know, you know." But it turns out that clarity isn't something sharp or sudden or stormy. It's soft and slow and subtle, much more like a prolonged sunrise than a shock wave.

"I'm sure," I say with a firm nod of my jaw.

Rory's eyes are getting watery, and he's crinkling his nose like he's trying to keep from crying. "Stupid allergies," he mutters with a self-deprecating smile that tumbles into a laugh.

In the movies, this would be where he'd match my speech with an equally sappy declaration of love. But that's not Rory, and I don't want it to be. It means so much more just standing here with each other, *for* each other.

"I can't believe you quit," he says, the bounce back in his voice.

"It was a pretty great moment," I tell him, reliving the livid shock on Harold's face. "You would've been proud."

"I'm always proud of you," he says with that awkward lilt that comes out when he's trying to vocalize his feelings. "And always will be."

It means so much more because I know he doesn't say it lightly. He's putting his faith in me, and I'm putting mine in him. And both of us are putting it in something bigger than ourselves that we'll have to learn from and lean on during the hard times and the inevitable moments when we let each other down because, though we'll try to be good to each other, we can't be gods to each other.

I want to love him with all the parts of me I've lost and found again. Like I'm trying to love myself with all those beautiful, broken bits too.

Rory kisses me right there, in the middle of the Thames path as pedestrians push by. I could keep making out all day, but I don't want his PDA-related stress to kick in, so I look around for an alcove of privacy. The nearby telephone box stands empty, door slightly ajar as if specifically placed there for this purpose.

Tugging him inside, I close the door behind us and we resume where we left off. His hands are in my wind-blown hair, and we're pushed against the glass-paned wall, making out like two teenagers who've snuck out of their houses.

And that's what our love story is, really. Rory's my childhood sweetheart, the one I didn't meet until I was over thirty years old. It was written in the stars the whole time, the stars we both looked up at from our backyards, just a few miles apart.

I didn't have to audition or fight for this love, so I was quick to discount it as something lesser. Something too simple. But the truth is that intentionally loving someone day in and day out is the most complex and beautiful thing in the world, with all the layers you unpack and the trust you build up. That's what I want with Rory.

We don't have to get there overnight. The growth can happen over a series of many dawns and dusks, noons and moons. There's a feeling that it will keep getting better, not in a linear sense perhaps, but in a cumulative one.

Abruptly, the door to the booth swings open. A tourist stands there, camera around her neck, clearly hoping to pose for a photo op with Big Ben in the background. She gives a start at seeing us tangled up together.

"Sorry," I say with a girlish giggle. "We'll just be another minute."

"Or another hour," Rory mutters as the flustered tourist slams the door shut and leaves us alone together.

The afternoon sun pokes through the London haze, transforming the splotched telephone box windows into prisms of stained-glass art.

EPILOGUE

It's early autumn in Islington, much like the day I first spotted Rory on the bus. Upper Street is shimmering under a fresh coat of rain, asphalt and cobblestones aglow with refracted headlights. It's late afternoon, that crossover period when the Victorian lampposts are already switched on, but the daylight hasn't yet faded.

Across the street, the King's Head pub still serves as a refuge for the weary, though Jules no longer works there. The awning of Gail's bakery flaps in the feisty wind as customers crowd in for the same scones, almond croissants, and flat whites I remember.

The fishmonger remains as pungently recognizable as ever, and next door, Marlow House is just as characterful with its red terracotta and sloping dormers. The aqua-colored door has been repainted a sleek black, but otherwise it looks the same.

Nostalgia rises to the surface, along with relief that I don't actually have to go back in time and relive that frantic stage of life.

It's almost like Islington is unaltered since I left, while just about every part of my life has radically changed. Except for the person at my side.

Rory's still there, still with that spring in his step and that softness in his soul, even as his hairline recedes and sun spots dot his skin.

It's fall break for Kalamazoo Public Schools, where Rory teaches fourth grade, and he surprised me with a trip to London—our first time back since we lived here. We're celebrating eight years since the day that we had our first conversation on the bus. It's not a date that he remembered, but I did, so he marked it in his calendar when I first mentioned it, and makes a point to always do a little something for it.

Or a big something for it this year. Trips like these mean more now that all my airline points have long run out, and we don't have a budget like I did in my consulting days.

We're at St. Mary's bus stop, waiting for the 4 bus to pull up so we can get on again for old time's sake. And so we can bring our two new travel companions along for the ride.

"Is that it, Mommy?" Anne Marie wants to know, pinching her nose to avoid the raw fish fragrance as she points at a red double-decker bus coming our way. She's inherited Rory's amber eyes, alongside my frizzy hair. I've stopped straightening mine since becoming a mom, and one of my favorite things is how people can look at our bushy ponytails and tell that we belong together.

"No, silly goose," James says. *Silly goose* is the closest thing to an insult that we let him say, and he uses the phrase liberally. "We're looking for number *four*, remember?" He looks enormously proud of himself.

Then, tugging on Rory's hand, James whispers for verification, "That bus isn't number four, is it Daddy?"

James is five years old, and Anne Marie just turned three. Dressed in oversized raincoats, with their wellies up to their knobby knees, they look far too adorable to be allowed. Sometimes I still have to pinch myself that I—that *we*—created these miraculous little beings who are growing up in front of our very eyes.

Becoming a wife and mother has been the greatest achievement of my life so far, though it took me a while to embrace this. Even after I quit Leo & Sons and started my life with Rory, the worldly paradigm I'd been worshipping for decades didn't just dismantle straight away.

The type of joy I found in caring for Rory, and then the kids, felt searingly shameful. I'd been conditioned to believe I was letting women down and letting myself down by giving up my high-powered corporate career to tend to a family. Sometimes I still feel that guilt.

But I guess happiness—*fulfillment*—isn't about feeling like you're doing everything perfectly all the time. It's just about knowing that the trade-offs you've made are aligned with your highest self. That you're prioritizing what you truly want to prioritize, not what other people have told you to. Blake has helped me see this too, and our friendship has grown dearer over the years that we've both been reconstructing what it really means to be a successful woman.

A buzzer goes off on Rory's phone, and I know what time it is. Anne Marie does too. "It's beautiful o'clock!" she squeals, beaming with glee through her gummy baby smile.

After all these years, Rory still sets his phone alarm every day to remind me that I'm beautiful. The kids have learned the routine and taken to joining in.

"You're one fit bird, as they say over here," Rory tells me, with a quick kiss on the cheek. "Beautiful."

Though my body has stretched and expanded since having kids, and my wardrobe is devoid of its former designer logos, Rory has an understated way of making me feel like I'm more attractive than the day we met. He doesn't shout his love from the rooftops or dip me in the street for a kiss. There are no ribbons or bows, no bells or whistles. From the outside looking in, it might look a bit dull, a bit lackluster. But from the inside, it's the most glorious love I've ever felt, deepening inch by inch, day by day.

"Beautiful, beautiful!" Anne Marie parrots it back in a higher voice as I reach down to wipe chocolate from her face, from the hot cocoa we got the kids (and Rory) at Gail's.

Life as a mother is more demanding than the corporate world ever was, but so much more energizing, filling me rather than stripping me. And though I have no interest in reentering the 24/7 rat race, I've found I'm a better mom when I'm pursuing some projects outside the home.

A few years ago, I founded a small consultancy to help local businesses with their strategy and finances. I do the work nearly on a pro bono level, making just enough money to add some buffer to Rory's teaching income. But the satisfaction that comes from the work makes me feel wealthier than when I was raking in a grotesque salary from sitting up in a skyscraper all day.

We don't have much, but our cost of living is low, and there's a harmony that comes from living modestly. We save on childcare too, as my parents and Rory's jump in whenever we need them (and sometimes when we don't need them). Now that I see the bond that James and Anne Marie have with their grandparents and cousins,

I can't imagine ever living anywhere else. And my appreciation for Michigan as a place—the open acres and freshwater lakes and slower pace—just keeps growing.

Rory and I might not have waltzed off into a once-in-a-lifetime sunset together in a royal carriage, but we face daily sunrises together from the Adirondack chairs on our back porch while the dogs splash in the water, then shake dry by showering us.

"Keep your eyes out for it, buddy," Rory mutters to James, nodding to a bus that's still a bit farther up Upper Street, snaking past the new lineup of boutiques and Tudor-house cafés.

Sounding the alarm, James taps his little sister excitedly. "Lookit, I found the bus!" he exclaims. "I see it, Anne Marie!"

Anne Marie claps and bounces on her toes as the bus huffs to a stop in front of us. The doors squeak open, and Rory and I shepherd the kids on and up the stairs.

James and Anne Marie marvel, as if this bus is singularly the most interesting invention of all time. I, too, feel my inner child squealing with glee at being back atop a double-decker bus.

That's the beauty of kids—how you get to experience everything through their eyes, like it's brand-new. Not only have I birthed new life, but it's made me feel reborn as well, like I'm perpetually mesmerized by the everyday enchantment all around. And I have so much more faith in good to triumph over evil.

With Rory's encouragement, I ended up reporting Harold directly to Turpi's board of directors after I quit. He was quietly pushed out soon after, as there had apparently been too many similar complaints to ignore. I didn't feel a sense of victory with Harold's departure, but it did help me close that chapter and release its chauvinistic grip.

On the top deck of the bus now, James and Anne Marie plop down on the blue-fabric seats in the row in front of Rory and me.

Anne Marie plasters her hands up against the window, smudging her nose too. "I'm queen of the castle!" she proclaims, staring down at the people, dogs, and telephone boxes on the street.

"Don't do that—it's gross," James condemns, peeling Anne Marie off the germy plastic as he, too, peers out curiously. "I've never been up this high in my life before," he professes, endearingly forgetting the airplane ride to London just a few days ago.

Marlow House is straight in view, the curtains to my old sitting room window drawn shut. It feels like yesterday, and also a full lifetime ago, that I was sitting at that baroque desk, hoping that my knight in shining armor might look my way and save the day.

With the skyrocketing rent prices, Jules and Nina have moved out, over to the quirky neighborhood of Hackney Wick in East London, filled with converted warehouses, but we met up for afternoon tea with them yesterday. The kids couldn't get enough of the English accents and "silly-goose words," and Jules and Nina were equally infatuated. Jules texted this morning—Me & Nina are trying to expedite our adoption process after seeing your American angels (no cockney slang there, they are literal ANGELS.)

That might be an overstatement, but I can't deny we've gotten pretty lucky.

"This is where you and Daddy fell in love?" James wants to know, looking all around like he's in the science museum we took them to this morning.

"That's right, James," Rory says. "It was love at first sight, according to Mommy." He grins at me, wagging his tongue teasingly.

Enough time has gone by that we can joke about our story now, and the whole Prince Alexander invention.

"What's love at first sight?" Anne Marie wants to know.

Rory looks over at me, like he's curious to hear my answer to Anne Marie's question.

"Love at first sight isn't actually a real thing," I say. "Just make-believe."

Both James and Anne Marie look highly disappointed in this answer. "No fun," James declares.

"You want to know what *is* real, though?" I ask, inspired by the emotion that's overflowing as I think of how close I came to not being Mrs. Cooper. "Love at *last* sight."

"What's that?" James and Anne Marie ask in unison.

"Love at last sight is when, at the end of your life, you look at the person next to you and feel how lucky you are to have done life with them."

It's not something I've articulated before, but once I say it aloud, I realize how the notion has been formulating in my heart for a while now, and I know it's what I've found in Rory.

Anne Marie looks bored, preferring to paw at the window again as the bus lurches down Upper Street. James, on the other hand, is digesting my answer with his typical gravity. "So you can't know it's love at last sight unless you're about to die?" he asks with a frown that's wise beyond his years.

"You'll know before then," I assure him. "You just might not know right when you first meet the person, that's all."

Rory slips his hand into mine, wrapping my wedding band. He proposed six months after we left London and moved back to Michigan at the end of his exchange program. He was going to splurge on the ring, but I made it clear that I didn't want anything fancy, so we decided together on a wooden band made from a fallen maple tree in my parents' backyard. Rory had it sawed and sized, and it feels just right—both the fit and the mission behind it. The low carbon footprint and the symbolic stability of a humble, homegrown promise, so far from mined diamonds that ravage the Earth and steal the show.

"Is it time for gelato yet?" James wants to know, moving on to a more exhilarating topic. The kids have taken to European ice cream very quickly, proving they have our DNA, if the striking physical resemblance wasn't enough.

"Do the beefeaters like gelato?" Anne Marie wants to know. We took the kids on a tour of the Tower of London, where they were enraptured by the ceremonial guards and tried to get them to break their statuesque postures.

"They'd better," Rory deadpans. "Or they'll be taken to that execution chamber we saw."

James looks concerned. He's quite the sensitive soul.

"Only joking!" Rory clarifies, and James relaxes.

After a long day of walking, it feels so good to sit down and rest. So good to move through this world as a family unit, a place where I'll always belong. "Can we stay on the bus a little longer?" I ask Rory.

"Sure can," he says, casting a firm please-behave-yourself look to James, who's starting to pout as he rattles off all ten gelato flavors he's going to get. "We can stay on as long as you want."

"Just a couple more stops," I say, leaning on my favorite pillow—my husband's shoulder—as we continue along the route where it all began, and is still beginning.

ACKNOWLEDGMENTS

Since I was six years old, I've dreamed of being an author. Of having a book published. The fact that I now have not one, but two "book babies" out in the world is pretty wild. I'm deeply grateful to everyone who has made this possible.

Thank you to my readers and supporters of my debut novel, *The Heart of the Deal*, whose success paved the way for this second book. To my literary agent, Abby Saul of The Lark Group, for being an extraordinary strategist, editor, cheerleader, and friend, all wrapped into one radiant human. To my wonderful editor, Faith Black Ross, whose thoughtful notes and love for London helped the story reach its final form. And to the rest of the team at Alcove Press for helping this manuscript become a book.

To my family and friends, for being there to celebrate during the highs and help me keep perspective during the lows. The book is dedicated to my grandparents, Bill and Rita Vullo, who have poured so much love into me over the years and made me feel like I couldn't do anything wrong. Now more than ever, with the noise of public praise and criticism, I'm so grateful for my family and my relationship with God for reminding me what truly matters. With your support, I'm able to keep my feet on the ground and my head in the clouds.

To Anne Marie Greig and my Goldman Sachs colleagues, who gave me the opportunity to work in London, where I lived in a characterful Islington flat while writing this book. Places are major characters in my stories, and the fact that I got to immerse myself in UK culture and pen these pages from inside quaint English tea shops still seems like something out of a dream.

For the "bloody good mates" I made while living abroad, who taught me the local lingo and traditions, especially the brilliant and beautiful Mala Mawkin. Our country-pub dinners and living-room dance parties filled my heart with so much love and inspiration.

To my big-hearted hometown of Kalamazoo, Michigan, for welcoming me back with open arms and for spurring me to write a book that explores what it means to come home, emotionally and physically.

And to you, dear reader, for choosing to pick up this book and for reading all the way through the Acknowledgments. My hope in writing fiction is that it might reveal truths in our hearts that bring us closer to other people's stories and our own. If you've connected with Kat's journey, I'd love to hear from you, so please do reach out.